THE GRINDER

A *Beowulf* Retelling

T. Carl Hardy

Paperback ISBN: 979-8-9902084-4-5
Ebook ISBN: 979-8-9902084-5-2

Cover and interior design by Taryn Costello

Library of Congress Catalog Number: 2024909542

First Printing: 2024
Printed in United States of America

Contents

Author's Note

Re-creating stories and mythologies from the deep past is a tricky thing. Many concepts and themes do not translate easily into modern parlance or even the modern way of conceptualizing the world. Other items from history have survived to today but have undergone the natural twisting and knotting that occurs over time.

I have sought to strike a balance between loyalty to the original *Beowulf* context and the necessities and conveniences required for a modern reader to fully engage or be subsumed in its re telling. For example, the more accurate (though not completely accurate) "Valholl" or "corpse-hall" is used rather than "Valhalla." The number of similar alterations and tweaks is extensive and too long and boring to list here.

I thus ask the reader to approach unfamiliar items with an open mind. Similarly, I ask the historically inclined to excuse minor anachronisms and modernisms. The past and the present both have their demands, and the storyteller can only favor one or the other so much before losing the trail altogether.

One comfort: the act of storytelling has always been familiar to everyone. At its core, the storytellers of the past and those of the present are doing the same thing, in much the same way.

Part One

Unferth and Wulfgar

The men who live in the cold north have twenty names for ice. Those who live east, in vast forests of pine, have fifty names for one type of tree. Sit with a rock long enough and it will become a hundred types of itself. We all have our ice, our tree, our rock.

Mine is the dark.

An eclipse of the sun is the first dark. It dims. Blots out the light. It shows you what dark can do. How it can change the world.

Descending, the next shade is night. The moon is out, the outlines of things remain. You can still rely on your vision. But this is not your world. This is the world of other creatures. With large eyes. And teeth.

And the bottom. Total dark. True dark. Darkness in which no man belongs, in which no man can survive for long. This darkness thrives in only one place.

Quiet. The hush of the underground. Water dripping in some unknown distance.

I hear them. Walking. Small talons on stone. Like a dog's claws scrabbling over rock.

More of them. The noise breeds. A stream of clicking. The river pours nearer.

We are to trap them. Kill them.

I suppress my fear. Sit. Just sit.

I hear them scratching above me, on the roof. On the walls, the floor. They crawl around me, past me. A river of beasts in the dark. Brushing my legs, my booted feet. A roar of footfalls. A click-clack waterfall. There are too many. They told us fifteen at most. There will be nothing left of us.

One slows. It sniffs. We had bathed, scoured our bodies, washed our hair and weapons and armor and clothing until scentless. But it smells something.

A small prayer to Odin: let it pass. Let it go. Turn its nose away. It sniffs closer.

It puts a clawed hand on my boot. It withdraws suddenly, makes the slightest noise. A fluttering meep. The pit-pat stops.

They have stopped.

Silence. The dripping of water.

Now, Wulfgar roars.

In the blackness, the metallic-sounding sheer of Wulfgar's sword scraping the stone floor. Blade-made sparks.

My hands move to strike steel against flint. The spark darts forward.

Wulfgar's sword finds something, reduces it to jelly. His sword, Hrunting, has whistles drilled into it that wail and sing when the sword is swung. It screams. The cave screams back.

My spark finds its target, igniting a pile of powder. I arm myself, sword and shield. I look up. Brief flashes of light. Svala looses an arrow. Yngvarr thrusts with a spear.

Darkness.

Another flash of yellow light. Wulfgar, stone-faced.

Darkness.

Light again. The powder sputters awake. Wulfgar swings his sword, spinning. Flinging orcnea bits into the air. The viscous drops fly from the tip of his broad sword.

More powder ignites, throwing light around. And shadows.

Orcneas. Next to me. On the walls, on the ceiling, stretching out like an insect swarm. Man-shaped but small. Like toddlers. I see them in the flash and then I don't. The powder flash blinds me, blinds us all, is meant to blind. Our vision returns faster than they who live their lives in the bottomless recesses of the world, their huge eyes tuned to catch a sliver of a sliver of light.

I step back and feel the cracking of little bones. The trapped orcnea bites into my calf. I blindly swing my sword down, finding its sinuous flesh. It bites harder. I kick and hack again. It holds on like a dog. Pain slices up my leg. I scream. I kick. I hack and hack and hack. It does not let go. I drop my shield, grope blindly. I grab its slimy torso. I hold it out long and sever it in one long slice.

My vision returning. A low glow in the room. The orcneas: green and black, man-shaped but small as children, scrawny with sinewed flesh and wide reptilian heads. Enormous, bulbous eyes. Rows and rows of serrated teeth in fast-chomping jaws. No snouts, flat-faced. Little three-clawed hands.

Wulfgar swings his sword long and low, catching them at the level of their heads, necks. He is coated in their black gore, his arms draped in ropey innards. Svala draws and shoots with quick grace, swinging her bow from target to target. Yngvarr throws a javelin, striking an orcnea, sending it flying and sprawling, the javelin passing through it and pinning it to the leg of another orcnea.

I am to hold one end of the chamber, keeping the orcneas from running blindly out of it and down the cave, deeper into the stone-bored world-mouth. I stand at the edge of the chamber, hacking down or kicking back any orcneas that come near.

One of them runs toward me. I swing my sword at him, sheer off a finger. Blind, he sprints down the tunnel, stumbling. I chase. He is too fast.

None can get away. They must all die. I stop, drop my shield and my sword, reach over my shoulder, pull out the throwing axe. It is for moments like this, which are watched by the gods.

I throw. The axe arcs up and down but its path is wrong. It pings on the stone floor, bounces and slides away. The eoten runs. I lose it to the darkness.

I run back. A few still scrabble blindly at the walls or run in circles, but the rest are trying their eyes. One of them turns its head back and forth quickly, searchingly. Huge black-slitted yellow orbs. It looks up. We lock eyes.

It can see. The others, too. Shrieks of monster glee.

Wulfgar drops his sword. He pulls out two cruel knives. To me, he bellows. He runs to the cave wall nearest myself. The orcneas chase him, hopping. A surging wave of bodies reaching with black baby hands. I run to Wulfgar.

They hop onto me, grasp me. Spine-crawl. They claw like starving children. I stop to wrench them off.

Wulfgar's hand, huge and powerful, hauls me by the shoulder to the wall. Wulfgar slams his curved knife through an orcnea on my back. He pushes my back against the wall. We stand, side-by-side against the assault, backs to stone.

I cut and stab. Their black blood wells up through slashed eyeballs, severed arms, sliced necks. They spread out over me like water over rock. I howl. On my arms, my face. Jaws and teeth everywhere. Snapping at my eyes. Ripping my ears. I go to my knees, my shield blocking my left side, sword futilely swinging at them. Stand, yells Wulfgar. He pulls me up by the throat. An orcnea chomps into his neck. He roars. Blood, theirs black, ours red, everywhere.

A piercing scream.

I look. A human form covered with orcneas. It runs, flails. There is a man-sized orcnea hive running.

Wulfgar leaves the wall. Four orcneas chewing him. He runs to the figure, hacks at the orcneas on it. It falls. It writhes on the floor. Limbs flailing. It screams. Horrible screams. Breathless screams, fast and urgent. Like it is on fire.

Crazed, desperate, Wulfgar slashes at the orcnea horde. Kills them in batches. Yngvarr. I can barely tell. Red, top to bottom. Chewed beyond recognition.

Svala. Where is she. The thought comes to Wulfgar too. We turn to look.

A mess. Blood and viscera. Piled orcneas. Feeding. Gore dripping from their chins. Their yellow eyes slathered in red blood. Bloody bits of scalp hanging from their mouths. Tufts of Svala's hair falling to the floor.

We round up the rest. Wulfgar pins the last with his foot, stomps its head.

The cave floor is slippery.

We stand. Dazed. Breathing in the flickering light.

My left ear is gone. I have a bad bite on my right hand, small cuts all over me.

Wulfgar has deep, semicircular bite wounds on his face, his neck, his back, his legs.

Yngvarr is a bloody ruin. His flesh dangles. He is missing an eyelid, both ears, most of his nose, his lower lip, two fingers on his left hand, three on his right, and the toes on his right foot. He is missing continents of skin. Vast stretches. The only parts untouched are the soles of his feet.

Of Svala, there is nothing. Teeth on half a jawbone.

The light sputters. The darkness returns.

We stand in the void, breathing.

Ð　　　Ð　　　Ð

I had not before seen any orcneas. Wulfgar says, you've lived nineteen winters and never seen an orcnea. They will make a good introduction to this place, he says in good humor. He says, the monsters that live in a place will tell you more about that place than anything else.

The Svear and neighboring clans have lost many of their slaga, their monster hunters. Hygelac and Beowulf are all who remain of them. Those two are nearby, even, in the land of the Geats. But Hygelac and Beowulf hunt eoten like a king hunts for game. They bring dogs. They do not soil their hands with small pests. So we, me and Wulfgar and Svala and Yngvarr, traveled half the world from the land of the Danes to come and kill the orcneas.

And now, just me and Wulfgar and Yngvarr. Most of Yngvarr. And Svala's bloody chainmail shirt. Wulfgar sifts it out of her flesh-mess, hands it to me. The dead expect it.

I drag the chainmail out of the cave. Trailing clotted blood. The metal shrieks over the stone floor. Wulfgar helps Yngvarr walk. I walk listless behind them. Bats fly past us from the cave entrance, back from their nightly feast. They dart past, their shadows thrown by sputtering torchlight. A flitting dance on the cave walls. We drip, streak blood the whole way to the surface.

Out into the day. Fall of the year 514. In the summer and fall, this northland is a land of green. The sun is in the sky all day and most of the night, warming all of those who emerge from its caves and recesses.

A night to rest. Back to the village the next day. Wulfgar's fury simmering, simmering, simmering as we approach. The townspeople gather.

This has happened to us before. The people who hire you on, the townspeople or the thane or the king or the warlord, give you a false account of what you will go up against. More ferocious monsters take more slaga and carry more risk. So fewer are willing to take these jobs. The thane or king or townspeople want to save themselves at any cost. Even the cost of dead slaga. Sometimes they get away with their lies. Most of the time they do not. This town told us that there were fifteen orcneas that attacked their village three weeks ago. We counted sixty-seven corpses. They always travel together, one herd.

Svala died. We did not know Svala well, so the death is not personal. But there are reputations to uphold.

We approach the village with our armor on and our weapons out. Yngvarr, bloody and ruined, has a javelin out. Behind his back, Wulfgar gives me the hand signals *kill if attacked* and *cover left flank*. I learned the hand signals two days ago. I'm not sure if he signals *kill if attacked* or simply, *kill*.

The thane of the village approaches us, looks at us like he is surprised that one of us is gone.

She's dead, Wulfgar says.

The thane blames it on us. But he knows he's been found out. Look at him, shifting around in that loose clothing. Probably his father's clothing. The thane is my age, nineteen or twenty, tall but skinny. Wulfgar is a grizzled thirty-nine. Wulfgar stands wide-legged in front of him.

Twenty-one pounds of silver, says Wulfgar. He has tripled the agreed amount.

The thane glares at him. Articulates his fingers. I look around, checking the odds of the fight. I am learning to balance forces. There are many more of them than us: the thane with a sword, four of his men with spears and axes, lots of men and women around. Three against twenty. But I like the odds of this fight more than the last one. Unlike orcneas, these men value their lives.

The demand has been made. There is no backing down.

Silence. Tension. I feel for the handle of my sword.

Yngvarr's tattered breath. The sound of breaths from a man who does not have lips. Shallow. Toothy.

We look like murderers. Filthy. Bloody. We stand lazily. Wulfgar looks bored, looks like he has nothing to lose, like he wants to die to be rid of the burden of life. But he is ready to fight. I've known Wulfgar to take life lightly, and death. But not his reputation. Reputation is the only thing a man can take with him to the grave.

Wulfgar looks ready to die and to take the thane with him to the corpse-hall. The thane looks around like an abused dog, bent neck and slumped back.

He crumbles. I would too.

Twenty-one pounds of silver. And a good meal.

Ð   Ð   Ð

The world sits upon the tree Yggdrasil. There are three women, three spinners who sit at the base of this tree, weaving the threads that make our fate: mine, Yngvarr's, Wulfgar's, Svala's, everyone. They sit and they spin, and I imagine that they discuss the weaving of fates. But I also imagine that they discuss other women who are not present.

How could anyone resist a little gossip?

Oh, how poetically sad you've made Uhtred's fate, says one.

I've never been able to suffer a braggart, the other replies.

Or: Why do you let Borgunna live, spinner? asks one. You usually weave enslavement or at least a disease into girls that pretty.

And the other spinner will say something like, oh, but I do so like to see women murder their husbands, and Borgunna was so good at following my subtle hints. Did you see the deathcap mushroom that I wove into her garden?

That sounds like great fun, says the other. Let's watch her do it again. Who could she marry next? It is too bad she is so poor. No one wants her. Maybe I can spin some wealth in for that Borgunna! Isn't Gunnmarr's silver buried near her house? Maybe I can lead her dog's nose over there.

But I imagine that, as the spinners sit around that tree, they also discuss each other in a calculated, pointed way. They have millennia to do it, after all. And I think that, when one spinner's beauty or worth is insulted by her fellow spinners, she weaves destruction into the fabric of the world. And if this is true, then the three fates must have been at each other for a long time.

Man has always been in chains. I have heard of men called Romans who found a way to pull themselves free of these chains. They lived a long time, they conquered the world, they were never hungry. They even built with stone. Entire houses, walls. I think that, for a time, the spinners enjoy watching men and women free themselves from hunger or pain or fear. They enjoy watching people build things, cultivate fields. But then one of the spinners will make an off-color comment about the wart on another spinner's nose, or maybe one spinner will cruelly tell another that maybe she should take her smelly self somewhere else to do her spinning. Or maybe it is more tragic. Maybe the long look given from one spinner to another, a look given out of love or lust or admiration is instead interpreted as hostility or dismissal. So the insulted spinner spins angrily and disaster enters the world through her fabric and men die and the Romans fall and the world is chained again and eoten wander the land, eating whom they please.

I imagine that if I were a different man I would use this as a lesson that says, watch what you do, you never know how far the pain you inflict will travel on the web-like fabric of fate, you may be hurting someone who is woven near you. But I am not a man who says this. I am a different man. I believe that the world that sits on Yggdrasil needs pain, that there is a reason for it. I don't know the reason. Maybe the spinners know the reason. Here is what I know: pain happens too often not to be central to the functioning of the world.

Somehow, Yngvarr does not develop a fever. It looks like he will live. But he cannot continue as a slaga. No toes means that he can't run. Wulfgar says that his missing eyelid is trouble, though he doesn't say what kind of trouble, and Yngvarr doesn't have enough fingers on either hand to steadily hold a weapon. We travel for five days across green plains dotted with black boulders to a large town to leave him there. He has no living kin. We take him to the village thane to introduce him.

The thane, scarred as an anvil, stands tall. I look into his eyes and wonder if he will take advantage of Yngvarr or if he will neglect him. He agrees to look after him for the price of six pounds of silver, provided that Yngvarr learns to support himself somehow within three months. We give him six pounds of the new silver: arm rings and torques. The thane brings us to the hovel of an odd but harmless man who is wimpy and round next to our mangled companion. Yngvarr will stay here.

The three of us then lead the horses far behind the house, over the next couple of hills, and Wulfgar takes out a leather sack and we stuff it with silver and bury it next to a tree that might as well be Yggdrasil, so grand and twisted and knotty it is. Across the world, men with power should be generous. As we bury it, it is clear on Wulfgar's face that he wishes he could do more for Yngvarr, but he cannot.

The two have fought through many spats together; who knows the depth of slaga knowledge they hold between them. Though Wulfgar may not be the absolute best trap-maker or best fighter, he knows more than any man in the slaga profession, the profession for which knowledge is more important than for a smith, shipwright, or king.

We go back to the hovel. I keep my mouth shut, scared to speak in this fragile moment. I am surprised that there is no talk about what kind of work Yngvarr could do. I guess that there are many tasks he can assist with on a farm, or he could do women's work. But he and Wulfgar don't discuss the future at all, though they had been slaga together for seven years. Wulfgar hands Yngvarr his weapons with a peculiar, sad, distracted look. Like he is injuring himself in handing them over. We know that Yngvarr won't be using them again. I detect something between them. I am learning to sniff subtlety. But I shrug it off.

Wulfgar ties up Yngvarr's horse outside the house. We are leaving him behind. We leave Yngvarr there at the doorway and walk to our horses.

It is short, just a few paces, but it feels longer than two days through rough terrain. The air is still. The world can't breathe.

I put my hand on my horse's bridle and put my boot, muddy and dripping, into the stirrup.

We are mounted. Wulfgar says goodbye to Yngvarr like you say goodbye to your brother. You cannot.

We turn away, ride to a gallop. I turn my head to see Yngvarr, mangled and broken, standing in the doorway of the hovel, leaning against its post. Looking at us. A hollow despair. He goes limp in the door frame, puts his destroyed head in his destroyed hands. I have seen enough. I turn to face forward.

We are away now, riding at a slow pace through the lowland hills. Wulfgar is not looking back, never did look back. He is in front of me. I can't see his face. He says nothing. He sniffs, a sniff that tries to disguise itself as a normal sniff. But it is not a sniff. I

can tell the difference between a Wulfgar sniff and a Wulfgar sniffle. It is a wet sniffle.

I realize it. It hits me like a hammer to the skull-cage. They had
not discussed Yngvarr's future because he would have no future.
We left the silver there for his afterlife. When Wulfgar handed
Yngvarr his weapons, that pained look on Wulfgar's face was not
out of pain for what had happened to Yngvarr but out of pain for
what was going to happen to Yngvarr, inflicted by those weapons.

There are depths to the bonds of men. Overcome something
difficult with a man and he will love you until you are in the dirt.
And after you are in the dirt, he will turn his sword hilt in his hand
as is his custom before he is to use that sword. And as he does this
he will remember you and will fight against your parting though
you have long ago parted. He will fight against your parting not
for himself and not entirely for you but because the world has
taken yet another of his treasures from him and he cannot bear to
do nothing about it.

We come over the rise of a hill. There sits the ocean, wide-
spilled, silver. Deep enough to house leviathans, to drown everything.

Ð   Ð   Ð

The wind is made by a huge eagle in the sky. This wind sweeps
over us, sweeps across the night-hued sea and up onto the dark-
ened plains. A silver moon is out, its reflection cut and chopped
in the churning sea. Wulfgar and I sit at a campfire in the lee of

boulders black as the sky. These boulders have been licked with caches of reflective stone. The reflective flicks catch the firelight, send it back at us. The rocks cast out dots of light, stars, that rest on us, around us. The campfire a center of a small island of comfort in a sea of damp and cold and darkness. The fire moves and dances, making the light-dots crawl over us, crawl over the sand, and then scurry back.

The sea is home to eoten that fin through the deep, endlessly hungry. It churns and ebbs behind us, blowing its salt breeze over the plains in front of us, the green and black marches, grassy and mossy and rolling and swooping. Wulfgar does not seem concerned with danger from eoten tonight. Maybe he can feel it. But they are out there, the orcneas and others. Eoten that burrow and dig. Eoten that make their broods in the recesses beneath ground or inside trees or at the bottom of mud ponds or in the gaseous hearts of swamps. They are growing, mating. The young ones that develop from pupae wait for their brood-mothers to return to their cave with some carcass. The newly-fledged eoten, ravenous and eager to grow, search the rocks and desolate marches for corpses or small prey. The adults, grown and twisted, hide in the rushes or behind stones, eyeballing the villages or campfires of men, envying them their warmth, their food, their friendship. They attack or return to their holes, whatever their mood suits. If they do not attack now, the hunger in their souls grows. It will encourage them next time.

Wulfgar holds something that belonged to Svala. It is her necklace, a Thor's Hammer. A bronze, hammer-shaped amulet about the length of a woman's smallest finger. These amulets hang upside down, the leather neck band running through the base of the hammer. It is covered in her blood. Wulfgar gets up from his driftwood log, walks around the rocks, over the shifting sand to the sea. I peer from around the rock to watch him. He crouches down and puts his hands into the water, his back a tiny mountain of black against the breaking waves and the myriad stars. He stands back up, slowly, and for the first time I think I see a sign of his age. I remember that he is thirty-nine. Old. I have seen a few his age in better shape. But not many. I stop watching, move back to my sitting spot before he sees. I hear his steps on the sand. He returns, wiping salty water from the cleaned bronze amulet. He hands me the amulet by its leather string. He sits back down.

He says nothing, letting the waves speak their language of crash and spume. And then he says, Svala is now in Valholl. Or Folkvangr, the other corpse-hall. He says, every morning, she will arm herself and go out onto the field of battle or to some eoten's lair and she will fight. She will do this for years and years. Training. Training for Ragnarok.

He pauses. He sits heavily. Wulfgar is a heavy man. Half bone, half muscle. He used to be a man with looks. His eyes retain the swift movements of youth, and one can imagine a woman reflected in them. He is a stocky man with long, dull blonde hair and a grey-blonde beard. He has taken off his mail and leather and now sits in his green shirt and faded red pants. His cloak, which is fixed at his shoulder with a metal brooch, is draped around him for warmth. But he wears it in token fashion. Wulfgar is never cold.

Just Wulfgar and me now. Svala and Yngvarr are gone. I wonder what he thinks about me, what I think about him. Isn't it always that way. Isn't it always that you don't know a friendship until it is over, don't know your mother until she is dead.

He looks at me and pauses in his speaking. Like he expects me to say something. Which hall will she go to, I say. How do you go to one hall and not the other.

He says, it does not matter. He says, either Odin or Freyja will choose you, and if Odin chooses you then you go to Valholl and if Freyja chooses you then you go to Folkvangr. All prefer Valholl but I am sure that the two corpse-halls are the same. Maybe the mead is different. I'm sure that if you really want to visit the other hall, you can.

Right. What if your friend goes to one and you to the other? You will want to visit them.

Svala will dress every morning, he says, and fight all day, along with all of the other dead warriors, all of those that have ever been sent to the corpse-hall through all time. She will fight with them against other men or against eoten. Or maybe she will die trying to defeat a fyrdraca or wyrm or some giganta. But she will rise. She will return to the hall each night and drink and wrap her legs around some man she chooses. She will have her choice of the men because there will be many men in these halls, all worthy and good. He says, and all of the men, all of the people, everyone who is in these halls does the same thing each day. They get up and they fight and they die and then at night they drink and mount Odin's maidens. There are plenty of maidens, too, and Valholl and Folk-vangr are the greatest halls. These halls are so big that hundreds of men can pass abreast through just one of Valholl's doorways. The halls will be warm and tall-ceilinged and full of cheers and taunts and boisterous bragging. You know these parties, he leans back and says with a mischievous grin, and I smile back. He says, the nights will be like that night we had but just a bit better in every way.

The days sound bad because I still hate fighting and am afraid of it. But the nights sound pristine. If something bad is paired with something perfect, do not let one spoil the other.

He says, this will happen every day and every night for as long as you can conceive. He says, and then Ragnarok will come and we will fight for Odin. And we will lose. This world will wink out of existence. As Wulfgar says this, he opens his palms and pulls his hands apart as if something were expanding. And then, he says, something new will be born. He puts his hands together, right hand wrapped around left fist.

He pauses again. A long pause. Like he does not want to wake from a good dream. He leans forward again and puts his elbows on his knees and says to the fire: so look forward to seeing Svala in the corpse-hall. Or on the battlefield outside Valholl. Maybe you will get the chance to kill her, or, during your first battle there, she will see you from across the battlefield and will work her way over to you. She will wait until you are not looking and then she will stick her sword into you and twist it and pull it out and spill your guts onto the mud and she will laugh with glee and as you are dying she will clap a hand on your shoulder and lean over and look into your face and she will say, welcome to eternity. She will say, welcome, and look out for sneaky bastards who deal low blows. They'll spill your innards. And then she will laugh her deep laugh. And then that night, when you feast with her, she will brag that she slayed you during your first battle near Valholl. And then the next day you will vow revenge and stand grinning on your tip-toes to search the battlefield for her so that you can pull her guts out, too.

I look down at Svala's amulet in my hand. I lift it and tie it around my neck. It will give you strength, says Wulfgar. Thor will look out for you, he says. Not as much as I look out for you. He smiles at this. But he will help, he says, and between the two of us you may live long enough to become a slaga.

I cannot help but smile at his chiding. I'm nineteen and I have something to prove, so I try to be dower, as many slaga I have met seem to be. But sometimes I cannot hide my smiles around Wulfgar. He pulls smiles from you like you pull a plant out of the ground, roots and all. He grabs your smile at the base, where it connects to that hidden, underground part of you. And then he pulls and up comes everything, flowers and leaves and stem and roots and all. And then he dusts off the roots and holds the whole thing upside down, roots skyward, and he lifts it up to the wind and the sunlight and he smiles at his success and gives you a look that says, look what I did, look at these little roots of yours.

Ð   Ð   Ð

Years ago. My mother looks at me.

What is this flower called, Unferth?

That is columbine, mother.

Yes, I know, but just for you and me, what will it be called for us? Look at it. What should its secret name be?

I tilt the flower up to face me. It is beautiful in the way that things are beautiful to children: its presence means that the world contains beautiful things like this, that more beautiful things could be out there, that more are waiting to be found.

It's purple and white. Like a moonlit lake turned flower. Two layers of petals reach out, twice-bursting. I sit on my feet in the way that children do, that ready-to-rise kneel, knees cocked, head forward. The day is warm. Breaths of wind billow over the spring-time hills, the colorful flowers, the emerald grasses. We come here sometimes, midday, when my father is far away and won't know it. Those days are the real pieces of my childhood, the pieces that I collect and piece together to make some sort of leaky pot.

I said, Mom, what's a secret that everybody knows?

That's a rumor.

Then let's call it rumor because it's our secret but it's also out here where everyone can see it.

There are slaga who do not travel. Wulfgar says that slaga who do not travel are farmers who club snakes. To make money, to stay keen, to make a reputation, slaga must travel. They travel on the wings of Rumor, that shrieker, manipulator of men and women. Me and Wulfgar are traveling and looking for work, which means collecting rumors and sifting through them, going from village to town to city to village, asking what people have seen, who saw it, where it went.

Rumor is rampant. I sometimes think that there are four spinners, not three. Maybe Rumor is so involved that she has become a spinner herself. Maybe the three spinners who sit at Yggdrasil and make our fate don't know about her. Maybe before their weaving bubbles up into the world, before it coats the leaves of Yggdrasil, Rumor, a fourth spinner, secretly grabs up that glowing fabric. She runs her eyes over it. She looks for any gaps in the fabric, for gaps in people's minds. The places waiting to be filled with something. She puts in little lies. These are what we sort through. We peel the lies of Rumor away from what people have actually seen, have actually heard.

Sniffing a lie is a skill of the hands – you have to feel a statement. Its shape, its roughness or smoothness. A statement that fits your hand like the hilt of a sword or like the roundness of a fresh apple, a statement that sits well with you, that you find comfortable, should be cast away. Those are the ones created by Rumor. Those are the lies. Her craftings have those marks on them: graspability, juiciness.

My mother, too, could coat things with her words to make them softer, rounder, easier to grasp. Whenever I imagine Yggdrasil and the spinners and Rumor, I imagine Rumor with my mother's face.

But those are of a different time, a different world. Maybe there was a time and place where rumors and silly lies could be followed. But not this time, not this place. We toss them out. We move on.

Instead, listen to the statements that are rough in your hand. Those that feel dirty and uneven and coarse. Those that feel sharp like the tooth of a bear, or sticky like sap, or gritty and coarse like mud. Those that you would not want to sleep on or eat. Those that you want to wash from yourself. They will lead you to the monsters.

Ð   Ð   Ð

Part One

The eoten rise from their mounds or holes or caves each winter day, stretching their hairy limbs. Their stomachs grumble. The deer of the northern lands are scarce and harder to catch in the winter, so the eoten head to the homes of men, to where they know food can be found.

The eoten of the milder south are calmer in the winter, so there is less to be done there. There is something about the cold that slows those beasts. But not so with those in the north. They thrive in the cold. It wakes them.

So the slaga go north for the winter. Slaga are a coarse bunch. Sometimes the villages of the north say that they do not know if the eoten or the slaga are a worse curse. But they pay for our services, after all, and better an enemy who you can murder in the night than one who murders you in the night.

We follow the rumors, sorting through them. Winter comes. We board the boat of a trader, rowing in exchange for passage to the far northern coast. And then we ascend, going up into the hoary mountains, climbing and then descending and then climbing again, north and north and north. We trot our horses over frozen dirt paths from village to village, traveling further and further. Trees on all sides, branches above you and pine needles below. We talk as we ride but Wulfgar scans constantly, does not take his eyes away from the trees. When I talk to him, he listens to the silences between my words. Listens for eoten. We build a fake watchman, standing tall in Wulfgar's armor, before we bed down in the snow.

Winter in the north is dark. Like Ragnarok has come early. It hangs low over the land. It wails at us with frosty breath. Cold, so cold. My urine freezes soon after I leak it out onto the white snow.

Over a rise and we look down. A village of twelve houses, scattered around like dropped bones. A few have smoke coming out of their roofs, and I can smell bread baking. Wulfgar eyes it. He sniffs.

We approach on horse. A few villagers come out of their homes, some of which are thatch and some log. They are ragged and wild like all isolated men. Among them, a girl my age. Pretty in the way that a fox or a mouse is pretty – some cuteness in her nose, and her hair falls well.

Wulfgar greets them, starts speaking to them. I have heard people speak with accents but these of the far and isolated north are hard to understand. They speak with a strange tone and the order of their words is jumbled. They pause between them, great long pauses, like crows pause between squawks.

Wulfgar asks them some questions. Past eoten trouble, past eoten killed. He asks about the moon and the stars and if they have been clouded over recently. He asks about the northern lights. He asks about eclipses. He asks about previous battles in the area. He asks about nearby caves, nearby ponds. None of what the villagers say seems to interest him. And then he asks about disease. A woman tells us that, in the spring, a plague had killed a third of the village.

Wulfgar detects something. I feel it too. Maybe. It is something in their eyes. Some expectation of death. Something else, too. Something changed when we came over that rise and looked down onto the village. The air became colder, thinner, less viscous. When you get out of water and into the air, there is a feeling of lightness. The air here is like getting out of air and into something thinner.

The woman stops speaking. It is time for Wulfgar to reply but he says nothing. He takes a deep breath and then breathes out steam. He turns his head toward me. His blonde-grey hair is wavy and thick, to his shoulders. His face is all nose and beard and blue eyes and scar-wrinkles.

He points. Buried over there, he asks in his granite voice.

She says, yes, most of them are behind that hill. Huge sores, says the woman. And mania.

He calculates. He looks at me. He looks back out there. Maybe he is measuring strength, our strength against that of some enemy. He looks over at me again, shifting in his saddle, his armor clinking. He wonders if I can handle it. The villagers stand there, bothered by his silence. They fidget, waiting for him to speak.

I sit in fear of what Wulfgar has detected, of what cold souls haunt this mountain range.

His face looks pained and sad. A rough beginning for Unferth, he thinks. The orcneas and now this, he thinks.

Wulfgar has the smallest twinge of hesitation to him. And then he firms up and his face is hard again. I am scared.

The usual agreement is struck: they feed us and we stay up nights guarding the people and their livestock. If we defend against anything that might have killed some of them, we get paid. But Wulfgar adds a demand: he will need fuel to keep the smithy forge hot all night, every night.

The villagers laugh at this. They think he is some southerner unused to the cold.

Wulfgar shifts his weight from one foot to the other. I can almost feel the earth groan under his weight. He looks at them, person by person, like a shepherd looks out over helpless sheep.

Ð   Ð   Ð

I wake beside the forge. In my chainmail armor. I step out into the snow, bringing my sword and shield with me. Wulfgar is making rounds. I go and find him.

We stand, backs to the village, facing out toward the empty night, watching the snow fall in big, soft flakes. I am taller than Wulfgar, standing beside him. My hair is darker, my skin is lighter. He often pokes fun at the blackness of my hair.

Wulfgar never tells me things. So I ask. I say, what do we go up against.

Draugr, he says. Men that neither made it across to the corpse-hall or to Hel. You will see them. Not tonight. But I think later.

Who knows why these men were rejected from the corpse-halls, rejected by Odin and Freyja, and also not taken to Hel. Maybe they refused to go. Maybe they did something to offend the gods. Or maybe they were just forgotten, their souls dropped like slippery fish into the void as they were being carried from one world to another.

We look out at the field in front of us. The silence of snow. It is the same as the silence of an owl. It is the softest of noises. It is nature's whisper, lonely and darkly serene. Snow is from the beer of the gods. Their beer is so cold that its froth is made of snowflakes. When the gods are in their mead-halls feasting, they blow this froth off of their drinks and it falls on us.

It is cold, but less so because of the nearness of Wulfgar. Trees come from seeds, violence comes from swords, warmth comes from Wulfgar. Draugr, he says like he is recalling a memory, and he looks toward the town graveyard where the woman pointed. When it gets cold enough, he says, they will rise. Not tonight, but soon. It is getting colder.

They died of disease, he says. Disease robs men of the corpse-hall because the diseased do not die in combat. You have to die in combat to go to the corpse-hall. And so they are restless in their graves. Even so, they would not normally become draugr. The thing that brings the corpses out of their sleep is the cold. When many people die at once, the town digs shallow graves. No one wants to dig a grave when half their family has just died. And the cold can penetrate these shallow graves. If it gets cold enough, the cold will reach through those shallow graves and shake them awake.

I wonder at how to kill something that is already dead.

Wulfgar's low voice rumbles the earth. He says, the cold wakes them and the heat kills them. We burn them. We heat them in the forge.

A pause.

Why don't we dig them up now and do it, I say.

Wulfgar turns his head and looks at me. Do you think that Odin or Freyja will want you in their corpse-hall, he says. Do you think that they will want you if you dig up the bodies of men, or if you destroy an enemy before he becomes an enemy? Heed the spinners. If the spinners drop a shovel from out of the sky, then we should dig them up.

I wish I could take my words away. He looks down at the snow, annoyed. There's a better way to do it anyway, he says. We'd turn them into draugr just exposing them to the cold. And waking one wakes them all.

Wulfgar looks at something in the trees, craning his neck. The perfect silence of falling snow. I'm hesitant to speak. To break it.

What's the better way, I ask.

He says, they will come together, in one group. We cannot handle fifteen draugr at once. We can handle three or four. So we make traps. To slow them.

Wulfgar looks at the trees. His brow furrows.

I look up. I see it. An owl, brown and white.

Ð   Ð   Ð

It snows. We are making snares between the village and the graveyard. Drive the stakes, wrap the rope. Twenty-seven snares. They will not all catch draugr, says Wulfgar. But enough. The draugr will walk straight into them, he says. He pauses. He leans to the right, like he's imitating one of them. He says, somewhat straight.

We do our work and keep watch in the evenings and nights and we sleep during the day. The village of twelve houses is planted in a valley between two ridged mountain veins. West of us are great plains. During the day, there are deer and wolves down there in the plains, wandering or grazing or hunting in their herds and packs.

We are in the village's largest hovel. This one has a rare wood floor. Dinner has come and gone and the men shoo away their sons and daughters, the pretty mouse girl among them. She looks at me as she goes.

It is the way of Northmen to boast in front of each other. It is our way of getting to know men.

The wild, strange-speaking men of the village say that they want to boast to Wulfgar, which really means that they want to hear Wulfgar boast. I am learning that he is a slaga of renown.

The drinking bowl is finally brought out. The men pry their iron wit under Wulfgar's stone slab of a tongue to get at what stories it holds. Ten of us sit around the stone hearth on furs or blankets. The men have removed the brooches that keep their cloaks on their backs. They sit in comfort after their winter's work of chopping, milking, and hunting. I sit leaned against a wood-post. The fire's warmth is a taunt to the cold night watch that I must soon keep. But for now the heat is in here and the cold is out there and the mead is passed around in a great bronze bowl engraved with the story of Loki turning into a salmon to escape the wrath of the other gods.

The men of the far north, more than any other place, are aware of a man's standing with other men. In a village with eight men, even the seventh most powerful man feels like he has something to defend. So the men boast and expect boasting from others. They grow tired of hearing each other boast because most have lived with each other in the same mud hole their entire lives. And so now their eyes turn to Wulfgar. Wulfgar the slaga. He is not a famous man but he is a known man. He has proven himself useful enough to earn him a place in the minds of kings. If you have some monster that is unknown or new or strange, you hire Wulfgar because he's shown that he can usually think up some way to kill it.

The drinking bowl goes to Wulfgar and he tips it up and passes it along and it makes its way to me. After honey, from which it is made, mead is the sweetest thing to be found anywhere. It has been months since I have had something sweet. It is magic in the mouth.

The men sit. Bearded. Broad. They watch Wulfgar. He savors this moment of attention. He sometimes complains about a lack of respect for slaga. But look at him now: he looks content.

He knows how to handle a crowd. Stories, says the eldest of the men. Of what, Wulfgar says. I have many. Give me a place to start, he says.

In saying this, he shows that his time as slaga has given him more than one thing to boast about. He makes us all think: what has this man seen? Is there a place he has not been? Wulfgar savors their attention; glancing at me, mischief comes to life somewhere between his smiling lip and his wrinkled left eye.

And we, the men and I, believe it. We believe that he has seen much. Look at him. He sits in that deeply relaxed way that masters sit, with that lazy posture of ultimate poise. We believe him because he has more scars than wrinkles. They crisscross his face and arms like he fights monsters made of blades day-in and day-out. Wulfgar looks like he pours himself a bowl of thorns for breakfast.

A story of trolls, one of the younger men says, a man somewhere near my age. I look at him. My experience, though small, makes me feel older than him. Wulfgar must feel as though a thousand years have gone by.

Trolls, repeats Wulfgar, and he says, let me tell you a story about how I – I alone – slayed two terrible trolls.

Two trolls. Impossible. None of us believe him. Smiles round the fire.

He starts, the two giants lived in the extreme southern tip of a peninsula in a cave next to the sea. For some reason, no one knew why, they began to eat the men and horses and goats out of nearby villages. So the local thane called on his king for help and the king called on me.

I was twenty-eight at the time, says Wulfgar, and sharp in the mind.

We are rapt. Now we wonder: is this a real story? Is he telling the truth? The firelight casts a soft orangeness onto the bearded men.

I went to where the giants lived, says Wulfgar. The cave was on the beach. The door to it was small, barely big enough for the trolls, which were each as tall as five men, to enter and leave through. It was the only way in or out. I knew that I would have to come up with some plan to end all plans, says Wulfgar. But then again, I am Wulfgar. Smiles all around. This man knows how to boast. I am Wulfgar. It is assumed.

Wulfgar says: I asked the thane how often whales wash up on his beaches. Once every two years, maybe, he responded. I planned to be in the area for at least the next year, so I told him: I cannot kill these eoten right now. No one can. But I can eventually. I will need maybe two years. The thane was distraught at hearing this. Because, you all know, a thane's land and his collection of people are his entire life, they are his bragging right and his source of income and his rank among other men. But I said, buy oil, enough oil for your entire village for one year. Set it aside. And when a whale washes up on your beaches, in a year or two, like you said, send for me again.

And then Wulfgar asks us: do you know how I did it. Can anyone guess.

Silence.

One of the men says: why wait until a whale washed up?

Wulfgar pauses and then says, the washing up of the whale was a sign. It is up to the spinners. A slaga leaves it up to the spinners to decide when and how he will face his opponents. And so in choosing an event that may happen now or may happen later, I left it to them. Because if they wanted me to kill these eoten, they could then make it happen. They could just wash up a whale and they could count on me going to kill the trolls. Or if they wanted for me to die against the trolls, the spinners could also wash up a whale and send me to the troll cave and kill me that way. Or, if they wanted the trolls to live in peace forever, all they had to do was keep the whales from washing up.

The men nod. Wulfgar is a man who knows how to trust the spinners. Men like these, men who can give up control to the spinners, are the best men.

Wulfgar continues: well, twenty months went by. And just as I was getting onto a ship bound for the Danes, just as I was leaving to hunt eoten elsewhere, a rider on an exhausted horse found me. I heard its hooves just as I stepped into the ship.

It was from the king. A whale had washed up.

Wulfgar continues: so I told the captain of the ship – it was a merchant ship – that he must right now take me to that village, a day's journey away. He refused but I offered him silver, and more silver and more silver until he agreed. It was worth the price because killing two trolls would bring in a haul. I arrived and then made preparations.

Wulfgar asks again, now does anyone want to guess how I did it.

He is gloating. I am proud to be under his wing.

He continues, we waited until night, when the trolls were asleep in their cave. And then I had the thane wake all of his nearest subjects, fifty of them, and told them to bring all their carts, their horses, their oxen to the beach. We butchered the whale. By now its smell had grown awful. Whales have their own special stink. They don't smell like dead fish. They smell more like dead cows. We loaded up the blubber, cut into huge marble-colored slabs, from the whale. We took it to the entrance of the cave and heaved it over the lip of it, heaved the blubber just inside the entrance. It slopped and flopped and came to rest on the cave floor, oily and bloody. We made four trips from whale to cave. This took all night. You can see a whale from afar but you will never really know how enormous they are until you are right up next to one.

And then I had the thane's villagers start a bonfire on the beach. We waited until it raged and raged. Morning had almost come. The giants would soon wake in their cave. I was nearly out of time. While the fire roared, good and hot, some men and I took the oil into the cave, the oil that the thane had bought. I could hear the trolls snoring; it was like the crash of waves and then a huge echoing slurp, like a giant child drinking from a cup. I poured out the oil, spreading it evenly over the blubber.

Wulfgar says, and then I got all of the villagers, children and women and all, to grab firebrands – logs, sticks, anything – from the fire. Anything burning. And we ran with those burning logs across the beach, panting and excited to the point of giddiness. That feeling of wobbly legs that you get when you are excited. And we threw them into the cave onto the oil and the blubber. They lit into a great, bubbling blaze.

Blubber burns smokily, so smokily, and it filled the cave with that black smoke. The sea breeze blew toward the cave's mouth, and the cave had small holes at the far end, so it sucked the smoke in. The trolls were deep inside. After a long time, when the cave was so full with smoke that it began to gush out the entrance again, the trolls began to wake. The villagers ran away when they heard them coughing, down deep in the cave's crevices. But I stayed near the cave entrance. I thought, I can't run now. Do I not trust my plan?

The trolls woke and yelled and coughed, their lungs pulling in that thick smoke. The very earth rumbled with their bellows. Then there was a crash in the cave. One of the trolls had keeled over. Pounding footsteps got closer and closer to the entrance and to me. I thought, the second troll will make it out of the cave and see me and crush me to jelly and eat me. But a second crash came. It shook the ground. Near the cave entrance. Very near. I peered in and, through smoke billows, could see the beast's enormous hand, large as my torso, spread upon the ground.

His story complete, Wulfgar looks down at the boarded floor.

He says, the hæftworld.

The mead cup goes around.

Part One

Silence.

A man asks, the whale was a sign from the spinners? Only a sign?

Wulfgar smiles. His smirk is keen as any blade.

Ð   Ð   Ð

Hæftworld. It is not a word that we tell to anyone.

The hæftworld is the slaga's name for this world, the eoten's world. The eoten that hide on the mountainside, that lurk in the fen, that squirm under our feet. The hæftworld belongs to the nameless hunger that resides out there. The hunger embodied that keeps people close to their villages, that makes parents clutch their children for fear that they will be eaten up. The hæftworld is the relentless malice of the draugr, the frenzy of gnawing orcneas, the lurking terror of the sceadu-gengan.

Here is how it is said. You are telling another slaga of how you fought this or that eoten, or group of eoten. Know that the telling of this story is more important to slaga than anything else. It is our most important tradition. So you are talking to them and you tell of the preparation and of the fight. But you do not speak of the terror and the pain, not directly; no one does that. You tell the story, which is hard to get off your chest. But you have to do it. And then there is a brief silence after the telling. The man or men who hear it take a good amount of time thinking over the tale, appreciating it in its fullness, appreciating the ways in which it must have been terrible for the teller, the ways in which the teller felt pain or lost a part of himself. The listeners sit and think on this, and the longer they sit and think, the more a compliment it is to the teller because it takes a very long time to think over and imagine and grasp the worst moments or the most dire moments, takes a long time to see how much those things must have pained the slaga, how much they will forever change that slaga, what ghosts that slaga will now see in the night, what nightmares will forever keep that slaga from good sleep. And then, after that long, honorable pause, the listening slaga say to the storytelling slaga, emphatically,

The hæftworld.

And saying this says, yes, we are in bondage. The world is in chains. It says, the chains of this world are in your story. I can see them and hear them in it. I also feel them around my own wrists, my own ankles. I, too, feel your futility, your bored but terrified resignation to its limitless capacity for torment.

But. When our world, the hæftworld, came into existence, Odin whispered another meaning for this word into the ear of the first slaga. Odin did this to give all slaga something precious, something that others in the hæftworld do not have. This second meaning has a wryness to it. It is a wink from one slaga to another. When you say to another slaga, the hæftworld, you are also saying, so you are still alive, eh? It hasn't eaten you yet, eh?

Ð   Ð   Ð

It snows. Night.

Wulfgar. He looks up at the owl. Every night, it keeps our watch with us.

When the draugr come, Wulfgar says, many will be caught in the traps but some will get through.

He looks down at my sheathed sword.

Fight them, but do not try to kill them, he says. I will. The forge is the way.

We stand at the edge of the village, looking out at the trees that separate the graveyard from the village, the light from our torches barely reaching those evergreens. We stand there silently, minding our vigil. The snow counts out the moments, falling soft and steady in large flakes.

I do not notice her first. Wulfgar does. His head turns. Mine follows.

The mouse-faced girl, peering from around a hovel. She is looking at us, looking at me. Furtively, calculatingly.

I cannot interpret signals from women. Interpreting signals from women takes years, at least ten years, to master. But Wulfgar knows what she's up to. He mouths to me, stay within earshot.

He walks away.

I don't know how to interpret signals from women. But I do know how to interpret signals from Wulfgar.

She approaches through the ankle-deep snow. Even her gait is that of a mouse – some light-footed scurry. I feel that if I move, I will scare her away. The snares we have set for the draugr could also be used to catch others and I am worried that she will get caught in one though she is not even near them.

The mood hangs in the air, unknown, undiscovered. And then her eyes flash. A hunter's prey-tracking eyelock. I freeze.

She approaches. She advances and then stops, determined but skittish. I am rapt, still unbelieving that she has an interest in one as nameless, as clumsy and fickle and bland as myself. I am not even funny.

We talk about the snow, the owl. We look up at the bird. Spotted brown and white. It has been there each winter night, all night, she says. Look at its talon marks all over the branch.

We stand together in silence.

And then she gives me a look that says, clasp my hand. I do and then she pulls ever so slightly, bobbingly, like a fish on the end of a line. I follow her. Her hair is bark brown, a faded, ashy brown. She wears a dress dyed the color of not red, but red hair, orange. She makes no noise in the snow and pulls up on her dress, keeping it from collecting snowflakes. They fall and collect on her hair.

We go into a stable with a leaning roof. We are alone. I've never done this before. I'm unsure of what to do.

There are yearnings that make me understand eoten. Maybe the things that I feel in moments of desire are what eoten feel all of the time. The uncontrollable urgency and the animal heat. The want that sparks into need.

I want to be closer, closer to her, but I am touching her, I am right up next to her. It is impossible for me to be any closer but still, still I want to be closer.

The next day, I again wonder what she saw in me. And then I remember how much I saw in her.

The next night is terrible. But it does not change my night with her, Gudny. That night glows orange and blue. It stays warm as skin, pristine as snow, and is locked into a crispness of ice.

Part One

Đ   Đ   Đ

The next night. Wulfgar sleeps at the forge. I'm making rounds, bored. The snow crunches under my feet. We have worn a snow-packed path around the village, Wulfgar and I, from our rounds. The snow came; the snow comes still. Every morning we have to clear it away from our snares. We have been here six whole weeks.

It is cold tonight, so cold. Wulfgar and I have borrowed a set of furs. One of us rests, one of us wears the furs, patrols. Each time that I pass the forge, I feel its heat on my face.

The snow comes tonight in big flakes. It weighs down dead branches, breaking them in the night; the cracking echoes through the woods, distant and forlorn.

The falling snow blots out the moon. My torch makes the only light. It casts furtive yellow rays; the owl's eyes reflect them back. Yellow-dancing, the eyes sit high on the branch.

I cannot decide if he is my friend or my enemy.

Is he hunting mice? There are no mice.

I continue my round. Walk, stop, look.

Listen.

Nothing.

If there is something, will I see it? I can see to the line of trees that encircle the village. Barely.

How fast are draugr? I've asked about them but Wulfgar sees no point in telling me. He gives the usual instructions: you will see for yourself.

Breath goes out. Cold comes in.

I continue my round. Village huts made of sod, snow-covered, on my right. Cold, wind, darkness, silence on my left. My feet crunch the snow. The wind whips my torchflame.

I stop. Look.

Listen.

Nothing.

I walk.

I'm almost back around to the owl. Gods, it is cold. Part of me wishes that the draugr would just rise from the grave so that

The owl is gone.

Spine-tingles.

Look. Listen. Nothing.

I step off the path and out into the field, just a little ways from the village.

The graveyard is beyond that rise.

Silence. The flakes fall, so silent. Like noise has never existed.

I look at the torch. It is sputtering, fighting to stay lit.

I look back out at the trees. I can't see anything. Looking at the torch has muted my vision.

But I hear something. Walking. It packs the snow.

I'm shaking.

I put my hand on my sword hilt. I quietly pull on its handle. But the blade is stuck. The frost.

I look. A ribcage, just a glimpse of one. Yellow torchlight barely shows it, lighting the bars of the bone-cage.

And now: full figures standing upright, some nearer, some further. Marching, slowly. A procession.

They stride and they stride, beautifully. A steady, determined walk. I want to be like them. I want to have that poise, that steady purpose. For a moment, I can do nothing but watch.

I pull hard on my sword. The frost. I wrestle with it. It will not come.

Wulfgar, I yell. I run.

The snow slows me. I stumble, kicking whiteness into the air. Wulfgar.

He is awake, sitting down on a bench on the other side of the forge.

The draugr, he asks.

Yes. My sword is stuck, I say hurriedly. The frost.

Wulfgar extends his arm over the forge, hand open. I wrench off my sword belt and give it to him. He grabs the scabbard and holds the sword over the warmth of the forge. The heat rises between us.

The heat wobbles the air to make it look like old glass. The light is yellow and orange and softly red. His forge-lit face is gold. The heat-waves move his features.

He has a look of resolve, embodied resolve. I have seen this look on the faces engraved onto helmets, onto coins, the faces etched into metal sword hilts. It has a silver beard, almond-shaped eyes, angled, cliff-rock cheeks, and a mouth straight as the sea's horizon.

He casts off his cloak. His chainmail clinks as a handful gemstones. The cleaned metal shimmers the light of the forge. He stands and, as he straightens his legs, his back, as he comes to his full height, as he brings his massive breadth to bear, Wulfgar says in his bottomless voice,

Bring them to the forge one at a time. I will wrestle them, one by one, into the cinder-pot.

Wulfgar hands me my sword. The hilt is hot. It burns me. A pain that's better than pleasure. I am burned to action. I run into the night. Around the forge, to the draugr. Villagers wake up, make noise, but they seem far away.

The draugr march. I turn to face them, wielding my sword, hefting my shield.

They advance. The forge suddenly feels distant.

There are six draugr that I can see. More coming out of the woods. Indomitable. Undefeatable. Some carry thick branches, one drags a log to use as a club. Two must have been buried with their swords. They drag the rusty weapons over the ground. The blades etch the snow.

Their cold blows over to me, some deathly hand of wind caresses my face, my body. I shake violently. A plea crawls from my mouth. The hollow eyes. They say, I will drink the soul from your dying body like wine from a gold-gilded drinking horn.

Our traps spring, grabbing. A snare catches one by the foot. The draugr looks down at it, bending its body and back, bones creaking like thousand-year-old doors.

A snare catches another, holding it fast. It flails at the snare with its sword, confused.

There are some over here, I hear Wulfgar yell. I will come when I can, he yells over the roofs of the village.

And then I hear Hrunting whistling through the air, meeting metal, whistling again, cracking into bone. It sounds like he is felling a tree.

Two in front of me are trapped but more come. Some are closer, some further away. One has unwittingly passed by the snares.

It sees me. It has hollow eye sockets, but it sees. It drags a hefty branch through the snow.

My back is to the village. I must make my stand here.

Closer, closer. I can smell the thing: dirt and mold and must. The draugr breaks into a run over the last stretch between us, sleepy movements, heavy-footed. Its tooth-mottled jaws open like it cries for battle, but the battle cry is silent. The crunch of the packing snow, the heaving of my breath are the only noises. Shield up, sword back.

He swings his branch, uppercutting. I move my oaken shield to block. I think, it is only a branch, I can block it easily, I will counterattack.

And then I am in the snow. Unbelieving. Falling. The force of the blow is impossible. I am on my back, wriggling to get up while the draugr recovers from its strike. That could have broken my arm.

I drag myself to standing, just in time to react. Forward it comes, the same strike, uppercutting with what is left of the shattered branch. I dodge back just far enough. The branch fans the freezing air at me, barely missing my chin. My sword-arm is primed: I bring it down on the draugr's collarbone.

Like I have hit a granite boulder. Pain in my hand, down my arm. The corpse does not even move. It winds up for another swing. There is no way to dodge. I have to block. The branch hits my shield and I am on the ground again. I am barely up before the branch thuds into the man-imprint I have left in the snow.

He chases me around the snowy field. Evade him. Keep him busy.

We do this clumsy dance; more emerge from the woods. There are six now within vision, three of which are writhing and wrestling with their traps. Who knows how long those things will hold.

Two other draugr have passed the traps. I now face three opponents. The draugr are aware of each other: they form a loose circle around me.

The villagers are awake, hiding in their hovels. They watch from out of holes in the sod.

The snow falls, muffling sound. I am breathing hard, very hard. Frantic.

A noise from the village. Thank the gods. A man is coming, coming to help. We shared ale. He has an axe. Running at a draugr. His yell breaks the silence. The draugr he's after turns and winds up to strike the man. The man hits the draugr with a heavy, two-handed blow of the axe. The axe bites into the draugr's ribcage, sticks there. The man stays to try to pull it out. I say, no, get away. But it is too late. The draugr flails at the man with a bony arm. It knocks him into the draugr's other arm. It grabs at him, closes its fingerbones around the man's skull. A vicegrip. The man flails. He screams.

I run from the other two, toward the draugr that clutches the man. I swing my sword at its neck, chopping hard, though I know it will do little good.

The blade pings away from the vertebrae and I stagger from the blow. I turn to look. It has both hands on the man's skull.

I can hear it whisper, as if directly into my ear. This, this that you see now. This is what you will be.

It tightens its hands around the man's head. It pushes its hands together. The man wails an inhuman shriek. His head shatters like a blood-filled pot.

A break inside me. There was resistance before. A forlorn defiance. But the pain and the horror. The courage drains from me like blood from a stuck pig.

I urinate. The other draugr advance on me. I start to run.

And then Wulfgar comes.

He is shieldless, wielding Hrunting with both hands, running, turning the corner around a hovel like a great boulder rolling down the mountainside.

The draugr, its bones covered in blood, turns its head to look at him. It charges. It swings its weighty arm, dense and pendulous, down. Wulfgar swings his sword up to block. But the heaviness of it: he will be crushed. Impossible. He cannot block.

Wulfgar plants his feet into the snow, getting his entire weight and body under the blow. He blocks. Staunch as a pillar.

He evades, dodging another blow from the draugr, and then grabs the eoten by the top of the ribcage. He drags it forward, pulling it off balance. It stumbles and falls and flails at him as he pulls it forward. He swats its dense hands away and he starts running, dragging the draugr behind him like it's a mere bag of bones. He runs toward the forge and calls out to me in joke-tone: I've taken five at once. He says, behind you.

I leap away. Without looking. I feel the draugr's jagged blade slice my fur coat. I look up, get my bearings. They have me between them. Blocking is out. You had better be fast, Unferth.

I dodge or half-block, shearing away their strikes. Left, right, left, blows from each draugr. I do not need to strike; I evade. This draugr, now that, now this needs my attention. I turn and shear. I turn again and dodge. I feel a smoothness, a flow, like I am anticipating their moves though I am not. It is like telling a story: I do not feel entirely in control of the story, it has a life of its own. But it is rooted inside me and grows under my care.

Then, again, horror: another draugr breaks from its trap. Hacking away at the snare with its sword, it has loosed itself. It comes now, gleefully, skull-grinning.

I am caught. I cannot run. I evade, dodge, but I cannot break away from the pair I fight. The third will come and kill me. My head will be crushed in a pair of cold, bony hands; my blood will steam on the snow. The deathblow is on its way.

But. This does not feel right. This does not feel like the coming-on of death. I have been told that there will be a rightness to death when it comes. It will feel like finishing a chore, or agreeing with a friend on some opinion, or laughing at the delivery of some joke. This feels off-kilter.

Oh, it is not death on its way to me. It is Wulfgar.

Out of the silence, out of the cold, hollow night. Intercepting the falling sword of the third draugr with his own sword, with Hrunting. He swings Hrunting back up over his head, pulling up for a massive strike. The sword lowly hums, deeply whistling, carving the cold air. The sword savors its keenness. Wulfgar swings it forward and Hrunting screams a high-pitched tune like a proud falcon. The impossible: the blade meets the dense arm bone of the draugr and shears it straight off. And the draugr, for the first time, seems to feel pain. It is shocked. It pauses to look at its even-cut stump. Unbelieving.

Hrunting is one good sword.

Its gaze is still fixed on its stump as Wulfgar drags it by the backbone through the snow and to the forge.

The rest of the fight is more chore than fight: the rest of the draugr, in the traps, are singled out, one by one, and taken to the forge. I keep watch over the trapped draugr until the last is taken. For the last, I follow Wulfgar back to the forge. I watch him annihilate it.

He holds it to the flame. Orange fire, blue fire reaches up at it, grabs it, licks those cold bones. And then, igniting the bone, the fire spreads and grows. It gives out the flame-stoking noise, a wind, a grunt. And then green fire, so much green fire. Pouring out of its eye sockets, pouring from the tooth-holes in its jaw, pouring from the cracks and fissures in its skull. Bones bursting and cracking. Withered flesh withering more, curling into flakes. The draugr thrusts its hands forward, tries to push itself away from the burning. But Wulfgar is sure as stone, his face stern and confident and malevolent, his hands unbudging from the back of its skull and its serpentine spinal bones. It is a transfixing death, a transfixing re-death. When you burn, when you die when you're already dead. What kind of pain is that?

The green flame hums and blows and flows explosively from the draugr. It flies, flames lapping out from the draugr's mouth and eyes and ribcage in great length – the length of a man or more. Fire and struggle and shuddering and green light blazing, greening Wulfgar's stern face. His hands stay firm, unburnt.

The skeleton goes limp. Its charred skull falls into the forge, breaks into black bits of char. Wulfgar releases. What is left, a pair of legbones, falls to the ground. Wulfgar breathes hard. Sweat on his face, his arms. Are you burnt, I ask. He shows me his hands, scratched but not burned.

The calm, low, quiet grunt of the forge. Thirteen sets of draugr legs sprawled round.

I can't get them out of my mind. The empty eye sockets. Breeders of nightmares.

The hæftworld will gulp down your soul and crush your body into the earth. And then it will pull your corpse back out of the grave so you can wander, kill others, perpetuate death.

Ð　　　Ð　　　Ð

Spring again. We cross the mountains. Travel the mountains in the spring and you get to see the snow melt and turn into its old self, the water of the mountain stream. The flowers of the mountain rise and bloom despite the snow around them, and their beauty is clarified by this white snow, their purple, yellow, red flowers quietly throbbing in the wind. The birds and the rodents have been awake a while. The squirrels and chipmunks are keen and loud with their chidings and chirpings. The mountain birds wake the other sleeping animals with unlullabies. They sing songs of wakefulness, rousing the larger animals with rising tunes. The great sleepers, the bears, are just now waking up from their lengthy slumberings. Wulfgar and I see a she-bear, groggy and slow-pawing, just out of long hibernation. Cubs with her.

There is all this color and sound as Wulfgar and I approach the highest point of the trail. It runs itself between two mountain peaks. We are leaving one kingdom, entering another. We approach the top. It rises and rises. We breathe heavily as we go. I look up at the view above us and I see only mountainside and blue sky. Reaching the top, panting, we look over the edge of the mountain and new valleys are there in front of us, sweeping low and long and gentle like the roots of Yggdrasil.

I am sad to leave the village because I enjoyed the company of the men who thought highly of me after my action against the draugr. And there was Gudny. But now, as I ascend this mountain, I do not feel apart from them. There is something about a mountaintop that changes missing. Miss your lover, your father, your brother, or your former self. Take this missing and spend all day climbing to the peak of the mountain. And then look out at the world. If you look out over it all, you will still miss them, but missing isn't so bad from up there. You can see so far that you feel like you can almost see all the way to whoever you miss. And anything you can see you can get to.

I am no wise man but I am a smart man and I have learned something: mind what you want. Tend it. Remember it. Wear it around your neck or have it tattooed on your leg or cut into your palm.

Though mountain birds and mountaintops are things to see, the thing that you really want, the thing that you live for, is the thing that pulls you down from that mountaintop.

Wulfgar. He's thick, heavy. Poised and relaxed. He starts again. Walks pendulously down the mountain slope in front of me.

Stern. Brave. Balanced. Strong. Better intuition than Odin. Harsher than he intends and kinder than he knows. Tender. But only if you can see it.

I follow Wulfgar.

Ð   Ð   Ð

I meet my rival Beowulf like all men meet their rivals: one man sees another man doing something unbelievable.

Wulfgar and I enter the land of the Geats. The country is blooming. Unimaginable amounts of flowers, purple and white and yellow. They grow out in the fields but they also grow under dense canopies of trees where there is no sun. In roads and foot-paths. Out of rocks. Out of sand. You trample them everywhere you go.

We are on our way to the hall of Hygelac and Beowulf, a king and his nephew, the most renowned warlords in the region and beyond, to see what other work there is. Hygelac and Beow-ulf receive pleas to kill eoten from all kinds of people. But they are usually too busy or too lazy or too proud to accept. So slaga come to them and hang around them until jobs come up. And so Hygelac's kingdom has become a kind of center for the eoten-tormented to find help and for slaga to find work.

Beowulf's reputation has reached the ears of all in the king-dom, and many outside it. Men know at least his name. Those who know him personally may know of his big boast, his claim that he will slay a fyrdraca some day. Beowulf will slay a fyrdraca. Yes, and someday there will be no eoten and warriors will rally out of their halls to slay the pink and blue flowers of the land, cutting them down with long, wispy swords made from strands of fog.

Hygelac is a good king. Proud, Wulfgar says, and a slaga descended from a line of slaga. He says, when kings hunt eoten, they bring hordes of household guards. They do more rounding up of eoten than real hunting. They don't have the skill to hunt something smart enough to escape, like orcneas. And they don't have the will to hunt those that are hard to find like the sea-prowling nicor or feonda, or those that require a man to be unafraid of caves and the subterranean world, like trolls or haugbui.

Wulfgar talks through his blonde-grey beard, wavy and kempt. He says, but these royal bastards are important because they can command large groups of men and so are needed for trolls or other big eoten. For fyrdraca, if one ever comes around. Hygelac is a cocky man but a good man. I last saw him about five years ago. His nephew, Beowulf, showed promise in continuing the strength of the house.

And so we ride, me and Wulfgar, myself in brown and black like some streak or slash of night in this uprising of flower-color. In front of me on his horse, Wulfgar, blonde-haired, full-bearded, flat-nosed. He's in his red shirt and green pants, fitting in with the flowers and the trees and grasses. We ride through the squirreled woods toward the hall of Hygelac. Eventually, we hear the blow of a horn. A mournful alarum. A boar hunt.

It sounds again. We turn our horses toward the sound and quicken our pace. It must be Hygelac and Beowulf, says Wulfgar. Wulfgar says, we are nearly there. It could be the pair we're looking for. He clicks his tongue, comes to a gallop on his horse. I kick mine forward.

We ride, swift but controlled. Wulfgar says over the hoof-rumble, have you seen a boar hunt? I have not, though I have heard of boar hunting, more dangerous than hunting some types of eoten. Wulfgar says over the hoof-rumble, there are a few ways to do it. Most men trap the boar against some boulder or rock wall, or inside a circle of men. The boar does not go willingly. It will charge. It will usually charge the man who shouts the loudest, or the man who has injured the boar, or the man who moves the most.

We duck a tree limb as it goes rushing by. Wulfgar says, but you can only kill a boar when it charges at you. So once the boar is surrounded, the men dismount and the man to kill it shouts and moves and threatens the boar, and the boar charges him. The man kneels down and waits for his moment. He has to time it perfectly. He waits for the boar to impale itself on his spear, which he will lift up in front of him just at the right moment. If he is too early, the boar will flinch and his stab will glance off the boar's skull or tusk or hide and the man will die. If the man is too late, the spear will catch the boar in the belly or the leg. The boar will trample him and tusk him and the man will die. But just at the right moment, the man raises a spear that he has laid on the ground in front of him, point toward the charging boar. He pulls up the tip and wedges the base of the spear into the ground with his foot. The tip must penetrate through the animal's throat or to its heart.

Wulfgar finishes just as we come to an old man on his horse. We rein in our horses. The old man's horse looks over at ours.

That is one big horse. Big and black. The man's grey hair streams out from beneath a helmet that covers his entire head and face. A helmet worth more than five good slaves.

Are we too late, shouts Wulfgar in his gravel-voice.

The other man looks over at Wulfgar. His voice comes slow but sure. His words are deliberate. He says, no, you're not too late, you must be why Odin has let this boar escape us at every turn. He wanted you to see it. Hail, Wulfgar.

Wulfgar looks around for Hygelac's nephew, Beowulf. He is not yet in sight, but hooves can be heard thundering toward us. Hygelac says, watch. You will never forget this. Wulfgar says out loud, bellowing, I don't see anything. Apparently I have already forgotten.

Hygelac's head laughs in its metal cage.

Hooves thunder, the horn brums. The boar approaches, running on its stubby legs, scuttering away from six horsemen.

I now see Beowulf. I will not forget.

He must be an eoten. He has the largest horse I have seen. But this man looks like he could wrestle it to the ground.

The men surround the boar on their horses. The boar snorts in frustration and turns around, looking from one horsed man to the next.

Beowulf stops his horse, dismounts.

He is massive. Freakish muscles. Thor has a hammer named Mjolnir that can slay anyone. I would rather have Beowulf's body.

He has no neck. More a head-root. His long moustache and cropped beard and head hair are well-tarnished gold: a dull yellow, with hints of dazzling red. Blue-green eyes.

He wears chainmail, but the armor has no sleeves. My eyes go to his arms. He has too many muscles. His arms are tangles of muscle and sinew. It is grotesque. The arms ripple with deep power. He dismounts from his horse and the stringy arm muscles flex and pluck like strings on a lyre. You can almost hear them sing.

He lands on the ground. His legs are enormous, each as big as my torso. It is a wonder that he can walk. I cannot see his stomach. Probably a range of valleys and hills.

His chest: a surging, rolling swell. The chainmail armor hangs from its shelf. And his mantle: those shoulders, bulbous and swollen. They rise like waves to make him look like he is crashing forward like a surging surf, like he is always hurling himself forward.

The boar snarls and hoots in rage, turning its hooves and its body to find a way out or gore the man who keeps it from roaming free. It is brown with bristling hairs on its ridged back. It has two yellowed tusks that could break through any armor, could gore the life out of men. Enormous and powerful. This circle of warriors. Bulky Beowulf. This writhing beast. An arena of muscle.

The men tighten their circle around the boar. It prepares to charge. It has picked a man opposite Beowulf. It paws and snorts and screams, riling itself up to kill.

Beowulf springs forward. Fast as a fox, arms pumping madly, feet tearing up clods of dirt. He leaps with a rumbling grunt.

The boar turns around to look at this noise. It squeals in surprise and anger. It gets its tusks around just as Beowulf comes within reach.

He grabs them. He grabs the tusks. The boar thrashes them in fury. There are no things more powerful than a boar thrashing its tusks. Beowulf holds on. He holds its tusks firm and, instead of it thrashing him, he thrashes it. He stands and shakes that boar by the tusks. He pulls it to the ground and he wraps it in man-limbs. He wraps his legs around its belly. He wraps his right arm around its neck, if boars have a neck. He grabs his right forearm with his left hand, making a vice of arms around that tree-thick neck to choke it.

He squeezes. The sinews under his skin pop up to reveal themselves like worms during rain. The boar wriggles and bellows and paws at the air. Beowulf closes his eyes. A calm comes over him.

He must be digging for strength, digging into some fathomless place. His face is serene except for his eyebrows, which are upturned. Like he is pleading for something. You'd have the same expression if you were soothing an infant.

His arm tightens and tightens around the boar's neck. It can't tighten any more. But still he tightens. I cannot believe it. The neck is squeezed impossibly small. The boar stops squealing. Its windpipe is crushed. But it still struggles, twisting itself and pawing at the air with its sharp hooves. And still, still he tightens his arm around its neck. Thor, the force. The force to squeeze the dense boarflesh so tightly. The animal's neck, before as thick as a goodsized softwood, has been squeezed down to the size of a woman's arm. Blood seeps from its eyes, its nose, its mouth. The animal's black eyes bulge. A last surge of urgency. It flails its limbs. And then something gives inside it and the boar goes limp. Beowulf lets go.

Hygelac looks over at Wulfgar, helmet off now, and smiles.

It is sickening.

I think about what Wulfgar has done. Wulfgar ambushed, blinded and killed sixty orcneas. Wulfgar knows how to find, trap, and kill men of bone that rise from the ground. Wulfgar killed two giants with a dead whale. The skill, the mind that it took to perform these feats. They are things to swell a man's chest. To give him comfort at any old age.

And then there is this man.

We must think better than eoten, Wulfgar told me once, because we cannot do anything else better than them. Wulfgar had said, but this is good. It is the eoten who rely on something as inelegant as instinct. That is what makes them eoten. He said we, you and me and the other slaga, Unferth, do what the gods want us to do: we think like Odin, we trick like Loki. And then when the time is right, we pound like Thor. We make the gods proud.

Will Beowulf make the gods proud? This man could kill eoten single-handedly, using just his muscle. He could and he will and the craft of slaga will never be the same. Wulfgar will never be first among the slaga; no one could be first above Beowulf's power.

I look at Hygelac from the corner of my eye. He watches Beowulf with admiration. What is it like to be related to some half-beast, some freak of muscle and ligament?

Beowulf, nephew of Hygelac and thus a prince, looks at me. The breeze plays with his blonde hair. He is maybe two years younger than me, but I am lanky and waif-like in front of him.

I have never before felt that I've truly known myself. But now I do. Here is who I am: I am the opposite of that man.

His name is Beowulf, his father says, introducing us.

It is our reputation only that endures. Beowulf will find fame, I can tell. I am jealous. I want a reputation. I want for men to talk about my cunning. At the mead-table, I want to speak words that honey the ears of men and women and set them to dropping their half-chewed chicken bones as they forget themselves, forget the world while listening to me rattle off my stories about the cleverness that I used to slay eoten.

Or maybe I'll just be Unferth, the man who opposed Beowulf.

Beowulf gives me a sarcastic look that says, well, who are you. He smiles a sharp, crooked-toothed smile.

I want to throw a rock at his face. Right at that slab of a forehead.

I already know how men keep their hatred going. I already know how men nurse and grow their hatred for each other over months and years and decades and generations. But in this moment I finally learn how that hatred begins.

Ð   Ð   Ð

Courtesy demands that Hygelac invite us to his hall and courtesy demands that Wulfgar accepts. It is strange that we listen to our traditions over our common sense. We'll be doing that forever. Everyone but me.

We group up to ride back. Wulfgar is on edge, like he expects Beowulf to reveal himself as an eoten, like he thinks Beowulf's body is just a husk taken on by some shape-changer. Beowulf ties parts of the boar carcass to our horses. Not to his own. He is too much for his horse already.

We leave the woods on the way back to Hygelac's hall, trotting onto the great plain. The ride is long for coming home from a day hunt. But it's always good to see a king's territory before speaking much with that king. You can't know a man without knowing what kind of landscapes he sees.

They are Geats, a proud people who have lost and gained much over the years. They are an all-or-nothing people. This gets them into trouble. They always love you or hate you. To them, there are never so-so men. Those who they love they treat as gods. Those who they hate they do not spare. But like I said, it gets them into trouble: if a man hates you fully, he'd never show you mercy. And you never want to show mercy to a man who would never show mercy to you.

The sun is setting. It throws our shadows in front of us as we ride up a long grassy incline to Hygelac's city. The sunset is all red, almost pink. Like the flesh of salmon. I crane my neck over my shoulder to look at the salmon-set as we ride east. My horse bumps into the horse of one of Hygelac's thanes. He grumbles at me like a drowsy bear.

Hygelac's hall is impressive. Tall-gabled and long, the walls lined with weapons and body parts. There are human skulls from slain warlords, other trophies from various eoten. Wulfgar points these out to me. Claws of a ketta, the rake-shaped nose of a haugbui, even the tooth of a brimwylf, a sea-prowler that even Wulfgar has never seen.

Me and Hygelac and Beowulf and Wulfgar sit, joined by some of their thanes. Hygelac can even afford a scop; the man sits across from us and strums softly on his lyre. Hygelac's wife takes around a bowl of mead. Breca, a long-time friend of Beowulf, introduces himself.

The bragging begins strong and early. Hygelac's thanes are tired of their king's bragging; I can see it on their faces the moment that the old turd opens his mouth. Hygelac's wife sits with so much patience and discipline that it frightens me. She looks morbid. Who knows what he expects of her, what he makes her do. Hygelac is a demanding king, and strict.

It has crossed my mind before that women cannot always do what they want. Unless maybe they are some outcast witch. Maybe if we are to make them obey, we should also ensure that they are happy. Men shouldn't miskeep their wives. Just as it is with horses.

Women can ask for divorce, but what woman can ever hope to divorce a king? What would her father say? Her brother?

Hygelac starts talking about the fame that his son Beowulf will win, that his son has already won. Hygelac's wife's ears perk up at this. So do Wulfgar's. Beowulf is stronger than any troll, a better swimmer than any scuccum or scinnum, says Hygelac. Unafraid of trolls, and anything else. We killed a troll not three months ago, he says. And the orcneas attacked two weeks ago but we sent them home wailing like babes.

Some of Hygelac's thanes are speaking to each other, ignoring him, but some are listening to what Hygelac is saying. I look around the room to see how the men take Hygelac's praise of his son. The young thanes are paying attention, which means that Hygelac's praise is sought by them, but the old thanes pay no mind. They have Wulfgar's bored-with-the-world look. Those old thanes are a rough lot, even for Geats. Scarred. Men with appetites for giving and taking pain.

Beowulf eats. He stuffs himself like a dog that found its way into the pantry.

Hygelac's wife is the wisest of the Geats, according to Wulfgar. She stares at Wulfgar. Maybe she thinks, I will learn something from him if I listen closely enough. Maybe I will learn something that can save my son Beowulf from some eoten. It is obvious that one will kill him some day. The strongest and stupidest men always die. Maybe she's thinking, how can I do anything to save this stupid man.

Wulfgar listens to Hygelac's bragging. Wulfgar drinks from the large bowl, now filled with wine, and passes it along. He lounges on his bench with that master's posture, that never-surprised but ever-watchful look. Like an owl. I look into his face. He is laughing inwardly. I can't tell for sure what he's laughing at. Maybe at kings and fathers and boasters and men in general.

When Hygelac's boasting is done, calm as ever, Wulfgar leans forward and puts his elbows on his knees and asks Hygelac some questions. He learns that Hygelac lost six thanes against the troll. And that the orcneas made it back to their hole, that they were not chased and rounded up and exterminated.

Six thanes. Does Hygelac plan on losing six men every single time a troll wanders up to his door? And the orcneas: foolish. If you don't kill them all, they only breed more. They will just hide and breed until they have enough. If you fight them, you have to kill every last orcnea. Every last one. And even still sometimes they come back. Sometimes you can't ever find their lair, their brood, their tucked-away eggs.

A moment comes back to me: my first fight with orcneas. Guarding the lower exit, told to not let any through. One had escaped. We had not killed them all. I told Wulfgar about it on our way back to the village but he just shrugged because he was angry about being lied to. I would do the same.

Now Wulfgar rebukes him. He implies that Hygelac is a fool. That his people will be attacked and eaten up by orcneas. That, with sloppy slaga work, his hall may not stand. It could be coated with the blood of thanes that deserve a better king.

Wulfgar doesn't fear this warlord, or anyone else. My heart sings for him.

It is a serious thing to soothsay something so damning. To ward off such curses, men sacrifice animals. Or more.

The thanes are tense. I am glad that it is the custom of the Geats to leave their weapons at the door. Hygelac slams his fist onto the table and roars at Wulfgar, maybe with hostility, maybe playfully, telling Wulfgar to outboast him if he can. It takes a skilled king to, in one phrase, seem menacing to his thanes but friendly to his guests.

Wulfgar stands up, his master's poise draped over him like a heavy cape. His beard is long and straight, flowing. It is grey-blonde with two silver stripes in his moustache, like the stripes of a badger. The beard frames his wrinkled face.

There is a reason that men have beards, and double the reason that a mature man has a grey beard. A man who is strong enough to have vigor in his movements but who is also old enough to possess a silvered beard is the finest of men, the best in the world at whatever it is he does. It is like the grizzle on a huge male bear, like the foam on a breaking wave. It says to its enemies, leaning over them and giving them a stern eye: steer clear of me. Jabbing a pointed finger into the chest of its enemies, it says, the only thing that can defeat me is time, and you do not look like time.

Wulfgar will now tell the story of the two trolls; surely he has no greater boast. But instead he says, have you heard of the Grinder.

The Grinder. Grendel. The one who grinds men. Shreds them with his teeth. Pulverizes them with his fists. If monsters had rulers, Grendel would be king. A night-wolf, a marauding, gluttonous, blood-drinking fiend. Strong, so strong, able to collapse a hall with only his taloned fists. He stands twice, three times the height of a man. He rips men in half and drinks their blood. Most eoten his size are slow and can be outmaneuvered. But Grendel's greatest strength is his quickness. He is faster in the fight than any man, as fast over land as the best of horses. He can smash anything and evade any blow. Unkillable, they say.

No one can say for sure what he looks like; all that claim to have seen him disagree. To this man he is slimy and frog-like, to that man he is a great furry bear, to another he is a giant, bony draugr risen from the corpse of a huge troll. But all agree on one thing: there is a light in his eyes. His eyes are seats and souls of malice that burn and broil, orbs that bounce in the night. They glow, lighting up his shadowy grin below.

Hygelac says dismissively, Grendel. If he is real, you could never kill him.

That sparkle enters Wulfgar's eye. That hint of lively mischief. He smiles. He crosses his arms over his chest, says, Thor, sometimes I think that it takes a hundred years for news to get up here.

Hygelac's wife looks at Wulfgar. With the slightest smile.

Wulfgar says, he is more than a myth; you would call him more than myth if you ever came face to face with him yourself. He says, you are right, Grendel may be unkillable. But I did just as good. I trapped the Grinder deep in the earth, between stone and stone and stone and darkness. In the land of the Danes. And I could take you to the cave that he is trapped in and we could pound on the stone that blocks him in and yell his name and he would roar mine back. If he is still alive. If he hasn't starved or been eaten by something even bigger down there in the depths.

Hygelac shakes his head dismissively. He does not believe.

Yes, he can speak, says Wulfgar. Wulfgar turns toward Hygelac's transfixed thanes. He says, I told him my name so that he can grind on it. And he is down there now, grinding away, though not grinding on what he's used to grinding. He shouts in his madness, tormenting himself, making himself more and more monster. But he will never get free.

Silence.

He shrugs at me. His shrug says, I suppose I forgot to tell you. And then he brings out that sly smile. His smile draws out my own smile like a budding leaf. You never told me. Wulfgar, you sneaky bastard. You sneaky bastard.

Grendel is a thing of legend. Grendel is an eoten that is too scary to not believe in but too unbelievable to ever think real. No one can possibly top this boast. Is it true? They all deny it, but they really believe him, to a man. I can see it in their eyes.

Hygelac has decided that he had has heard enough of Wulfgar's talk. He says, my boast is in my nephew. I will show you my nephew's true strength. There have been no eoten in my area of late, but there is another way that I can show you. Tomorrow, we will have a swimming contest. He will show his quality.

We all look over at Beowulf.

Face-down over his bowl. Feeding his mouth. Somehow, through some feat of gluttony, he is still eating.

Silence. The whole hall looks at him. He doesn't look up.

Ð   Ð   Ð

The sea will take many things. Try it. Give the sea something and see if it takes it. It accepts almost anything. Sometimes, it will only let the thing float on its surface. But the sea is hungry. Generally, throw something into the sea and it will gladly swallow it.

But there are some things that the sea will not take.

Like a fool, Beowulf offered himself to the sea and I thought that I would be rid of him as soon as I found him. But the sea spat him back out.

Generally, if a man enters the water wearing chainmail, he dies. If he has hold of something, some rope or oar or piece of wood, he will maybe avoid drowning. But chainmail will drown a man surer than any flood, any sea-storm.

So when Beowulf decided to enter the water wearing chainmail, I thought, thank Odin that this fool is foolish in a way that will kill him.

A swimming contest with Breca. Wearing chainmail.

Beowulf smiles vacantly as he warms up his arms. His front two teeth are yellowed and slanted; one nudges in front of the other in a way that makes him look like a child.

Breca is limbering his arms too. I know that he is smarter than this but I also know that his pride pulls him into it. I do not fault him terribly. But Beowulf is different. He's performing for his father, which is worse, much worse. Even if it is false pride, it is much better to own your own pride than to carry around the pride of your mother or father or uncle.

Breca and Beowulf have been friends since childhood; they have done this before. Breca has a swimmer's body – tall, with long arms and wide hands. But Beowulf. Can he swim?

Hygelac stands on the mud-rock shore in his armor, ever in his armor. His wife has come too. She does a poor job of hiding her glances at Wulfgar.

The contest is decided as any contest between grown men is decided: on the spot, with clear objectives. Swim out to that rock.

A few of Hygelac's thanes row out there to judge who arrives first and to take the swimmers back. Beowulf and Breca strip down to their skin. Hygelac gives them their chainmail. They put it over their naked bodies. Beowulf is one hairy man.

The chainmail is heavy, so heavy. Breca puts on the weighty metal tunic like he goes to his execution. If he doubts himself, he's doing a hero's job of hiding it. I almost feel sorry for him.

All I want for Beowulf is for his idiocy to drown him, as it should. He hops up and down twice in the sand-mud to test the weight of the tunic. His feet sink deep into the black, rocky earth. He looks right, left, not looking for or at anything. Just looking because he feels like he should.

The two men ready themselves, standing at the waterline. Hygelac looks at them and hesitates. And then, amused, he gives the signal.

The men are off, running through the mud and into the sea. Beowulf runs powerfully, easily taking the lead. The men stride into the water.

I gawk, mouth open. Beowulf cannot swim. Was he never taught? Or: can you be dumb enough to forget how to swim?

Breca shoots ahead, somehow, despite the chainmail. Beowulf flounders. The splashing and crashing of water. He struggles with it like he is trying to rape it. His arms flail in opposite directions. He digs down through the water to the mud-rock beach.

Wulfgar and I sneer at each other. We giggle as Beowulf's arms start digging into the gravel. His swim-digging kicks up sandy clods. They come lobbing through the air, plopping down all around us, around Hygelac and Hygelac's wife and the other thanes. Hygelac's wife dodges one gravel clod but they are as unavoidable as turds from a flock of scared seagulls. They speckle everything on the beach – me, the royal braggarts, their horses and thanes. Mud rain everywhere. Beowulf's struggle intensifies. The clods become bigger and fall on us in large, fist-sized globs. Hygelac's thanes curse and Hygelac's wife shouts and Wulfgar and I hoot. Wulfgar yells at Beowulf: is there a shortcut down there?

And then Beowulf seems to figure out how to swim or at least how to propel himself through water. He moves forward through the sea, his powerful arms heaving over each other. Breca is a distance away from the shore by now. Beowulf looks around for where to go. His vision is poor and he has a hard time seeing the island. So when he sees Breca churning the water out to sea, Beowulf just follows him.

Ð   Ð   Ð

Beowulf lost. He caught up to Breca, and even passed him. I should have expected this. But Beowulf swam like some writhing animal. Think of a struggling fish and the sea-predators that perk up at the sound of it. They think, easy prey. If you were a scavenging shark or prowling eoten and you could hear the thrashing of what sounded like the biggest dying meal you had ever heard, would you not go try for a bite?

Breca arrived at the island first, desperately heaving for air. Beowulf was nowhere to be seen so we went out looking for him. I thought maybe he had used all his energy flailing around. Or maybe he accidentally swam down to the bottom of the sea and drowned. Intelligence told me that, yes, he drowned. But wisdom said: no, you are not done with Beowulf. He is too good an oddity and too great an annoyance for him to depart so soon, Unferth.

We find him thrashing around with a shark. There are corpses of sea-beasts floating in the brackish water all around him. Well, if you kill one sea beast, others smell the blood and they come too. So they came and came and attacked Beowulf and he killed them and then more came and he killed those too. So there he is, treading water and wrestling with some shark, grabbing it by the head and the tail and trying to fold it in half to break its back. But it's a slippery thing. It flops out of his grip. He grabs for it with clumsy hands but it's thrashing around too much and Beowulf gets a tail-slap on the face right before the shark plops into the water and swims away. Beowulf scowls.

The water around him is filled with beasts of all kinds. Floating, bobbing carcasses. Sharks, but also things that I have never seen. Wulfgar points them out and tells me their names. But there are also some he does not know. He grabs the corpse of one, a long, spiny, red-green eel-like creature with a big, armored head. Beowulf broke its jaw off. The jaw dangles by a single sinew. Wulfgar pulls the dead creature into the boat to get a better look. Hygelac's thanes pull Beowulf into the boat, sopping and heavy-breathing. Frustrated as a cat stuck in a water barrel.

We row away from that floating carcass-hoard, leaving it for the water-wanderers who would come next.

Ð   Ð   Ð

We row over a calm sea, through a cold misting rain. Back to Hygelac's hall. The mists hide everything but the shore, which Hygelac's steersman keeps on his left. The sand is black.

The shore of the sea is where I first met Wulfgar. He was coming to my village to kill an eoten. And then, four days later, on the same beach, as I was looking down at the black sand, he spoke to me in his rocky voice. He offered to take me with him because he did not save my parents.

Ever since, the sea has reminded me of death. The smell of it, the rhythm of it. Death, death, the wind whispers to me over the waves, death, the waters say as they lick the sand from the shore. Most men love the sea. But when I am near the sea I feel that I am just waiting to drown.

Ð   Ð   Ð

Wulfgar and I have not forgotten what Beowulf's strength means for Wulfgar, for slaga everywhere. But we can forget for now: he's bringing out the drink.

Hygelac settles from angry disappointment into resignation. It bothers him that his favorite kinsman, his nephew Beowulf, has made a fool of himself. Hygelac grabs up a horn of mead. He orders a pig slaughtered. He is a man who comforts himself in this setback; he does not torment himself with it. No one ever admits loss, no one with a reputation. But there are setbacks. Kings had better know how to handle setbacks, says Wulfgar. Some kings hit their women. Some kings drink. Hygelac eats.

So there is fresh pork at the meal. Hygelac also has a taste for the exotic. His women boiled some fruit and mixed that with mead and a strange brown spice that grows in the shape of curled, brown sticks. A trader brought them from the east. Hygelac gave the trader a thick silver arm-ring for four sticks. The bread is good, too, and we have the first of the season's berries. Eat a tart berry after a long winter and your jaw paralyzes in that pain-tingle.

No one speaks of Beowulf's failure in front of king Hygelac; his thanes are all man-gossiping: talking about neighboring factions or threats, where the next war will come from. The Jutes, they say. No, it is the Danes that we should worry about. Hygelac watches them absent-mindedly. He doesn't want to hear it. He calls for his scop to tell a story.

The scop is old but not decrepit. He has perhaps a year left to him. His cloak is fastened over his shoulder with a great brooch, big as your hand, made of silver. It is heavy, so heavy that he has to wear it almost on top of his shoulder so that it doesn't pull the cloak forward off of his back. It is an impressive token. I don't think he earned that brooch in a battle. Some king gave him that for doing something great.

The man gets up, solemnly drags his stool closer to us, sits back down, puts his hands on his knees and leans on them like he cannot at the same time support himself and also tell his heavy tale.

But the story flows out of his mouth smoothly and evenly and well-paced. He is a word-fountain. He says, a little girl once found a branch of Yggdrasil, which stuck up ever-reaching from the ground into the sky. The branch was this world's link to the rest of the worlds on the tree Yggdrasil. She tore at the bark of that branch and broke a bit off. That piece of wood, on its own, twisted itself into a lyre. It bent itself into the perfect lyre shape, cracking and reaching. It splintered to form the strings of the instrument, which sung like the voices of trees, and it was always in tune. The girl became the first scop, and to this day she whispers into the ears of scops everywhere, telling them their stories. I can hear her now. She is still a child, and impatient. She wants me to get on with it.

It is the story of Ragnarok. Ragnarok, the time of the firing of the sky and the melting of the land and the upheaval of all that is rooted.

He says, someday, all of the troublesome gods and eoten will finally be trapped. The gods will finally trap Loki, the trickiest of the gods. And we do our own trapping. We trap the eoten by killing them, by sending them to Hel. They will keep coming and we will keep killing.

But then time will end.

And after time ends, Loki and all of the eoten – all the fyrdraca and the draugr and the trolls and the orcneas and the scuccum and scinnum – will all escape from Hel and the places where they were trapped. They will fight against Odin. But others will fight for Odin. All those who have been taken to the corpse-hall will rally out and fight for their lord, fight for Odin against Fenrir the wolf and the uncountable eoten.

He says, Odin will be devoured by Fenrir the wolf. And then Odin's son, Vidar, will kill Fenrir. Tyr will die, and so will Thor, after he has split Midgard, the World Serpent, the beast that shores up the seas. Thor will split the serpent and it will spew poison onto Thor and Thor will fall. Heimdall and Loki will kill each other. Surt will kill Frey and then Surt will burn the universe. The stars will fall from the sky and clutter the ground. The sun will be blotted out and the sea will surge over its banks and drown the world.

The scop says, the world will get darker and darker and it may even get dark enough so that light can no longer exist.

He says, and the only thing that will exist will be one person. One of Odin's warriors. He will despair because he has lost everything. He will be cold, hungry, friendless. The light of the world will fade and fade and sink and the dark water will rise. The universe will soon be beyond hope: it gets darker and darker and colder and wetter. Eventually it will forget that it can be warm, that it can have light.

The man, shivering and sulking, will give up. He will think: what did we do, Odin? Or: what did we not do?

Years will pass and the man will watch the universe darken and darken. He will shiver in its vacuous coldness. It will diminish, then diminish further. The man will get his sword out to kill himself.

This man has the habit of turning his sword hilt in his hand before he is to use it. He does this now. He does this and he remembers. He remembers Odin. He wants to fight against Odin's parting though the god has long ago parted. He wants to fight against Odin's parting not for himself and not entirely for Odin but because the world has taken the last of his treasures from him and he cannot bear to do nothing about it. But there is nothing to do. Odin is gone.

And the scop says, and what will come next? Even the little girl who whispers in my ear does not know. Even she, the peeler of the bark of Yggdrasil, cannot tell. She says, though, that she can feel it. She says that it feels like the meeting of opposites. It feels like a cold heat, like a waking dream. It is like a cavern that fills the earth instead of emptying it out. It is like an ocean of air.

She says she cannot know what will come next just as she cannot touch her own water-reflected face without distorting it, without sending ripples rolling over its surface.

Đ   Đ   Đ

The next day. Wulfgar and I begin our wait to be called on to kill eoten. We don't wait long.

The door to the hall opens and four of Hygelac's thanes, fully-armored, walk in.

Spine-tingles. Danger.

Would Hygelac dare?

Is he so protective of his nephew's reputation?

They escort a man into the room. I relax. A messenger. It is a messenger.

The guard announces that the man is from Hrothgar. We all know Hrothgar: a king of the Danes. A man known for generosity.

The messenger frowns. Sad news has to overcome a lot to put a frown on a messenger's face. If a messenger ever looks sad, it is very bad news indeed. Because a messenger is usually happy to arrive: he has food and warmth and sometimes women waiting for him at a king's hall.

Hrothgar wants help, the messenger says. There is a sceadu-gengan.

Sceadu-gengan is what we call any eoten that we do not know the name of. Something new. Something that walks in the shadowy corners of men's minds.

I look to Wulfgar. Wulfgar detects something in the man's words. And, yes, I think I hear it too. The man has bottled up the king's fear and now spills it here in front of us, spills it all over us. Fear from a king like Hrothgar is no passing thing. Hrothgar does not fear plague or invasion or the death of his children; they have happened to him and he has weathered all. But Hrothgar fears now.

Wulfgar looks intently at the messenger. Sniffs the man with his eyes. He smells something dark, something that chews the bones of men.

Tell us about the sceadu-gengan, says Beowulf, sucking a hard-boiled egg.

The messenger describes it: huge, tall as a troll but not so thick. Stealthier than any creature. Consumes men whole. Raids Hrothgar's hall when his people gather in it. Tears them up and drinks their blood and plays with their corpses. Massacred thirty men at once.

Beowulf guesses, a troll?

Thirty men at once. This is no troll. Though many warriors could die fighting a troll, thirty battle-hard thanes could kill any troll. This is something else.

The messenger's thoughts go to something remembered, something else. His face contorts. He himself has seen it.

His mouth molds into something that might create a wail. He suppresses it. The pain is great. He fights for composure. He lost someone to this monster. His father, I think, or a favorite brother. He pushes his brown hair out of his eyes and forces composure onto himself. He continues.

Hrothgar's hall is called Heorot and the sceadu-gengan hates this place, he says. Any time we are inside it, the monster comes stalking. He kills sentries before they can yell out. The doors of Heorot burst open under the slightest touch of his claws. His power. He walks and things wither at his feet; he touches men and they become meat-pieces.

He says, the thanes fight and fight but it is always to no avail. Three times – Heorot has been attacked three times, chock-full of armed-to-the-teeth thanes, and three times the hall has been bathed in blood. The timbers of the hall have been so soaked with the fluids of men that they are now red even after they are washed.

The messenger says, and in the morning the corpses are wide-ranged, pinned on their own spears or broken in half or chewed. Many go missing, those who the sceadu-gengan has taken to his fen. The sceadu-gengan has an arm-pouch, a vast skin flap that he stuffs men into and carries away. Who knows what happens to them. There are men's teeth buried so deep into the floor of Heorot that we would have to pry up the timbers to get them out. But there they stay because men don't even go inside. They fear that, if they go in, the sceadu-gengan will come again.

All of us, surely even Wulfgar, we are all thinking: it could be the Grinder, Grendel. Or his kin. It is the same area that he used to haunt. Wulfgar trapped Grendel in the ground only a half-day's journey from Hrothgar's hall.

Hygelac says to Wulfgar, so much for your big boast.

Wulfgar looks at Hygelac. He wants to ask for the king's help. They are arrogant, cushioned royal bastards, but they could help. Though Beowulf is dumber than a log, he is still powerful and would make a good distraction. It would take a lot of time, a lot of wringing and twisting to pull Beowulf in half.

Just as Wulfgar opens his mouth to ask something of Hygelac, Hygelac raises his hand and says, tend your own pets, Wulfgar.

Wulfgar turns toward the door. I follow. We walk, heavy-footed, out of Hygelac's hall. As we walk, Wulfgar looks at me, gives me a nod. It is a man's nod. Outside, Wulfgar says, now you know the difference between slaga like them and slaga like us.

Đ Đ Đ

We board a trading ship to the Danes, agreeing to row in exchange for passage to Hrothgar's kingdom. To answer his call.

Wulfgar and I row next to each other. He sticks his head up, sticks it out over the side of the boat like he wants to get the full whiff of the sea, to feel its spray. The boat struggles forward in the blue chop. Wulfgar sits back down, grunts in pleasure. He pulls his oar like he's pulling himself toward a new beginning. He loves it, this pre-fight feeling, this challenge-to-be.

I am coming to know the feeling. It is felt by the dusty craftsman on his way to his workbench, by the rough blacksmith as he walks to his forge, by the scarred soldier on his way to the battlefield. The knowledge of work to be done, and it feels good because it reminds the man that he has molded himself around a craft, that he has grown to love it, that he has let it grow into him like tree-roots into stone. Returning to good work is like going to visit the side of yourself that is still pure.

Đ　　　Đ　　　Đ

The moon of the Danes, which is to say no moon, is out. The night sky matches the water: black, with only the sparsest bits of shine. The shine-bits are on the water's surface during the day. They move up into the sky at night.

The soothing slag-slop of ocean waves. We search for a landing spot. The merchant captain knows his trade; I can tell by the tone of his voice and the dry floor of his boat.

He slows the ship. It beaches, grinding the gravel. Wulfgar and I step out. He gives the merchant some silver for his trouble though we rowed to pay our fare. He was happy to have us. We are slaga.

Me and Wulfgar bring our horses ashore. They are hesitant. They do not like stepping into some void at night. The merchant puts off, leaving us.

We bed down. We'll hike to Hrothgar tomorrow.

There is nothing to see but the stars.

I wonder at all of the eoten out there, all of the eoten that live in caves and swamps and in cindering volcanoes. All the twisted horns, the teeth, the bristled fur and the armored carapaces that I have not seen, that no one has ever seen. The deeper you go, the farther you travel, the longer you live, the more you see. Wulfgar sees five new kinds every year. The eoten are unending. You can't ever count them all. You'll never know why there are so many, what makes them, why they are here. You can't ever really know.

Look at those infinite stars.

Ð　　　Ð　　　Ð

Morning. Wulfgar still asleep. I check on the horses and then go inland to see if I can find anything fresh to eat. The land of the Danes is the best land. It is a land of plenty. Its farmland makes the best ale in the world. The hunting is not so good as across the sea, but there are roots and fruit if you know where to look.

A berry bush. I taste one. It tastes like renewal. I take off my shirt to make a bag for the berries. I ransack the bush. I walk back to our camp over the soft, green earth. There is nothing but hilly green and grey sky and blue ocean and the hearty black of Danish soil as far as you can see.

I wake Wulfgar. We sit and watch as the surf pounds the black shore.

Wulfgar eats his first berry. His eyes go big and he chews and swallows. He pauses. And then he says, in morning-gruff, that was one sweet bastard of a berry. He picks up another berry and looks at it thoughtfully with his brows furrowed. He holds the berry between finger and thumb and he straightens his posture like he's speaking to some king and he declaims: I will copulate with the thing that made this god damned blessed little blue fruit. And then he pops it in his mouth.

Later in the day, the weather clears and the sun throws its golden warmth around like a generous king. Wulfgar says, Unferth, I feel incapable of telling this weather how god damned beautiful it is.

A slight smile over my mouth. Wulfgar knows I smile but does not look at me; he draws the moment out. He says, I would gladly stick my head under Thor's great hammer and let him split my skull into bits of brains and bone if he gave me just one month of days like this damned thing, like this day which is more beautiful than the best drunken, desperate sex with a silver-bodied queen.

Wulfgar has a taste for queens.

He says, well, maybe not as beautiful as that time with Hygelac's wife.

He puts a surprised look on his face, like he has let a secret slip. But it's no accident. I see through his act. It's even more endearing because I see through it.

You can predict every single action, each and every little movement that Wulfgar will take for an entire month. And then he'll tell you something like that.

I say, you sly bastard. You tricky bastard.

His cheek tweaks and that bit of roguery goes from his eye to the corner of his mouth. The slightest arc of a smile. And then he turns his head to look at me and he smiles his full smile, cheeks ridging along scar-lines.

He has done it again. I smile from the marrow of my bones.

The weather goes as Wulfgar hoped for; a little breeze rolls itself over the hills and marches to blow at our backs. We are out of food and we ate all of the berries because they were so good. So when it is time for lunch, we don't eat but we stop anyway to let the horses graze.

You can tell a lot about a man by how he names, uses, and treats his horse. A man who treats his horse well will treat you well. If you can be as valuable to him as his horse.

Leaf Litter is the name of my horse. I call him this because of his scatteredness. He cannot seem to look at one thing for more than a second; he is always swooshing his head back and forth, getting a different perspective on things. Most horses graze by sweeping their mouths back and forth over the grass, grabbing up all the blades that are near. Not this horse. After each bite, Leaf Litter pulls his head back and tilts it to get his right eye into full view of the grasses available to him. And then he'll stretch his neck toward his grassy choice and he will bite. And then he'll pull his head up again and turn it to the side to look for the next good bit of grass. It takes him an eternity to get full.

Wulfgar has commented on the rarity of such a horse. He says, I think that he is a good horse. He says, it is good to have a horse with some character because then you know it and it is less likely to surprise you. It is the same with men.

We ride in the long afternoon. We sit in that lazy horse-rider posture. Our tongues are loose in our heads.

I ask Wulfgar something. I would normally not ask him something so probing. But sometimes, when things change enough in a short period of time, either in yourself or out in the world, you throw out things to see if they will be caught or if they will be thrown back. You test things to see if the world reacts like it used to.

I ask him what he misses most of all things.

I look at him. He rides, his blonde, smooth beard catching the wind, his mail clinking in time with the steps of his horse. He holds his gaze on the horizon. He answers plainly. He says, I miss it all. He says it in a way that makes it sound like he used to live in some golden world, some place without chains. Maybe he was orphaned like me. Maybe it was worse and maybe that's why he picked me up.

I don't ask further. There are men that scare questions away.

And in the next moment we crest the last hill and Hrothgar's proud hall, Heorot, is there upon the hill in front of us.

Ð   Ð   Ð

Wulfgar and I ride up to the king's palisaded city. It is the greatest concentration of people I have ever seen; there are maybe a thousand people in this place. A thousand people churning the streets of mud.

The slaga have heard Hrothgar's call for help. They have flocked. We make our way through the mud streets and the slaga stick out like red streaks on salmon heads. They have swords, axes, spears, seaxes. They wear animal skins, they have designs carved into their sword-hilts, their leather helmets. Tattoos all over their arms, their faces. Wulfgar knows almost all of them. He greets them: wrist-shakes, rough slaps on the shoulder, insults delivered over smiles. They greet Wulfgar and then they look at me, sizing me up. If you meet a Northman and he does not size you up, he is either a weakling or he thinks you're not a threat.

Someone calls out, Wulfgar the Strategist. Wulfgar looks over. Here comes a slaga. Rrodi is his name. A tall man of lean muscle and harsh features. His head is shaved bald and he has no beard whatsoever; I have never seen such a hairless head. Wulfgar introduces us and says, Rrodi is a woad from across the sea to the northwest.

He carries a spear and he looks like a spear. His arms are long: his reach in combat must be perilous. His spear is an unusual thing, two men long, with an ash haft and an iron tip. The tip is not large and broad like most spearheads. It is thin, shaped like an arrowhead but bigger. It looks very, very sharp. This man could kill me in half a heartbeat.

Wulfgar immediately asks him, have they tried to kill him yet.

Not yet, Rrodi says. They say that they are about to, but I think that they wanted to wait for you, he says, smiling.

Sometimes you think you know someone and then you see

them in a different place, or with a different group of friends, and then you realize that you did not in fact know that person, or that you only knew half of him. I say to Wulfgar: Wulfgar the Strategist?

He evades the question: look at all these men he must greet!

Word must have gotten out that a renowned man is here because the villagers and slaga are coming out of houses, groggy or naked or drunk, to see him. Most of the slaga are men but there are women, too.

All of the villagers are women. Wulfgar is busy getting mobbed, so I ask Rrodi why there are only women living here. Are the men off on some hunt? He says, no, it is because all of the men have tried to kill Grendel.

I hear Wulfgar promising rematches of old contests. He looks over at me, smiles deep in his blonde beard. He beckons me to follow him.

Wulfgar walks among the slaga like Thor himself. He has some new energy in his feet. The mud sucks my boots as I walk through the town, but it springs Wulfgar forward. We walk by four men with matching shields, round shields with black and white spirals, a team of slaga. They have beads and bones braided into their beards. They are short like southerners. They give him nods and they say his name. And then they look at me with mud-crusted, bloodshot eyes. I straighten up. I have put on more muscle by now and so I am by no means small. But I don't have the relaxedness that impetuous men carry. Nor do I have a beard. I have sparse, black seaweed tendrils.

A woman and a man, she a big woman with an axe and a shield and he a similarly sized man with a bow. They greet him and call him by that name, Strategist. Wulfgar grabs their heads in greeting with his thick-fingered hands.

I did not like the sound of Grendel. The Grinder of men. Has he really killed a hundred? But now it seems like maybe it was just the cowardice of Beowulf and Hygelac that stuck to me, making me afraid. Now I feel like a wolf, one who hunts. Look at all of these slaga. We're all wolves. This sceadu-gengan will be dead before dawn tomorrow. I do not know of an eoten that we could not destroy. Just look at them: these slaga could bring down a fire-spewing fyrdraca.

We continue down the muddy road. Heorot stands in the distance. It is the grandest hall I have ever seen. It stands tall, so tall, tall as four or five men. And it is long, spilling over its hilltop. The hill is not long enough, so a foundation has been built to shore up the front and back of the hall.

We stop. Grendel has forced Hrothgar out of Heorot; indeed, only those who dare go into Heorot have died. If you are outside of it, you are safe. It is like the Grinder has found territory that he likes and wants to defend it. Hrothgar has moved to a temporary small hall, which is just ahead. Modest but decorated. His banners fly at the door.

We approach. Wulfgar says, are you ready to talk to a man with real influence. I shrug and say, yes. Wulfgar looks me over doubtfully. He says, take off your boot. I look at him. I say, which boot. He says, it doesn't matter. Take off your boot.

I take it off. Left boot. I stand, one-footed, in the street. Wulfgar bends down, picks up a pebble. A little jagged thing. He holds out his other hand, motioning for me to give him my boot. I hand it to him. He drops the pebble in, gives it back. I say, what is that for. He says, you walk like you've never had an injury. This will help.

I look at him, standing there, holding my boot. He raises his voice, says, put it on, you walk like a little boy. It'll put some pain in your step.

I put on the pebbled boot.

He turns around and stalks toward the building. I follow. That is one sharp rock.

He says, stand up straight. I say, but there's a rock in

He interrupts, says, act like you are trying to impress a woman.

A look of hesitation on his face. He looks at me again, looks at me doubtfully. Wulfgar says, appear more confident. But don't let him see that you're trying to look confident. I ask, don't I usually look confident? He says, no.

Now that is a puzzling thing.

We walk to the door.

Men are to leave off their weapons in the presence of the king; we leave ours with the door guards. Wulfgar puts his hand on the door. He stops again. He says, and smile more than you usually do. You don't smile enough. You'll make him nervous.

I say, I don't smile enough?

Wulfgar says, no. You don't.

I say, maybe there isn't anything to smile about.

Wulfgar silences me with a look.

We enter. I step up, the jagged stone burying itself in the arch of my foot.

When a man meets another man who is skilled in the same way as the first man, he is disgusted. When a man meets another man who is skilled in a different way, he is inspired. Hrothgar. He is a man beyond myself. He sits. His sitting posture reminds me of a great black rock that sits along the coastline of the Danes. The sailors and merchants call it Thor's Anvil. It sits defiantly, locked in eternal combat with the sea.

He wears no helmet and no armor. Like a king should, he saves armor for the battlefield and cloth for inside the hall. I can tell that he swings a sword every day: his right hand is callused. He is scarred; one of the scars is a cruel slash across his entire neck. He is taller than me, and I am tall. He has reddish brown hair and a bright red beard. He wears a grey shirt and faded blue pants, nothing kingly. Ah, there it is. His king's boast: a golden Thor's hammer dangles from a silver chain around his neck. It is big as a hand. In a pinch, you could use it as a bludgeon.

We have come in at no special time; Hrothgar converses with his wife.

Wealhtheow. I have come to learn in my few days that a man's fame always dwarfs the actual man. But a woman's fame – her fame understates. While a man's fame is usually built around lies, a woman's fame is always built on hard-won merit. Wealhtheow is famed for her beauty. It understates.

She has a cold cutting beauty, a face of sharded ice. The bones beneath her face are angled. No. The bones beneath her skin are where angles became angles, where lines learned that they could come together to make sharp-pointed corners. Her face has been cut from something, honed from something. It could slice through water faster than the prow of any ship. Her skin is the color of creamed snow; her eyes, beautifully deep blue, the color of the sea on a sunny winter day. She wears a fine, coal-black dress. Her limbs angle down toward the floor; her dress touches the ground and I cannot see her feet and she sits lightly, floating in the air. This woman could never be drowned or frozen. She is too intimate with the sea.

Intoxicating. Frightening.

Next to her, Hrothgar sits with his red beard and hair like a flame. Wealhtheow dropped from the sky in particles, gathering in the sea and freezing into one body; Hrothgar pushed up from the depths of the earth, knotted, rooted, bark-skinned. I wonder at how they could ever get along; they seem to come from different worlds entirely; they must speak different languages.

We approach and salute. I stand tall. Breathe.

Hrothgar, too, calls him Strategist. Wulfgar is familiar with them; smiles chase each other round the room. The conversation goes quickly to the sceadu-gengan.

The Grinder has escaped, says Hrothgar.

Wulfgar looks doubtful. But he holds his tongue.

Silence visits us. Hrothgar looks at me, sizing me up.

A slight tilt of his head. His lips make the smallest movement. He has sniffed something behind my eyes.

Is now the time for me to speak? Wulfgar is silent. What do I say?

I am about to speak just to speak. And then I see that Wealhtheow has been staring at me. I stop. Her eyes are welded to me. A heavy silence. Like when you walk by a frog pond and they stop croaking or when you search for the noisy cricket in your home but when you approach, the thing stops making noise. We break our stares. And then we look again, exchanging glances. My glance says, you were looking at me and I know it. The return glance says, and I wanted you to know it.

The room feels cold.

Wulfgar says, are you sure it is the Grinder. Hrothgar gestures to a wooden pillar of the hall. We approach. Deep cuts in it, deeper than even bear claws could make. A pall comes over Wulfgar.

Wulfgar ends the visit with pleasantries, touches my elbow to remind me to follow him out, like I wouldn't have otherwise remembered.

Outside. Putting our weapons back on and picking up our shields. Wulfgar says, what in Hel did you do.

I say nothing.

He says, you didn't do a damned thing. You didn't speak. But something happened in there. Be careful, he says. And yes, it is Grendel.

He pauses, buckles on his sword belt. He says, I am liking this less and less.

I say nothing. I am lost in my thoughts. This would be another of those moments that Wulfgar refers to when he says that I do not talk enough.

But all I am thinking is: how does a man keep her out of his dreams?

Đ Đ Đ

Wulfgar the Strategist has arrived. Hrothgar hosts a feast.

The women of the city prepare Heorot for the feast. I ask, doesn't Grendel come to rampage and massacre whenever there are men inside Heorot?

Wulfgar says, he comes after a while. We will leave the hall before he comes. He will find it empty. And then Wulfgar lowers his scrape-voice to a whisper. He winks at me and says, and then we will get a look at him.

The fire pit is started. Sweet-smelling wood is piled on to give Heorot fragrance. Extra benches and tables are brought from homes and other buildings. Much of the city has contributed to the preparation of the food. The day turns to night. Our mood ascends with the stars.

It is all there. Ale, mead, wine. Pork, lamb, beef, chicken, fish. Roots and tubers and vegetables and fruits and even a spice from the distant south. A dish is prepared with this special spice. The slaga try to outdo each other in eating it; they are game for anything. But it is so spicy that they all sweat and swear and cry. They gulp ale and milk to wash it away. Vifil the slaga tries to stuff some into Rrodi's mouth. Vifil ends up with an eyeful of it. Spice-crying the rest of the night.

There is a scop. The scop's lyre fills the air with a tune that makes me feel united to the men around me, makes me feel like loyalty was bred into me.

Wulfgar eats deep and drinks deeper. The mood is light all around as the men stuff themselves. The dessert is passed out. A mixture of fermented fruit. This is undoubtedly the best meal I have ever had. I cannot believe the pleasures that have come to me today.

There are twenty-three slaga altogether. Wulfgar points them out to me as we chew. He loves his beer; it has loosened his usually tight movements, so he gestures lazily. He says their names. Vifil, Regin, Helgi. He says, you remember Rrodi, with the spear. He continues, saying their names and a bit about each. There are honorable slaga. There are slaga who will cheat you. This one lost his hand to a troll. That one hates Hygelac, too, like us. This other one killed a scinnum and he will tell no one how he did it. I don't even know how to kill a scinnum. That one saved my life and I saved his not one breath later. That other one has over twenty children with twelve different women and brags about it like it were an achievement and I still do not understand why he would brag over such a fool thing. He owes a lot of money.

The men slosh their way through stew, gnaw pig bones and toss them to the floor, dribble beer down their beards. Wealhtheow the queen brings the wine around in a great silver-fringed walrus tusk. She stops with each man and woman, offering them wine, dripping her smile into their eyes.

She stops at Wulfgar and me and offers the horn to him and then to me. We drink. The wine is good. She and I avoid each other's eyes. It is obvious that there is kindling built between us, kindling just waiting to be lit. She goes on to the next man. Wulfgar frowns at me, says, you are taking after me too much.

He takes a bit of meat out of my hand and pops it into his mouth.

The eating eventually slows. Hrothgar rises to speak. I look at him. That is a man who has something on his mind.

The mood is light, but he begins solemnly. He says, Grendel, the Grinder. Do you see the redness of the wood? He points to the spattered red pillars, floorboards. The Grinder has decorated this hall, he says. It is Grendel's hall. Heorot stands as a tribute to Grendel. The timbers are covered with the blood of my men, with the blood of my children, the blood of our families.

I am suddenly ashamed at having ignored the blood as I ate.

Scorn in his voice, he says, I will burn this hall down to spite Grendel. I will burn it down.

Murmurs run from man to man like quick fingers over the strings of a lyre. These hard men and women do not like this talk. They think, Hrothgar must have lost his nerve.

But I can tell that something is afoot. I can see it in his face: there's something underneath that scowl. Hrothgar knows what he does. He's laying the foundation.

I will burn it down, he says, because Grendel has killed enough in this hall. I will burn this hall down and I will move my town away from this eoten.

The slaga get visibly riled. To relocate a town is dishonor to any lord. It is second only to begging for mercy. They shout at him. They say, don't give up, Hrothgar. You cannot. The people would never obey you again. They say, the gods would make you suffer.

Hrothgar shouts over them, quiets them down. He shouts, he has killed a hundred men, he has ground their bones to bits, has impaled them upon their own spears, he has broken down the door to Heorot so many times that the entire hall now leans backward, look: look at how the pillars lean, Grendel has bent the entire structure of our proudest creation, my great Heorot. He's bent it backward into weakness and shame.

We snarl and out-yell each other, at the point of a riot. We look only at Hrothgar. He stops. He does not speak. He lets us rile.

And then, right on time, that look comes over his face. Disgust. Indignance. Hate. He jumps up and kicks over his table. He stands, his hands curled into fists, his height impressive, his beard a roaring fire. His voice rises and rises and ignites into rage.

He screams, a hundred men. A hundred men. A hundred exactly, more than any eoten has slain since Nuenemator, since that black, boiling fiend rose from the swamps and laid waste. That was forty years ago. Do you remember who slayed Nuenemator, he asks with fury.

Bodvar, we yell.

Bodvar, he says. Is Bodvar remembered, he asks.

Yes, we shout. Aye, we shout.

Who wants a reputation that will outlive that of Bodvar, he asks.

We yell but Hrothgar keeps talking. He points at his scop and he roars, who wants my scop to sing your story? Who wants a reputation that men will sing of for generations, for millennia, a reputation that Thor himself will envy?

We curdle the air with screams.

Bring me Grendel's head, he roars. Spit flies from his mouth. His frizzed red beard collects the spittle. He screams, bring me Grendel's head and I will give you more gold and silver than a warrior has owned ever before. Bring me Grendel's head and give me back my hall. I want Heorot back, he says, hammering his fist on his chest. He says, I want Heorot back, if for nothing else, to repaint its timbers with the blood of the Grinder, of Grendel. Will you do this, slaga? Will you, ring-brothers, do this?

And in saying ring-brothers, Hrothgar puts the edge on the blade of his speech, for it is a word to honor us. It raises us to the level of his brethren, the brothers that he would bleed for from his own veins.

We shout. We shout ourselves hoarse, and it feels like belonging. It feels like I have found a new family, Wulfgar its father and

Hrothgar its grandfather and the other slaga my older brothers.

Like metal bars, men must be heated so that they can be forged into one. The heat of rage, or confidence, or loyalty, or the heat from a friend, Wulfgar's heat. Any heat will do. Anything that makes men blur themselves, makes them adhere to each other. Hrothgar feeds this fire with beer and wine and women and meat, and then he stokes it with his words, making it white-hot and primed. And then he places us into that fire and we melt faster than ice in the palm and then he uses his words to hammer and pound us into a blade. And then he looks at his finished work just as he looks down at our faces now. He smiles because he knows that he is a master smith.

We scream, yes, Hrothgar. We will do this.

And then, just as smiths do to temper the blade, to cool it, to harden it, he says something to fortify us. He sticks this glowing blade, sticks us into a bucket of cold water. Steam shoots out of it like salt spume over a sea-rock. The cool water hardens us to the task ahead. He does this tempering and hardening by dipping us into this cold, reflective, simple statement:

Good, for I have lost enough sons.

Ð   Ð   Ð

The king's hall has quieted. The women are asleep and so are some of the men. On benches, on the floor. But none of the slaga are asleep. No, they cannot possibly sleep.

Wulfgar and the other slaga rise. They wake the sleeping men and women and tell them to go home. They empty the hall. It has held merriment this night. The Grinder will soon come.

The men cast the logs of the fire around, leaving them disorganized so that they will burn longer and so illuminate the hall longer. Wulfgar surveys the room, looks satisfied, gestures to the men to follow him. He walks out the door. They follow. I stumble after them. I am eager to get out. The floor nips at my heels.

We file out of the front door of Heorot. We walk around outside to the back of the hall. The men drill holes in the walls of Heorot with their swords, knives, axeheads. I stand next to Wulfgar. He finds a weak spot in the wall and drills a small hole by twisting his knife between two boards. The light from inside the hall licks out of the hole. I peer in with one eye. We will get a good look at him in the flesh, if it really is flesh that this eoten is made of.

The eye of Odin, Wulfgar says.

The eye of Odin – the eye that the god lost in exchange for the gift of foresight. We will look, each of us one-eyed, at Grendel. Odin intends this, he intends for us to do things as he did. He helps the spinners spin these moments. These god-spun moments are one-eyed winks from the gods to the men. They remind us. They say, yes, we are here watching.

Wulfgar drills another hole for himself. The men have all done this. They peer in and then sit back and lean against Heorot. Now the waiting begins. It begins to rain, softly.

Like I have said, I am familiar with darkness. Each night has its own character. But tonight is different. Tonight, my mind will not alight on what kind of darkness it is. It is a man without a face.

The weather is fair but the crickets do not chime themselves out. The wind blows but the trees do not rustle. Rain falls on the ground but the soil does not soak it up; it runs this way and that way over the dirt. There is some upheaval in the way of things.

We feel it. I look at Wulfgar. He nods, points at the wall of Heorot.

Thor, that eoten is stealthy.

I know without looking that he is in the hall. He has snuck in. Not a man of us heard. I have not yet looked in to see him but I know that he is there. I can feel him in Wulfgar's short, shallow breaths. Suddenly I do not want to see the monster. I want to know no more. I do not want to see it. I know without looking that it is a malign shadow, a wrecker of men. Whatever this eoten looks like, Wulfgar's previous victory over the Grinder was an act of impossible valor: Grendel's mere presence is more than I can handle.

The smell finds us. It is like a wolf's vomit, a chunky spew of coagulated cowblood. We gag, struggling to keep quiet.

He pounds around the hall, speaking some incomprehensible language, cursing in devil-talk. His voice dark, deep. He hisses between words. He is frustrated at finding no men or women to feast on. He wrecks the mead-hall, breaking the tables. We, the slaga, look at each other and listen to the shattering of wood. I put my hand on the splintery surface of the wall of Heorot. It feels thin.

Wulfgar is the first to look inside.

Quietly, impossibly calm, Wulfgar whispers: he has grown bigger.

We are all drunk. Fill up your skins, says Wulfgar as he carries the bucket of ale around for us. I obey and open up my waterskin and drink the remaining ale and let him fill it again. All of the slaga, all twenty-three of us, fill our skins with ale. Rrodi comes back from out of the darkness, a goat over his shoulders. Wulfgar looks around and makes sure that we have everyone. We light torches and we start walking.

We walk away from the town. I can still hear Grendel heeling and hasping in Heorot. Wulfgar says, the town is safe. He will rage and go home. He does not want to obliterate the town, only torment it. It is Heorot that hounds him.

We walk and walk and I am second in line, just behind Wulfgar, but I do not ask him where we are going. Nor does he want to speak. There is a slight breeze.

We walk for half the night. Finally Wulfgar stops at the top of a rocky hill. The ground below the hill is soft and has trees and bushes but the sides and top of the hill are rock, save one patch of dirt and a lonely, sickly tree that grows at the very top.

The no-moon is out; our torches make the only light. We sit in a circle. Wulfgar is on my right. There is a slaga I do not know on my left who has a forked brown beard and a red face and a turned nose with boils on it. Rrodi puts the goat down. We let it wander inside the circle of slaga. We plant the torches in the ground. The men watch the goat as it paces, nervous.

It is Unferth's first fáh, says Wulfgar, nodding his head toward me. The other slaga reply in salutes, greetings, grunts. There is no man or woman here who looks like any other man or woman, except those who are in teams, who have a badge or marker that indicates their fellowship. They are otherwise dressed strangely, wildly.

There are tall men, short men, men with potbellies or stomach muscles that can grate cheese. There are five women among us, three of whom are oxes, and the other two look tough as wolverines. There are tattoos, beards of every shape and length and color, every weapon that you can name and more. There are skins of bear and fox and badger and deer and elk and ox and one man wears a soft-looking, yellow, beautiful spotted cat pelt that I have never seen. Wulfgar and I are the most normal of them all, or the strangest of them all, if strangeness is normal. He and I wear dyed pants and dyed shirts and cloaks that are fastened over our shoulders with brooches. But one thing is similar between the garb of all of us: we all wear chainmail armor. To the last slaga. I am glad that I took Svala's mail from her flesh-pile.

Gatherings have colors. A battle is red, a king's hall is gold, a campsite is rusty orange. This one is brown. The color of leather, of skin and cooked meat and dirt. But somehow it is more elemental than even brown. It is more basic. Who knows how deep the brown soil goes, but the color of this gathering is the color of the stuff that you would find when you have dug past the bottom of the brown dirt.

I do not know what we are doing. But I do not feel like I have to find out; I feel like I know already, like anyone would know. Even that goat knows.

I am drunk so I don't pick it up at first. But then I listen more closely. The men are murmuring.

I cannot tell who murmurs and who does not. If I look at one man, it seems that he is maybe speaking softly, or singing, but when I look at him longer it seems that, no, he's not, he's just sitting there. I look at another man and I see the same. It is a murmur, something from the gut and the bowels.

Wulfgar skips me because this is my first fáh, but the man next to me is called on. Vifil, Wulfgar says. Vifil speaks, voicing his opinion on how to kill the sceadu-gengan. He prefers to kill the beast as others have tried: lure it into Heorot and trap it and kill it with swords and spears and axes, like you would kill a troll. He is big like trolls, is he not? Some slaga nod, some slaga don't.

We go around the circle. The men voice their stratagems. A few, like Vifil, want to trap Grendel in Heorot and kill him in combat with their weapons. They trust their sword-arms.

But others argue that a hundred other men have tried the same and were massacred. One man says, the eoten is too fast, did you not see his speed. Who knows how thick that bristle-armor is. Maybe, as some men say, it is warded against cutting.

There are a few men, Rrodi included, that say that however Grendel is fought, he should be trapped, should be held fast by something to give us time to kill it. But there are many eoten that can shrew their way out of traps; some that can become immaterial, some that can change shape and slither away. We do not know how Grendel escaped his rock prison. Maybe he can turn into vapor, or into a louse.

We go around the circle. The men rally around a few favorite ideas. We drink heavily from our waterskins. The goat beds down in the middle of the circle. We all look at it, throwing out ideas.

Dig a giant hole in the floor of Heorot and get him into it and then pour boiling oil and molten metal on him, one man says. Make a tree into a huge spike and rig it to fall, pull it up to the rafters and get him under it and drop the spike, another man says. Feed him a poisoned cow corpse, one man says. But how do we get him into the pit? What if the spike misses? What of his sharp nose? He will smell the poison.

One man, an older slaga with a braided beard and five remaining teeth, is more afraid than the others. He says that he has an apprehension to everything said so far. Block him into Heorot and burn the hall, he says. It is the best way. Another man gruffly assents.

Wulfgar sits and thinks and looks at the old man steadily. He likes the idea. But a shadow comes across his face. He shakes his head and says, Heorot must be saved. That is what we are here to do, he says. The other men say nothing in support of this but it is obvious that Heorot must be saved for the slaying to be counted a victory. So burning is discarded.

You trapped him before, Wulfgar, says the old man. Speak to us. How did you do it.

We collapsed a cave on him, he says.

Silence. The goat looks at Wulfgar. He looks back at it.

You may know the cave, he says. The one to the north of Heorot a half-day's journey. The one with the entrance that has a peak to it like the top of a mountain.

Rrodi and others nod. Wulfgar says, we, myself and five other slaga, looked around for three weeks in that cave. We found a dead end vein and mined around in it to make the roof weaker. We lost two men to that cave while preparing it. Rockfalls.

The men are silent. It is bad for slaga to die that way because they did not die in combat. They don't go to Odin's corpse-hall.

Wulfgar says, but we made a good enough spot. We lured him there and a third man died because Grendel caught up with him on the way to the cave. But luckily Grendel kept following the scent, the scent of me and the other slaga and the two goats that we put at the end of the cave, in our trap.

Wulfgar says, we nearly got him where we wanted him. He was deep in the cave and we were about to follow him and collapse the ceiling behind him. But he must have smelled human behind him because we heard him stop. He started coming back toward the mouth of the cave, toward us. And so the other slaga, whose name was Halfdan, told me: cave it in when I say. And then he slapped me on the shoulder and said to me, the hæftworld. And he ran from out from our hiding spot to lure Grendel back into the deeper reaches of the cave. He must have dodged or sneaked past Grendel somehow because I could hear them both going deeper into the cave, both letting out their roars and yells in the world-throat. And then Halfdan's yells turned to screams. He screamed, cave it in, cave it in. It sounded like he was being flayed, like Grendel was eating him from the feet up. I ran out from our hiding spot, carrying the great axe that we had set aside. I ran to the trigger beam that was to be chopped to bring down the roof of our trap, the roof that would crush Grendel or trap him forever.

Wulfgar says, I hated the Grinder so much that I yelled to him, it is Wulfgar who brings your doom, you spawn of demons. I chopped and chopped. Stroke by stroke, the trigger beam withered under the axe. I could hear Grendel catching on to what was going on; he came loping up the cave, loping up to me, gurgling on Halfdan's blood. I yelled my name. I shouted, Wulfgar. Do you hear me, demon spawn, do you hear me, cursed one. And with this, the trigger beam broke and the rest of the beams gave way under the weight of the weakened cave roof. It fell with a roaring crash and rumble. I heard Grendel yell my name over the din, could hear him yell, Wulfgar, in that demon-speak, and it sounded like he had hollowed out my name and filled it with something that cannot be removed. Some curse. Some mark.

Silence.

The hæftworld, we say.

But obviously this did not work, continues Wulfgar.

Rrodi, intensity on his intense face, says, I still think that we should trap him. Is there a way that we could trap him like you did, Wulfgar, and be sure that the trap would kill him?

Trap him in a lake or in the sea, I say. He might drown.

No way to be sure, says the old five-toothed slaga. But no one has tried drowning yet. Many eoten can be drowned, he says.

Wulfgar looks doubtful. But he says, I had hoped that we might have a better idea. He puts his head in his hands. He says, alright. Find a boulder and drag it to a sea cliff. We'll bring bait – lots of bait – ox blood and goat blood. And we will need runners to help lure him, to goad him. Fix chains to the tottering boulder and then run those chains out and attach them to a grab trap. Rrodi can make that. When Grendel steps into the trap, we push the boulder into the sea and the chains drag him down to drown him.

Silence.

Wulfgar says, I wonder if this is a battle that we can win. But if twenty-three of the world's best slaga cannot kill the eoten that live in their own land, then what is the use of us, he says.

Rrodi and the old five-toothed slaga nod. Rrodi says, I believe in this plan. In a flat tone, he says, who else believes in this plan. The slaga go around and affirm consent. Some do not like the idea, but many are united behind it, so the rest agree. To be united behind any plan is much better than to be divided behind a good plan.

It is agreed. Chain him to a rock and throw it in the sea.

Rrodi gets up and pulls out his dagger and approaches the goat. It sees him and stands alert. He grabs the goat by the horns and pins its body between his legs and he hugs its horns to his chest and reaches in front of the goat's neck with the dagger.

He slides the dagger over the throat. The goat twitches. Blood pours out over the ground. The animal struggles but only for a moment. A quick death is a good omen.

As the goat dies, Rrodi says, Thor: we give you this blood and body. Feast. We ask you to let us slay the Grinder. We hope for one muscle of your arm, a splinter of your strength.

We bury the goat under that dying, cracking tree on the hilltop.

We walk back to Heorot and to our fate. I'm still drunk.

Ð   Ð   Ð

Wulfgar the Strategist plans our attack. We are given our tasks. The trackers and beast-men, those who know how Grendel might think, are charged with planning the route that Grendel will be lured along to the sea cliffs. Wulfgar is in this group. Two men that could build a trap to catch your soul are working out the best design for something that will snag, bite, wrap, or otherwise bind a chain to Grendel. Rrodi is one of these men. Some, those with a hand for smithing, are helping Hrothgar's smith make a great chain that will be attached to this trap and will bind Grendel to the rock, which will be placed at the edge of the sea cliff. The right sea cliff is scouted out by more slaga, and yet more slaga look around in a boat at the base of the cliff. These slaga below will measure the depth of the sea to make sure that it is deeper than the length of the chain plus some: we do not want to throw Grendel and the boulder into the sea to have the Grinder tread water until he wriggles out or chews through the chain. The rest, those who have none of the previous skills, are to find a right-sized boulder and drag it to the chosen cliff, where all of our plans will converge and where we will drown Grendel.

I do not have the skill to help with any of these tasks except for looking for the boulder. While other slaga tinker away in the dark after-hours on an ingenious trap, or while they look for good terrain and depths of water that create the perfect combination for a precipitous murder, or while they bend their minds to mimic the mind of the eoten so that they may recreate the precisely tuned bait trail that will lead it to our trap, I am given the highly esteemed task of looking for a big rock.

Vifil is in charge of the rock-finding party of five slaga, the turds of our twenty-three man group, Vifil himself little smarter than any stone around. He says, split up and look for boulders for the day and then come back. There is a stony hill near where we have set up camp but Vifil says don't bother looking on that hill because the stones on that hill are not of the right kind and would float. He says, I've been up there and checked.

There is a stone that can float?

I say to Vifil, in front of the other three slaga, maybe it's worth looking up there again. But he snarls back that I am not to waste my time and his time by climbing all the way up that hill, and I am instead to go northwest on the marches on my horse to look for one.

Shrug. Maybe they do float.

We are after a boulder that is round and that comes up to at least my navel or maybe a little taller. That is one big rock.

We have bad luck looking for boulders. We find quarries of stone but the stone would need to be dug up and chiseled out. This would take weeks. We look for a good boulder for three days and we are supposed to be done by the fourth because that is when we will integrate and smooth over our plans.

But there is nothing. Who would have thought that there are no big rocks near Heorot? I have scoured northwest of our camp but I have found nothing that is the right size: everything is either an immovable behemoth or the size of a fist.

Odin knows I cannot depend on the other four slaga to find it. One of them, Riordan, sees things that aren't there and doesn't see things that are there, like some kind of useless seer. As I ride back to the camp after each day, I wonder if Riordan will have brought back a cow or a fat man or even a big, fluffy sheep, saying, look at this perfect big rock.

But no, to him I am usually saying something like, no Riordan, no, you didn't need to empty your waterskin on me. No, I was not on fire. I was asleep.

The other two are brother and sister. I think they are inbred. The boy looks like a fish. One of the girl's eyes swims in its socket.

It really is just me who has to find this rock.

It is on the last day that I decide that rocks cannot float. I will check the damned hilltop.

Morning. Vifil is as grumpy as ever. I ride away as he gives his morning rant, telling us we're lazy and don't cover enough ground. As usual he himself does not go look because he says that he must wait at the camp in case word comes from the other slaga. So he waits there, gets bored, eats our food.

I start riding toward the northwest like I am supposed to but then I go over a hill and I turn and loop back toward the hill of floating rocks. I ascend the hill on the back side so that Vifil cannot see. It is a big hill and it takes me and Leaf Litter the better part of the morning to reach the top because it is steep and rough and there is some innocent-looking shrub that Leaf for some reason does not like to touch so he takes winding routes, picking his way all the way up the hill. I cannot fathom how a horse becomes so particular.

The top of the hill is a strange landscape of jagged stones and large puddles. I step down from Leaf Litter, setting foot on the rock-scape.

Thor. There are two big rocks right there, just the right size. They are of a height that I can lean on, resting my elbow on them comfortably. The two big stones are about fifteen paces apart on this pocked hilltop. I look at them to decide which would be better.

They are of two different types. One of the stones is red and coarse with little holes all over it. The other is black and rough with lichens growing on it and is, on second glance, a little smaller than the other rock, the red rock, which is the perfect size. Ah, I will use the bigger rock then, the one with the small holes in it.

Don't tie the boulder to your horse and drag it to the camp yourself, you'll crush yourself, said Vifil. But so far, doing the exact opposite of what Vifil has instructed has been the correct thing to do. Let's roll it.

The rock looks like it needs some dragging to get it rolling down the hillside. So I go over to Leaf Litter. Ready to finally pull your weight, horse? He is drinking water as he always does in his strange way. He doesn't drink like a horse usually drinks, full snout in, but instead he tries to keep his nostrils out of the water. So to drink while keeping them out of the water, he has to crouch down and drop his neck as low as possible and stick his mouth out over the water like he's just trying to skim the surface. He sucks the water into his mouth with those big horse lungs and makes great slurping noises.

I grab Leaf Litter's reins, pull his water-skimming mouth up to bring him over to the stone so he can help me move it. But as I pull him over to me, his snout brushes a stone and knocks it into the puddle and, unbelievably, the stone floats in the puddle.

I gawk.

I lean over and pick up the stone and turn it in my hand. It has holes in it just like those in the rock that I am about to send down the hillside to be used to sink Grendel. Thor, they are the same kind of stone. Will the big stone float too? No, it is too big. Maybe it is only small stones that float. I start to bring Leaf Litter over to the big red stone.

I pause. I can't get it out of my head. What if it does float?

I look at its porous surface. And then I look at the other rock that I thought about using. Though it is not quite as big, it is maybe big enough.

Will that stone float too?

Do stones float? My world is a cracking egg.

Unferth, the man who doesn't know his stones.

I stand there, puzzling. I am glad no one else is here.

I have an idea.

I pick up a small pebble off of the ground. This pebble is the same type of the big second stone, the black one with lichens on it, not the porous one. At least I think it is.

I pick up that black pebble and I drop it in the same puddle that the red, porous rock fell into. I put it in this puddle and not a different puddle because maybe different puddles make different rocks float?

I extend my hand over the puddle, pebble inside, ready to drop. I look over at Leaf Litter. He's watching me. Staring at me bug-eyed with a look that says, are you learning a lot from those rocks, Unferth? I drop the pebble. His eye follows the stone as it plops into the water. Man and horse watch to see if it will sink.

It sinks.

I fish it out of the puddle. I move to another puddle, a bigger one. Maybe bigger puddles make different rocks float. Leaf watches me do a strange man-dance, hopping past the smaller puddles. I lean over the big puddle. I extend my hand. I drop in the dark pebble.

It sinks.

I do the same with the little red, porous rock.

It floats.

Black, lichened rock it is.

I walk over to the black rock. I imagine telling the other slaga: yes, here's the rock. You might want to check and see if it floats.

The rock is near the side of the hill facing the camp. The camp is far enough away so that you couldn't sprint all the way to it but not so far that you can't see what Vifil is doing. He is looking into my pack. Vifil, that is not your cheese.

The black rock is buried in the dirt a little so I dig it out. It's close to the sloping hillside. It looks like it just needs a good nudge before it tumbles down and away toward the camp.

I name the rock Vifil because it sits and does nothing as he does. I tie the rope around Vifil and pass it in front of and then around a rocky outcrop that projects forward from the side of the hill. And so, when Leaf pulls on the rope, Vifil will be pulled toward the rocky outcrop and also toward the slope of the hillside, where it will tumble in the general direction of our camp.

I knock and smooth the edge of the outcrop with the hilt of my sword where the rope will rub it so that the rock will not fray or cut the rope. And then I loop the other end around Leaf Litter's chest, putting my saddle between horse and rope for padding.

Like its namesake, Vifil is a stubborn stone. Leaf Litter's attention shifts from our task to other things, flying birds, insect noises, so I must always remind him of what we are doing by yelling his name and slapping his rump. He is not strong enough to pull the boulder himself, so I help, pulling on the rope as well. We pull and pull and Vifil the rock shifts ever so slightly, popping its bonds with the rest of the ground. It slides forward. Look: it's rolling. But it must clear a very small rise before falling down the hill. So I yell for Leaf Litter to pull, pull. I pull, too; the veins on my arms pop out. Vifil gets over the hump and starts to roll down the hill and in the same instant out comes my sword from its sheath. I chop the rope so that Vifil will not drag Leaf Litter over the side. Vifil rolls down the hill, light and free. Happy rolling.

Vifil, the dumber of the two Vifils, sits at the camp, munching my cheese. I watch as Vifil the boulder rolls down and, yes, yes, it is going toward the camp. It picks up speed. I can hear it thump the ground. I feel its massive pounding. The stone Vifil runs through our camp and knocks past the fire pit, sending sparks and chaff everywhere, and the other Vifil screams an absurd high-pitched scream and scrambles away just as mighty Vifil goes rumbling by like charging cavalry.

Later that night. I am finishing the telling of the story of Vifil versus Vifil. And at this point in the story, bass laughter comes out of the slaga ranged round the fire. And then one of the slaga women reaches over to the groin of the man next to her and grabs his stones and raises her cup of ale and says, to Unferth, the man who knows his stones.

Đ   Đ   Đ

Morning. Tonight, we move to kill the Grinder.

We start at Heorot. We will fake a gathering in the hall, yelling and causing commotion to lure him there. And then, when the time comes, the men will ride out to take their positions at the sea cliff.

Wulfgar and another slaga, Regin, will be Grendel. It is good to have two separate beast-men do this because they will each take their own path along the monster's thoughts. Two men give you a better idea of what could go wrong.

The two of them get themselves worked up, putting themselves in the færeng, the trance that induces men to take on the mind of a beast. They start by glugging Hrothgar's ale.

The city has gathered to watch us. The other slaga ride to their positions. One slaga takes up his position at the end of the main road leaving the city, within earshot of Heorot. This rider will be the first rabbit in a relay of rabbits that will provoke Grendel to chase them. One rabbit will pass Grendel to another, and they will lure him all the way to the sea cliff. Good hiding spots and the sweet smell of animal blood make sure that Grendel switches from one rabbit to the next. We need a relay of many rabbits because we do not want a horse to slow one bit while it runs from the Grinder. Bad things happen to tired horses: missteps, stumbles, falls. We are not even sure that the horses will be able to keep ahead of him.

Hrothgar's scop plays his drum: a quick rhythm that strikes a chord with your primacy, grows your claws, strengthens your bite, makes you hungry. Wulfgar shakes his head and moves his feet to the rhythm. He riles himself up for the færeng. Between shakes of his head, he looks out of the corners of his eyes for prey.

Hrothgar's villagers gawk, wild-eyed. They stand in a circle around the two man-beasts. Hrothgar himself stands near, arms crossed, taking it in.

Wulfgar had told me that this riling up feels like getting in a fight with yourself, which is hard to do. You have no opponent to anger you as you do in other fights so you have to do it all yourself. You must have rage in you, he said. You shake your rage until it froths and blots out everything else. Feel what it wants. He said, you will know that it is beginning to work when you start to drool and you don't care.

The drums pound madness into our hearts. Wulfgar and Regin beat their chests with their fists. They push each other, slap each other around. They rile up the crowd, too. They push them, growl at them.

Wulfgar pushes a woman, yells at her. She yells back and slaps him. He howls like a wolf. Those near him raise their mouths up and howl back.

The circle tightens. The beast-men grab us, pull us closer. The drumming quickens. Its beat is irresistible now; we seethe like an angry ocean. Wulfgar and Regin grab us, pull us in even closer. The circle tightens further.

They grapple with each other, shaking their heads, yelling. The circle closes and closes. And then, as if direct from the mouth of a monstrous bear, Wulfgar lets out a guttural howl.

It is time.

We put the men on their horses because we want them to have Grendel's speed for this test run. We do Regin first; Wulfgar looks impossible to handle.

Regin is drunk and livid; he fights, he is hard to move. But he still retains enough sense to let us push him onto his horse. We get Regin on. I turn and look at Wulfgar.

He is looking at me. He snarls. Spit-strings drop from his mouth. His hands move strangely – his fingers curl themselves in and pop themselves open like he tests a set of claws. He lowers his head and arches his back, readying himself for the pounce.

A glow coming from Wulfgar's eyes. Like a little flame. This glow sends shadows over his lips and forehead and under his nose and these shadows make him look inhuman, like a wolf or a bear or a cougar.

He speaks. Like Grendel. He says in that hollow language: Wulfgar. Wulfgar, he says.

I could never put this thing on a horse. But Hrothgar is suddenly behind me, having squeezed his way through the crowd. He says, let us do it. Wulfgar scratches and flails, gnashing his teeth and kicking us away. He bites Hrothgar at the collar, throttling him. Hrothgar's bodyguards push into the crowd, swords drawn, but he tells them to stay back, and he punches Wulfgar heavy-fisted. Wulfgar loosens his bite, letting Hrothgar tear himself away. We push him up onto the horse. Blood on Wulfgar's teeth. He spits Hrothgar's blood back at the king. He opens his mouth wide as it can go and he screeches. The taste of blood stirs his hunger.

I slap the rump of his horse. It plows through the crowd. The man who will be the first rabbit yells and waves at Wulfgar and Regin. The two take off after him on their horses.

I ride as fast as Leaf Litter will take me. I am to join with the slaga that stand ready at the sea cliff and the rock and the chain and the trap. Tonight, when it is Grendel instead of Wulfgar and Regin, I will already be there.

I take the fastest route, not the route that the Grendels will take because their route is intended to keep them on a scent, on a hunt, and this type of route avoids things like rivers and rocky, barren stretches where scents are easily lost.

I ride hard. Just as Leaf Litter begins to give me signs that he won't keep going, I see the sea cliff. I dismount, tie Leaf with the rest of the men's horses in a bramble of trees.

I rush over and sit next to Rrodi, who has a chain in his hand: the trigger to the trap. He says to me, don't worry, I have lessened its snap. It will not break his leg. It will only hold him.

The blow of a horn: the last rabbit approaches. The howls of

Wulfgar and Regin follow on the heels of this blow of the horn. Twin notes from a two-headed wolf.

I see the last rabbit. On his horse. The horse sprints across the last stretch of ground toward the trap. The rabbits have been chosen for their horsemanship. His horse is expert; it follows his command exactly, diverting course from running off the cliff just at the last moment. He stops it there, next to Vifil the boulder and the edge of the cliff.

Wulfgar comes next and Regin shortly after him. Their horses foam, wild-eyed. Wulfgar jumps from his horse and runs loping like a beast toward the last rabbit, who stands at the cliff edge.

Rrodi pulls on the chain. The trap springs and two large, semicircular metal bars come up and grab Wulfgar by the legs. He shrieks and falls to the ground, writhing, pulling up grass and mud with clawing hands. Wulfgar looks at the last rabbit like he will do nothing with the rest of his days but hunt that man.

Three of the slaga run out from behind one of our hiding blinds. They carry stout spears and run up to Vifil the boulder, which is at the edge of the cliff. They put their spears under its near side and pry it up. The boulder nudges forward, precarious. The chain around it goes taught and pulls Wulfgar toward the cliff. And then Rrodi says, good, and the three men stop prying the boulder over the edge. It falls back onto safe ground. The slaga come out of their hiding spots. They tackle and pin Regin. No one wants to approach Wulfgar. We stand in a circle around him. We watch him as he writhes.

Looking down at Wulfgar, Rrodi says, if something goes wrong here, we draw and charge.

But it will go well, he says, and smiles. He says, it's a good trap, and we have tested it on what might as well be Grendel.

Wulfgar foams and claws at the contraption. We must restrain him when he tries to chew off his legs.

Ð Ð Ð

Night. Hrothgar's scop helps us wake Heorot. Wake up, Heorot, it is time to summon Grendel. Wake up. Let us end your bad dream.

Maybe Grendel attacks Heorot because he despises the merriment that men can make in it. Tonight, we will rub salt in this wound of his so that it will drive him mad and he will come to kill us. We chant and clap and slam sword and spear on shield. We pound our feet on the floorboards. Wulfgar bellows his yawp out from between his twin iron moustache-fangs. The noise of his voice shakes the very ground.

Time to go to our trap. We ride out, putting hoof to heath, our horses kicking up clods as we cross the dark marches. The no-moon is out. Our torches light our way to the sea cliff and to the rock that I found that will drag Grendel into the deep and extinguish the malicious fire that resides in his eyes.

We arrive and tie the horses up in the blind of bushes. I tie Leaf Litter to a branch that looks strong enough to hold him but weak enough to break if he pulls as hard as he can. It is a good thing to tie a horse in this way because the horse will remain there unless it is about to die, and if this is true then it will struggle like mad and release itself. One of Wulfgar's tricks.

We divide ourselves between two rock formations that flank the boulder Vifil. I crouch between Wulfgar and Rrodi, who has his hand on the chain that will catch and hold the leg of the Grinder.

Four of the slaga are not with us; they are the rabbits who will run for their lives.

We wait. We are primed for this kill.

That feeling hits us. The feeling of un-being, of unnaturality and of the perversion of things. The hair stands up on my neck. The stars disappear though there are no clouds. The summer air is warm but I feel cold; I can breathe fine and yet I cannot get enough air.

The final rabbit blows his horn. A sad call in the distance. Here they come.

The scent. The rotted blood scent. It is worse than ever. The beast, in his agony at not taking home any manflesh from our luring him out the other day, must have slaughtered animals that range over the marches and he must have rubbed their entrails on himself, rubbed them into his fur. They have begun to decay. We are nauseous, gagging.

Torchlight. From out of the woods. It is the last rabbit. Grendel is on his heels.

The eoten's shady image lopes from out of the tree cover. Seeing Grendel is like when you see, very quickly, some horror in the corner of your eye. But with Grendel this is in every moment that you see him. He is the scare-moment at all moments; even though you know that he is there, every time that your eyes sit on him anew, you are spooked just as you would be by some sudden jolt. You look at him for a third and forth time and still you jump.

And so you dread even to look.

He lopes from the trees. Here he comes. He is big. Very big. Tall as two men, heavy and strong. He runs barreled over on four feet. The monster is tan and black in some patchwork of the two. He appears fuzzy at first. It is not fur. Spines.

Wulfgar says, his eyes are lit. He says, they light up when he eats the flesh of men. He must have caught one of the rabbits.

The Grinder hoops and hurls after the last rabbit. The man's horse is foaming. That horse is tired enough to die at the end of this chase, caught or not.

Grendel lets out a morbid scream. I bend forward and vomit. He screams again and I wretch heavily. We vomit out our dinner, trying as best we can to keep quiet in our hiding spot as we unload it onto the ground. Rrodi vomits without looking down. He must watch. His bile falls out over his lips and onto his chest and armor.

I look up over the boulder at the last rabbit, stomping nearer and nearer.

Grendel's body is a cluster of spines. They originate at his head and they sprout all the way down his body, down-pointing from head to feet. Each of the spines is long as a man's forearm and thick as a finger, each its own shade of brown.

Finally, as the horseman is almost on us, almost to the cliff wall, Grendel pulls his head up so that his face comes into view. As Grendel does this, Wulfgar puts his hand on my shoulder because he anticipates what I will do: I look into Grendel's eyes and I try to get up to run. It is not something that I think through. It is impulsive. But Wulfgar's hand keeps me there. Just before the springing of the trap, he says:

It is alright, son.

The men light their oil-coated torches.

The last rabbit tries to rein in his horse and turn it but it runs, terrified, full-tilt off the cliff. The rider yells in desperation. He follows his horse into the deep.

Grendel runs after the last rabbit but when he sees the cliff wall he starts to backpedal, digging into the earth with his talons to stop his momentum. Dirt and rock fly into the air around him. Grendel snarls as he sees our torches, sees the ambush he is in.

My hand hurts. I have been vice-gripping my sword handle.

Grendel slides to a stop in the trap. Rrodi pulls the chain and the trap shuts beautifully, snapping up with a metallic thwack. Its sharp teeth catch Grendel by the leg. Rrodi pulls harder on the chain and the trap turns and bites harder. The metal bows under the strain.

Grendel squeals like a boar. He wrenches his head over to look at where the chain comes from, to look at who holds him in this trap. He looks at Rrodi.

Grendel's face. The beast's eyes are flames of malice. Unnatural. They throw bright orange rays. The light from his eyes is caught by the spines on his face. Pointed shadows are cast by these spines. The spine shadows turn as his head turns. Though he must be in pain, he grins. His teeth protrude. The black-lipped mouth is filled with teeth of torture. Teeth not for chewing but for extracting pain. He laughs a joyless laugh. The air of his breath rushes between the teeth and it sounds like the whooshing of swung blades.

The three slaga rush out with their spears to tip Vifil off the cliff. Grendel turns his head to see what the men are doing. The spine shadows turn with his head. The men jam their spears under the rock. They being to pry it over the side.

We shout and throw spears at Grendel to distract him from what the men are doing. He glances at us but then quickly looks again at the men prying the boulder.

It rocks forward, back. The chain from the trap to the boulder, which was hidden under branches on the ground, rises into the air.

Grendel watches the chain rise.

Grendel's eyes go wide.

No. It cannot be.

I turn to look at Wulfgar's face. It is stricken.

We rush out from behind our rocks to distract him, to keep him busy long enough for the boulder to be pushed over the edge. We charge.

I lift my sword high. I yell and run.

The Grinder does the unthinkable: he picks up the chain. But it is too late. The men send the boulder off.

But Grendel pulls. Terrible strength. The boulder hangs in the balance, perched on the corner of the cliff.

We reach him. Our assault is ferocious. Each strike is aimed, well-placed. I hear Hrunting's whistle.

But the spines. They are like wood. My sword does nothing. I look over to Wulfgar. Hrunting has broken through. Blood wells up from Grendel's hide, reddish-brown blood, but the wound is not deep.

It is desperate. I look to see if the boulder has gone off. I see the three men trying to push it off with their bodies, with all their strength, but Grendel pulls and pulls. His might is unmatched.

Grendel pulls the boulder onto safe ground, rolling it back.

One of the men howls as the huge rock rolls over him, heels-to-eyes.

Wulfgar brings Hrunting down into Grendel's foot, all the way through it and into the ground. Grendel yelps in pleasure.

Grendel swipes around with his thorny arms and taloned hands, pushing us away. He grabs Hrunting, stuck into his foot. He casts it away. With his other arm, he grabs the nearest slaga and brings him to his mouth and bites off his head, and then drops the body. He picks up another man and bites off his head, drops the body.

Wulfgar leaves the circle to retrieve the thrown Hrunting. The men close in for another attack, I among them. Grendel lifts up his fists and brings them down, smashing the slaga Vifil, and then another slaga, and then another, one at a time. The blood coats his spines to join the old carcass-blood already on them. His orange eye-light dances, flashing over us as he turns his head.

We heave and stab but his armor is too thick. Thor, let me stab harder. Where is Hrunting? It is the only blade that can do this work.

Grendel lays waste to us, smashing men, picking them up and twisting them in half. Blood everywhere, flinging, splashing. It is futile, it is futile.

My hatred grows and grows. I stab and stab and scream. Finally, Grendel turns his attention to me. He reaches down and grabs me by the arm and picks me up. His talons enter my forearm. I howl with pain and I can see his other hand coming toward me to rip me apart.

A yell. Grendel. I am Wulfgar. Do you remember me, you Hel-bear. I am Wulfgar. Do you remember me.

Grendel looks up, drops me. I grab my forearm, pierced deep.

I crawl away and look around. There are four of us left. Wulfgar says, I am ready for you, Grinder. He stands, sword out and shield up.

Rrodi sees me crawling and comes over to me as Grendel turns to face Wulfgar. Rrodi helps me up and drags me toward the horses. I hit him and tell him to let me go and he says, it's over. He says, Wulfgar is buying us time. I wrench away from him. He looks back at me as he runs toward the horses.

Grendel gathers his wits. He keeps his eyes on Wulfgar. He cackles, his laughter leaving his mouth in great gusts that whistle through the winding chasms between fangs. He grasps the two bars of the trap that enclose his leg. He pushes down, prying them slowly open. His gaze remains on Wulfgar as he does this. He says in happy, twisted non-words, Wulfgar. He stares at my friend. Hungrily.

Kill him, Wulfgar. Hrunting wants to sing and drink.

Wulfgar sees his opportunity. He charges while Grendel is pushing open the trap.

Grendel takes his leg out. Just as Wulfgar's blade reaches Grendel, the Grinder springs backward and away. It is impossible that an eoten so large can move so quickly. Grendel lands on his feet like a cat: soft and balanced, poised. He then stands at his full height on two legs. He towers over Wulfgar. He readies to spring forth. But then his radiant eyes lock onto Hrunting. He hesitates. The sword catches the light of Grendel's eyes. It reflects sword-shaped orange light onto the ground. Wulfgar attacks, swinging, and the reflection dances and flies.

Wulfgar goes forward and so does Grendel, counter-charging.

Wulfgar anticipates Grendel's swing, ducks it, gets in close. Grendel brings his other arm down. Wulfgar plants his feet in that steady Wulfgar stance, that balanced, low stance that could not be uprooted if the world turned upside down. Grendel's down-rushing talon meets Wulfgar's shield and the force of the blow is enormous. Bone-shattering. The shield cracks. Somehow, impossibly, Wulfgar does not fall. He absorbs the blow.

Grendel attacks again, swiftly bringing his other talon back down to strike. Wulfgar counters with Hrunting. Spine-covered arm meets family-forged blade. The force is great and the blade shears through Grendel's enormous spines, cutting into the flesh of the Grinder, but Grendel's arm carries through the swipe and hits Wulfgar. My friend is off balance.

Down comes Grendel's other claw again. He is so fast, so fast. The huge claw comes down. Wulfgar sees it but he can do nothing about it: he is off-balance and shieldless. He screams out of defiance and doom. Down comes the claw, whooshing with speed, raking over Wulfgar, shearing along his helmet, meeting his chainmail, splitting it, smashing Wulfgar's knee. It buckles. Wulfgar yells in pain. As he falls, he swings Hrunting one last time but Grendel sees it coming. The monster swats the blow away. Hrunting flies out of Wulfgar's hand and bounces and slides not an arm's length away from me.

If ever there was a time that the gods showed me a sign, this is it. I reach down and pick up the blade.

Grendel picks up Wulfgar with his huge paw, drooling, casting yellow light on Wulfgar with his radiant eyes. Wulfgar still has not given up. Out comes his curved knife. But Grendel just pins Wulfgar's hand down with his giant paw. He holds Wulfgar between his huge paws. Grendel will crush him. I let out a yell. I yell, Wulfgar.

Grendel turns his head round, slow and smooth and too far, like an owl. You know that word, don't you, monster. He looks at me and cackles. His eyes and fangs are horrifying. They are twist embodied. His eye-flames dance and flicker.

In Grendel's eyes, some corruption deeper than can be known. Roots that strangle and leech and grow.

Grendel breathes. He watches me, only breathes and watches me, pinning the writhing Wulfgar between his two paws. He watches to see what I will do but does not act. He watches curiously. Observing. Thinking.

Wulfgar yells, go. I can hear the blood in his mouth.

I see it again: Grendel thinking. An idea comes to him. He delights in it. He laughs, yelping like a dog. He turns his right arm a certain way and out from under it falls a skin-flap, a vast leathery tissue. Grendel bends his arm to make this flap into a sort of pouch, and he drops Wulfgar into it. There are injured men scattered around. He begins to collect them. They wail as he drops them into the thick flesh-bag.

I run forward. Grendel's head snaps up, his grin widens again and as I reach him he swats me away with the back of his talon, sending me backward end-over-end.

I get up. I run forward again, my punctured arm throbbing. Hrunting sings through the air as I run. Again the beast swats me back. I fall heavily. He giggles. I am insane with anger.

Grendel grabs up the last of the men, stuffing them in the flesh-bag. Rrodi has come back on his horse. Leaf Litter as well. He speaks quietly, tells me in a vehement whisper, go, it is time to go.

Grendel pulls his arm up and twists the flesh-bag like you

would twist a net full of fish to keep them in. The muffled screams of men inside its thick wall. Wulfgar shouting that he has dropped his dagger. He pleads, a dagger. A dagger to cut my throat.

Rrodi drags me up onto Leaf Litter, who is shaking like a branch in the breeze. One of the surviving rabbits comes riding full-speed from out of the tree cover to see how the trap has fared, nearly running into Grendel. Rrodi yells, run, run. Grendel springs after him, the eoten's flesh-sack bouncing and full of men. The Grinder's talons dig into the soft soil for purchase and the monster springs forward, its hindfeet ripping up dirt and grass and treeroots. The rabbit turns his horse. Grendel descends and rakes down the horse. Grendel grabs the man and crams him into his mouth. The Grinder disembowels the horse with one quick swipe. The horse screams and neighs. Grendel picks up its guts with one claw, opens his pouch up, shoves the horse entrails into the pouch. Screams coming from the bag. Grendel twists it back up again, closing it, leaving the hollow horse on the ground.

Leaf Litter's eyes go wide at the smell of horseblood. He shudders and bolts. Rrodi rides after me, hard and fast, and Grendel sees us. He yelps, laughs, lets us go.

True malice knows when not to kill. True malice knows that some victims suffer most if left alive.

I turn my head. Grendel recedes behind me. The last thing I see is his bag, low and sagging with men and horse guts and Wulfgar. The Grinder's meat-hoard.

Part Two

Unferth and Wealhtheow

The boat rises and dips with the swelling waves. The grey sea rolls angrily, daring us to row in sync. I lift my hand from the oar and look at it to make sure I am not bleeding. I'm not. I can pull an oar for three straight days.

Our three ships prowl the sea in loose formation. Our wooden prows jut proudly into the air as our boats crest the white-capping waves. Our three ships come sea-swooping around a jetty and there, barely visible through the misty fog, is a coastal village. Uhtred, the leader of our raid, turns to look at us, thirty-two men, from his spot at the front of the ship. He catches my eye and he points to the village. I nod to tell him that, yes, it is a town that we have not hit yet. He nods, spins his forefinger in quick circles: row double-time.

Five years have gone by since Wulfgar's death. The year is now 520, I am twenty-five, and the sea still whispers. It still whispers to me, death. But the sea no longer whispers it into my ear. Now death is at my back. The whispers of the sea, the churn and crash of its waves and its wind now push me forward. They speed me.

The villagers should see my face. They should see the black smile stretched over my skull.

They spot us and begin to run. They will not get far.

Ð   Ð   Ð

The Grinder

I once heard that there is a way to trick predators. A slaga told me how he once did it. The man was a slaga of some renown because of his ability as a beast-man, a man that can twist his thoughts and hungerings to mimic those of eoten. A man like Wulfgar. This man was eaten by ketta last year.

As a child, he was out with his father learning to trap rabbit and fox. There had been a drought that year and the hooved and antlered animals had been scarce. The wolves were starving. Wolves attack men when they are starving. They attacked the boy and his father.

He had never seen wolves. He thought them mysterious creatures, svelte and graceful. And so the boy stood there as the wolves charged. But the boy's father ran.

And the way that the slaga told the story, and I agree, is that his father was eaten because he acted like he was supposed to be eaten. He ran. But he, the boy, stood and marveled at their speed and their beauty. They stopped to sniff at him. And they ran after his father.

I know how those wolves felt. There is nothing in the world like chasing some young village girl.

Almost every person, almost all the girls and boys and mothers and fathers that I have chased in my five years of raiding have run away. They all run. I suppose there is nothing svelt and graceful about our lot.

Our ship grinds onto the beach. We hop out into the surf and storm onto the beach and up to the village. Prey.

I have grown into a fast man. I am taller than the average man by a head so I am maybe the second- or third-tallest man of all of Hrothgar's thanes. I have joined Hrothgar, that wrecked king, who is still hounded by Grendel. I am faster than all of his thanes; fastest on foot and quickly becoming fastest by hand.

We could use horses but they are not as good because they take longer to prepare and in this delay you always lose some of the people that you intend to turn to slaves.

I am shieldless, Hrunting slung over my back, with a short wooden club in one hand. I wear no armor. I heave my legs and pump my arms. The whole village runs in front of me. I pass the lagging villagers, the old and the sick. I pass the people that carry their small children. I pass the slow women and the men who stay with their women to defend them. The other wolves will get them.

I am after the ones who will get away. I am after those boys and girls of the age where they can run quickly and only look after themselves. The almost-men, almost-women.

I am gaining on them over the grass. The dirt is soft and supple; my feet dance over it. The breeze blows in from the ocean at my back, pushing me forward. There are three of these younglings. Stupidly, they don't split up. Two girls and a boy. One of the girls is heavier; I am gaining on her. I think, don't hold back on blows to the upper leg. She's thick. You won't break that bone. Let her have it.

The girl hears me approach. She turns her head in time to receive a hard swat from my club on her left thigh. Right on the muscle. She shouts and falls in pain. I keep running.

Two more. The boy is slower than the girl. I gain on him. He looks behind him. He stops to fight. You fool.

He tries to tackle me. I lean in with my shoulder. He has grown into his full height but his muscle isn't on him yet. I barrel into him. He goes down, sprawling. I stand over him, looking him in the eye. I give his head a knock with my club, pulling back on the blow just so because I don't want to kill him or make him an idiot. He paws at the air and falls, disoriented.

Now. The last girl. If we grab every last one of the slaves, I get my own to sell or do with what I want.

She is fast. It could become an endurance race. I don't want that. I will not win a distance run because I carry a club and Hrunting. I put in for one last sprint to catch her. And look, I am gaining.

Into the woods, the green and the brown rushing by. She hears me coming. She turns her head and looks at me in disbelief. She's muscled, with narrow hips and a straight frame. No wonder she does not believe it; she must be the fastest of the entire village, maybe the fastest girl I have chased.

She sees that I am catching her. Eyes wide in terror. I yell to her, stop now and I'll just hike your skirts but not club you. She looks back with gritted teeth but does not say anything. A fighter. A fighter always tries something.

She's quick. Fakes left, stops, turns, sidesteps. I barrel into her fist. But I have been in fights with harder nuts than this. I regain my balance and lunge at her. I swing my club slowly and grandly overarm at her head. She puts her arms up to absorb the blow. But anyone who has been in more than four good fights would see through my bluff. I pivot my arm a little, sneak my blow in from the side instead of over the top. The club connects with the side of her head. She crumples faster than you could drop a fish. I say, well, you tried. I stand there, catching my breath, looking down at her. Her head bobs, her eyes swim. Helpless. I won't even have to pin her down. She may vomit. Keep clear of that. I am excited, almost giddy, because though she has a man's figure, she is prettier and less used than most. That little nose.

Ð   Ð   Ð

Before. I scoured Hrothgar's land. I looked under every rock. I combed the flat, rolling marches on Leaf Litter, and then I waded through the murky, death-smelling fens, keeping Hrunting, Wulfgar's sword, raised and out of their filth. Looking for him. Each night, night after night, I returned to my cold campfire.

I looked at the horizon, a border between black and blue. My thoughts slipped down some slope and arrived at some tender spot, some place in which any thought or movement at all might tip me over, spilling me everywhere.

I thought: is this how a man becomes an eoten? Maybe eoten are created when hardship chains men to sorrow, and then the men run off with this sorrow into some cave and in that cave they undergo some slow metamorphosis. Maybe Grendel broods in his den and nurses some ancient injury. He goes and inflicts that injury on others. And in this way the injury perpetuates itself, breeds.

Now. We are rowing back to find a place to put in for the night.

I pull my oar and look at the slave girl. She sits down in the bottom of the boat, glares at me, her foot chained. I say to her, you would cut out my heart, wouldn't you. She says, of course. I smile back. I say, I like your spirit.

I think: maybe I'll free you, slave girl. Maybe I'll pick you when we're deciding who gets the loot. And then maybe I'll let you go. Or maybe I could convince you that I'm a different man than this and you can come with me and we can find a village somewhere away from the coast, and we can hide ourselves away.

I break her locked gaze, putting my eyes out to sea. That same dark horizon. That line between blue and black, between the freedom of the sky and the weight of the world.

You thought you would be free, girl, but you were going to be chained all along. You just didn't see it.

Đ   Đ   Đ

Uhtred picks a spot for us to put in. We get out and drag our slaves ashore and tie them to a tree. Time to pick our spoils.

Uhtred, Uhtred the Hungry, is Hrothgar's chief raid leader. He is a berserker from deep within the forests. He is big with sandy hair and a broad forehead. A man of strange appetites. Uhtred the Hungry does not only mean hungry for food. He has eaten one eyeball of every man he has killed. He says he will eventually grow eyes in the back of his head so he can see any blade or blow sneaking in. I do not believe him, but some men do, and I have seen this or that odd comrade bent over a killed child. Carving out an eyeball.

We line up the slaves and we make a pile of the booty. We will each choose one thing and then Hrothgar, our king, will get the rest. It is clear to all that I prefer the girl that I caught. Uhtred will pick first but he knows that I have had her once and so she is half mine already, and besides, one of the women, a young farmer's wife, is just as pretty. And then I will pick next after Uhtred because not only did we get all of them but I captured three slaves myself.

Uhtred walks, heavy-shouldered, forward-leaning, from one slave to the next, looking them in the eyes. The slaves look down. All except for my girl. Of course she doesn't.

Uhtred stops at her. She looks back into his eyes. If she wants death, she is staring down the right man. The girls that Uhtred beds. Sometimes, we find them later. Alive or dead, always missing an eyeball. Maybe Odin found his first Valkyries in a similar way. Maybe Odin raped women and tormented them and turned the best of them, those that resisted, into his Valkyries.

Some have killed themselves rather than be submitted to the appetites of Uhtred the Hungry. She looks him in the eye. Each moment she taunts him will be another moment of torture for her. But she does not care. She is honorable. A Valkyrie.

Uhtred picks her. He states in front of all the men that she is his. The other men look at me to see if I will protest. Half of all arguments among warriors end in fights and all of the fights with Uhtred the Hungry end in death and none of those deaths have been Uhtred's death, so I don't say anything. I am boiling over, furious, but I don't speak.

Uhtred drags the girl off by the arm. She tries to wrestle away from him. He hits her with his fist, hard. She falls and spits out blood and a tooth and the other slave women gasp and wail and the slave men are now wishing that they had fought us to the death. Aye, fathers and brothers and sons, you should have.

Uhtred says, carry on with the picking. He drags the girl to her feet and then he pulls her past me, stumbling. Odin draws my eye to her.

The brightness of the blood on her lip and cheek, the soil-brown half-kempt hair, the set jaw that misses its lost tooth not one bit. You could knock all her teeth out and she would still bite your finger off. Those eyes.

I should have let her go. Let her get away. I think: the gods will take my head for cursing her with this fate.

As she passes I incline my head down, just a little bit, drawing her eye to my hand. I hold a thing I keep in the small of my back. A knife. A thin slice of steel. I pass it off, palm-to-palm. She keeps walking, hides it well.

It's either crazy or genius. Sometimes, if your plan is clever or poetic or reckless enough, the spinners will see it through out of their eternal desire to make unlikely things happen.

The rest of us choose our loot. I look over the women but I no longer have the appetite. There is one helmet lying in the loose pile of axes, spears, bows, coins, animal skins. I do not have a metal helmet. So I choose that. Not even Uhtred has a helmet. It's not very old. Maybe twenty years. It sits snug on the head and leaves the face open. It doesn't protect the neck, but it is of sturdy metal and it has two broad circlets that go down and around the eyes, round-framing them. It has a slightly raised metal crest, arcing from front to back, which is in the shape of the world serpent, Midgard. Midgard is the giant serpent which encircles the world with its body. Its head ends back at its tail and bites its tail, holding it to make a continuous circle, to keep the floods of the oceans from falling into the void. On the helmet's eyebrows are metal workings that depict Sköll and Háti, the wolves that chase the sun and the moon across the sky. And on the back of the helmet is the face of a third wolf, the greatest of wolves, Fenrir, which has jaws that are so large that they touch the sky when he opens them. Fenrir will someday devour Odin. It is a good helmet.

Uhtred always sleeps a little away from camp when he has a woman for the night, though we can always still hear screams. It is getting late, though, and we hear no screams.

Maybe he'll come back with a malicious grin, holding the blade I gave her, saying, who gave her this. He'll look at me.

Maybe she has done it already.

We hear it. Not a woman's scream, a man's. She has botched it.

The men grab logs out of the fire for light. I think, I could run now, while I can, but curiosity and the whispers of the fates get the best of me. We rush to where Uhtred has camped out. He is on his feet and so is his girl. She holds the bloody knife. She stands her ground, between us and Uhtred. Our leader holds his throat, stumbling toward her. His windpipe, which she tried to cut, is intact. But he is badly cut. The neck is not a good place to be cut. He clasps his hands over his throat to stop the blood but it is too much too fast. His hands drop and the blood coughs out of the wound and he falls in the night.

The Valkyrie looks at us. She stands straight and tall.

The men lust for her blood. Torture. Uhtred's choosing her has fated her to torture and she must get it.

It's over for her. She knows this.

But I owe her. I can hear Thor's rumbling discontent in the distance. She looks at me. No one has ever glared like that and been wrong.

I wink at her. She nods an unseeable nod.

She raises the knife and runs for me. She is so fast that my own speed is challenged. This is good because it makes it look like she really is out for my blood. Maybe so.

I draw Hrunting faster than I have ever drawn it. I knock away her arm with the flat of the blade. She looks me in the eye, searing her face into my mind. Hrunting comes back-swinging, whistling toward her neck.

I bed down at the fire, setting my helmet next to me. I think about the girl's chains, still in the boat, and how they will be empty tomorrow when we row home.

I'll row and I'll think about her. Has a man ever killed a woman that could have been his wife?

Greet Odin for me. Do not tell Wulfgar what I am doing with myself. Whatever your name was, girl, I look forward to seeing you in Valhalla, in Odin's corpse-hall. If I myself am ever worthy to go.

Đ   Đ   Đ

The next morning. Today we will get in our boats and head back to Hrothgar.

I wake up in the early dawn surrounded by snoring men.

I ascend a small hill next to our campsite to take a look around. It is good to get a broad view of things in the morning. There is a pond in the middle distance. I go down to it. I dip Hrunting into the pond to clean the Valkyrie's blood from the blade. The whistle that is carved into the sword always fills with blood. I clean it out. I wipe down the sword in long swathes. Like comforting a dog, petting it.

Wulfgar used to turn the hilt of this sword in his hand. He would spin it a couple of times. It was his custom before he was to use the sword. Similar to how a man will rub his hands together or clap them on his thighs when he is about to do some task that will require much of him.

I stick Hrunting's point into the ground and I look at its pommel, which is swirled with engraved waves, waves of water or of heat. They look to me like waves of water in this moment.

The work of the last five years, the raiding and raping, was easy-made-easier by Hrunting's sharpness. I take to this kind of work. It is in my bones. I've been doing things like it since I was a child. Back when I had a brother.

I look down its length of steel, which was made from metal bars wrapped and hammered together to make one long, sturdy rod. These spiraled bars can be seen on the flat of the blade, wrapping. They give it a feathered look, like the sword is made from the feathers of some iron falcon, some steel eagle. The sound of it, too. Bird-like.

The sword screams silently. I can feel it, vibrating down the blade and through the hilt. This is not work that Hrunting should be doing. I am not a man that Hrunting wants to be with. It wants to extend its wings. It says, let me be free.

I take off my scabbard and I toss it into the bushes next to the pond. I step back from the shore a few strides. I turn to face the pond. I hold the sword up, level with the ground, straight, pointing out at the pond's silver face.

There are men that follow you, lurking in your gear. I carry some dead man's comb; he peeks out at me when I groom. I have inherited another man's flint striker. He only comes out to see how inept I am at making campfires. The brooch that holds up my cloak is from some other man who sees all of the poor weather that I trek through. I have my father's belt. He is tucked inside it, peeping out of its belt holes. I have Wulfgar's sword. He stretches himself out comfortably on the edge of the blade. He sees everything that I cut, sees every move of every fight.

I spin. I run toward the pond, twirling in a circle, the sword in my hand screaming and screaming and spinning with me. I turn and turn and heave the blade as hard as I can into the air. It screeches and whoops through the dawning air, rising and flipping end-over-end above the glassy pond. It drops. The screeching whistle wails out a long, low, relieved moan and the blade hits the water out at the center of the pond. A splash that sends ripples toward the shore. As I walk back to camp, those ripples glide toward the shore where I stood. But I do not see them. I have already turned around. I will never know just how big those ripples were or how fast they came or if they also bounced off of the shore and rippled all the way back out to the center of that pond, where Hrunting cut its way in.

Ð　　　Ð　　　Ð

Before. I rode back to Hrothgar and his city, following Rrodi on horseback. We had escaped Grendel. Once I realized that we escaped I thought: have we escaped? Because I am still in that flesh-sack. My soul has been cut from my body and is in that sack with Wulfgar. I am back there, Rrodi, I am back there. I have lost myself. Like a dog that has lost its way home.

When we returned and told Hrothgar the news of the failed ambush on Grendel, he quivered. He lowered his head into his hands, running his long fingers through his red hair. He sank into his throne, which he must cede to Grendel before the night comes. Wealhtheow's edged face was breaking, shivering and shattering like stomped ice.

Hrothgar looked up with a red face. Barely able to sit. He said, what is left for him to eat but my wife, my own body?

Now. Heorot stands, grey and moldering but still strong, a monument to the dead.

I look into the hold of the boat. The plunder. Cups and figures in silver. A gold torque, a necklace with swirling filigree. Thirteen slaves.

We bring them up to Hrothgar. The door swings open and we enter. He's drunk. Wealhtheow refills his cup endlessly. Her face breaks just a little more each time. The lines of her face now run through each other, no longer creating neat angles. They are now a bird's nest of twiggy wrinkles.

Her face is losing its structure. Bits split off. They waft out into the wide sky.

Before. Just after returning, failed, to Hrothgar. Rrodi and I walked out of Hrothgar's hall.

Rrodi said something but I didn't hear it. I thought, it is getting colder. The balancing blade of the seasons has begun to tilt toward winter. It is a matter of letting the season fall.

Something nudged my shoulder. I thought, I will find him. The nudging on my shoulder turned into shaking, and my eyes came into focus and Rrodi was in front of me, grasping me.

He said, you have nowhere to go. You are professionless and untrained and you will probably be caught and killed for your weapons and armor or taken by slavers and made to row some trader's ship until your back gives out and you are tossed overboard.

But his words were clouds in the sky. I fanned them away like smoke.

Unferth, he said. He switched from pleading to demanding. He said, you have nowhere.

I was not listening. The last thing I wanted was to fill Wulfgar's void with Rrodi, like some child whose pet cat has died and the next day asks her father to find her a new one.

Dawn. The sky was changing. The sun cracked over the horizon in crimson and yellow. The clouds gathered the sun's rays and smeared them across the sky.

I went over to Leaf Litter. I mounted. I thought, a cave. That is what I am after. I am looking for Grendel's cave.

The sun's rays finally met the tops of the city buildings and me upon my horse. The top half of me was bathed in yellow and the bottom half in shadow.

My thoughts drifted in. Like they came from somewhere else.

What is left for him to eat but my own body?

Ð　　Ð　　Ð

Now. We drink, all of Hrothgar's thanes, with another group of foolhardy slaga who are here to kill the big puppy, as they call it. They are my age, but I must be decades older.

We drink in Heorot to bring the Grinder, then leave the slaga to their fate. Wake up in the morning and clean them off the floor. Do it again. I don't mind this. I don't mourn men who go digging for their own death.

This is what cuts me: Wealhtheow feels the brunt of it. Hrothgar still expects the slaga to win. He still calls on men to kill the Grinder. He is enraged at their failure. He hits his wife. If you give a man a mountain he cannot climb, he will find the nearest hill and stomp his boots all over it.

Next day, cleaning up their blood – their flesh has all been eaten or taken away. Hrothgar comes in, half hungover, half drunk, Wealhtheow cowering behind him.

Wealhtheow suffers her burden like a grinding stone: just as the stone becomes smoother as it is used, Wealhtheow's body shapes itself to the work. Her posture is spear-straight, her brow hammered down, her lips fixed, and her eyes are those of a man on his way to the chopping block.

My eyes go to her when all eyes are somewhere else. She catches my gaze, meets it, holds it for a long moment, and then pulls her eyes somewhere else. And then, one drink later, I look at her again to see how she fares, and there she is, looking at me again. Challenging me with a long stare.

Do I dare stare back?

I do.

A flame ignites.

I admit, as any man would admit, that I am proud that I am stealing a queen from under a king's nose. Aside from slaying Grendel or out-wrestling Beowulf, snatching a queen is the most impressive thing a man can do. And the most foolish.

The next night. There is a shallow cave just outside of town that is used by travelers and children. There are animal teeth, bones, bits of hide around on the floor. I have built a cot in it. The roof of the cave is black from old fires. My sputtering fire adds to this layer of soot.

I hear her horse. She ties it up. Wealhtheow comes in, timid at first, peeking her head in.

She says, a cot. And a fire. Look how cozy you have made it.

She sits on the cot without a thought, flopping down on it like I'm close kin. I sit across from her, leaning against the cave wall.

I say, you act very different at Hrothgar's feasts.

She says, did you expect me to act the same way here?

I say nothing, shrug.

She says, how did you expect me to be?

I suppose like other women.

Queens are not women.

She lays down on the cot. She says, I want to be your lover, but I do not want you to misunderstand me. I love my husband. I will tell you about him now, briefly. And then we will act like he does not exist. She says, women who sleep with other men usually still love their husbands. Many who truly love one person are apt to love another and another.

I nod. I say, fine by me.

She says, Hrothgar is a good man when he is winning.

She says, before Grendel, Hrothgar would wake in the morning, turning with the rising sun into a hard man. She says, his eyes would steady themselves in his head as he thought on strategy or war plans or judicial matters. And I knew that what came from his mind would be full of all of the best things. Honesty and surety and deliberate honor. He was a king who found kingship like a woman who finds love: it filled his chest and made him massive, made him big and made his footsteps weighty and yet made them bounce. He will get it back, some day.

Her talk on Hrothgar's walk brings Wulfgar to mind. His pendulous walk, his rooted stance.

A silence.

It comes to me that we both mourn the warmth of good men.

I hand her a drinking horn and fill it with mead. I open my waterskin, full of mead too, take a long drink, wipe my mouth.

We look at each other like we did in the hall: a long gaze. Intense and solid. If you were to cut this world from the world tree Yggdrasil, you could tie the two back together with this line. It would hold them fast.

The fire glows and snaps. It is ready to be neglected. We sit opposite each other, a few paces away, she lounged on the cot, me sitting against the cave wall. The space between us pulls like a long fall. She drinks from a wooden cup, I from my waterskin. The mead is good. It stokes the fire. The Hæftworld waits like a patient guest outside the cave.

I look at her. She is pretty in the way that a flaw, positioned just right, is pretty. Like a chip exactly halfway up a sword or a fish-ripple on a glass pond.

So.

The thought, that thought, comes to us simultaneously. She grins; I contain mine long enough to act the man. I can't hold it in for long. It skips onto my face. I lean forward, get up. I take two steps to the cot, put my arms down and lean on the edge of the cot. My face is close to hers. I look into her angular eyes.

It aches, this brief separation, this potential.

Come, she commands.

I lean in closer. She doesn't lift a finger. She doesn't move her head forward to meet mine. She waits for me, waits for me to lose my traction and slide down into her kiss.

Down I go.

Đ   Đ   Đ

Before. I looked and looked. There are many caves around Heorot. There are caves that drop straight and deep into the ground, black abysses. There are caves that the sea has bored into the rock near the coast. There are caves that begin from tidepools and reach under them and then up into chambers inside the sides of hills. Some caves empty their water during low tide and fill up again at high tide. I explored them all.

Roping and rappelling into them, stumbling over boulders that obscure their entrances, swimming down into large puddles that turn into caves, waiting for an hour in the dark for my torch to dry, lighting it and descending into the cave's cool depths.

Ascending a mountaintop will make you feel new, reborn. It makes you feel that, when you descend again, you can be whomever you wish. Caves give the opposite.

Climbing a mountain makes you feel new because there is potential as far as you can see. But in the earthen compress of a cave, your sounds reflect back at you. Your shadow dogs you. Your smell is the only smell. Everything is up to you: you must choose this way or that. You feel only yourself, you smell only yourself, you hear only yourself, you see only your shadow. It is you and the rock walls and the water droplets and nothing else, except maybe the eoten that waits for you at the end of the tunnel. A mountaintop tells you who you might be. A cave tells you who you are, who you will be, forever.

To escape seeing and hearing themselves, to forget themselves, cave creatures turn into transparent, quiet ghosts. Transparent centipedes, transparent fish, transparent salamanders. They avoided me, skittering away. No, light-bringer, we do not want to see ourselves.

Trolls and orcneas. Ylfe and deor. I found them in their caves, sleeping or grousing around, or on their way to the surface to hunt. I scrubbed myself down to remove my scent and I padded my boots and wrapped myself in leather, leaving only slits for my eyes and mouth, and I left my chainmail with Leaf Litter at the surface so that I could be silent. The sputter of the torch was loudest, but I carried a leather bag into which I could thrust it to extinguish it if I encountered a huge lurker of the deep that was not Grendel. I sought Grendel like a knife seeks exposed skin.

I evaded the eoten. The orcneas clicked past me without noticing, their small claws hard on the rock. A troll, hairy and moist, padded around as I hugged the wall, torch in its extinguish-bag and my hand upon the hilt of my sword. I did not breathe.

I descended for a full day into one of the caves. It was massive. I came upon a lair, full of bones and scat. I thought, Grendel was here. I turned to let my torch show me the walls. And then I saw. Just in front of my face.

Wulfgar had told me about them. Mound-dwellers, cave-dwellers, sniffers in the dark. Poisonous. Huge. A haugbui.

It breathed next to me, a mound of fur rising and falling. Asleep.

It was rolled into a ball but the spines on its feet stuck out from the wrapped fur. The spines were yellow and orange and red, intense hues, and long as my legs. Foot-barbs, the haugbui uses them as defense. They are ground-snifters, eating nothing larger than a salamander. It had a massive, wide, rake-like nose for smelling out carrion.

Trolls and orcneas and other nameless predators hunt the haugbui. An adult haugbui can puff itself up to fill an entire cavern passage so that the predators cannot get around it. It keeps predators behind it in the passage and the spines on its hind legs strike anything that dares bite into its thick hind-flesh. Men have killed them before but you have to surround them on both sides of the cavern passage and they taste bad anyway and always kill men, especially when the haugbui gives up defending and instead charges the men to crush them.

This haugbui, full-grown, was too large to be eaten by anything. It slept and had nothing to worry about.

I went deeper but I soon turned back. I went by the haugbui's passage on my way to the surface. I could hear it waking up. It let out its mournful call, alerting the underworld that a great grazer of the deep had awoken to feed.

Now. A raid to a small island. We heard that this man has gold. Where is it hidden? Two men hold him and the rest of us threaten him. I'll cut off your fingers, one joint at a time, says one. I'll cut off your cock, says one. I'll impale you, ass-first, on the butt of my spear.

I point my dagger at his face and I say, I will eat your eyeball.

He's a hard man, one of those squat, solid old men that are impossible to knock over. He looks me in the eye with all sixty of his years. He spits. Disgustedly, he says, no you won't.

I take his head in my hand. The others hold him still.

Where is Uhtred the Hungry to watch this? My old leader would be proud.

I speak but I do not hear my voice. I hear Uhtred's voice.

It says, the great grazer of the deep has awoken to feed.

Ð   Ð   Ð

Before. That cavern was massive. There were so many side passages, drop caverns, long-reaching halls. I explored these halls; they led to more forks, more passages, more rooms that spidered into more passages and yet more rooms that branched off into more tunnels. I could have spent months looking through that cavern, maybe more. I thought: is Grendel in there, deeper than men can go?

Where does a thing like Grendel hide itself? Where do nightmares go when you are awake?

I came out of the cave. I mounted Leaf Litter. I turned him around with the reins. This way to the Svear, that way to the mainland forests. There is Hrothgar, too. He might take me in.

A feeling of misplacement, like going for your sword and realizing that it is gone.

Ð　　　Ð　　　Ð

Now. Another night at our meeting spot. I marvel at how she escapes from right out of Hrothgar's bed. Danes can sleep through anything. I heard of a Dane warrior who was killed in his sleep because he slept through a man cutting his wrist. Slept and bled.

I tell myself, you know that being caught means death for yourself and maybe for her, too.

She enters the cave. I greet her and she takes off her cloak and she smiles because I have put some purple flower onto the cot for her and I have fed the fire with scented wood.

She looks around, takes it in, sniffs the fire. It's our second time so we are still getting used to it. She says, I know why I'm doing this, but why are you?

The question pushes me off balance. I search, grousing around for something to say that will move us on, that will tread this question underfoot. But she's looking at me straight. A frontal assault.

Before my silence lasts too long, I say, your beauty. But she doesn't bite, her silence says, say more.

You can't just come out and say, because I already love you, because you have put me under some bittersweet spell. So I say, because you're Hrothgar's wife.

She smirks. Look at her, amused. I think, what are you gloating over, woman. Why are we talking about this.

She sways forward and backward, standing tall, her hands behind her back like a girl playing the queen in a child's game. She says, Unferth? Unferth who stings anyone if they brag about the smallest thing? Unferth himself wants to be able to brag about stealing a king's wife?

It is a good thing for a woman to see through the lies of a man. It is even better if, after she tells him that he is a liar, she smiles.

When we are laying together, I rest my chin on her collarbone. It is a certain spot. Not right on the collarbone. It is a little bit behind. In that small, rounded, hollow space behind. In that little grove, that little cradle.

I fit there. Not one shred north or south, up or down. Just there, right there.

It is perilous to search for these small havens, and they are rare as white stags.

Ð   Ð   Ð

Before. I had just left the giant cavern. I was on Leaf Litter, deciding where to go, what to do with myself. The desolate marches stretched away in all directions.

I came over a rise. It was that last hill with Wulfgar on our way to Hrothgar's hall. It was the day that he ate the berries and cursed at their delicious juice, the day with idyllic weather.

A dark spot catches my eye. Cavalry coming over the road, from a distance. Forty or more.

Rrodi said, you will be killed for your weapons. He said, you have nowhere to go. Maybe the spinners liked Rrodi's suggestion. I thought: if this is the fate that they have for me, then I will not refuse it.

But the riders looked familiar. Hrothgar. Going out for a hunt?

They approached, spears leveled. Hrothgar rode up, put his horse's face right into Leaf Litter's. My horse shied away. Amused, Hrothgar said, I wondered where you had gone.

Leaf Litter stirred and nickered. They were in their battle gear, armed to the teeth with swords, shields, axes, seaxes, bows, throwing weapons.

He said, we are paying my neighbor Thorkel a visit. To collect something that is due. He said, would you like to come?

I thought, if I don't, the only good I am for them is that I have things for the taking. A horse. Weapons and armor.

Leaf Litter shook; he seemed to shrink between my legs.

I nodded.

Something rang in my head like a horn sounding the alarum. I thought, I have crossed a barrier.

Hrothgar extended his arm. He pulled on one of the many arm-rings around his bicep. Silver. He slipped it down and off. He held it up. He said, as long as you wear this arm ring, you serve me.

I thought, I do not know what lies behind the barrier but I

know that it is important.

He said, it is time I made up for what Grendel has taken from me. Fight well and I will put more of these on your arm. I am a generous lord.

I thought, it is a threshold, a waterline. I thought, some slaga fall into this other place, this other life. Some slaga fall into it and do not come back.

You thought you were free, but you were chained the whole time. You just had your eyes closed.

Now. We load up what we need. Hrothgar stands there, mead in hand, to see us off. Wealhtheow at his side.

Last to be loaded are the slave-shackles. They are handed to me. I turn to drop them into the ship's hold, but Wealhtheow catches my eye. She's the only one I've known to disapprove of taking slaves.

Let me be.

Hrothgar approaches. He stands next to me in silence.

And then he turns to look at Wealhtheow.

We are on my cot, after our lovemaking.

How many times have me and Wealhtheow done this? I had better go to ground if, some months from now, she pops out a little one with my black hair.

We usually drift to sleep now, after the heat and luxury of each other. But we're both awake; some god or spinner keeps us up. I pay attention to when there are unexplainable breaks in your routine. You can look into, you can open up these little fractures. You can find hints of what goes on behind the fabric of fate, things that you were not intended to see.

She angles her head down, into herself. Her silver-gold hair sprawls unbraided. There's something on her mind. Wealhtheow is eight years older than me. Thirty-three. If someone eight years older than you has something on their mind, you let them say it. So I wait.

She says, you could go if you wanted.

I wait.

I say, do you want me gone?

She says, no.

I think, we are both stuck with Hrothgar, but I have a way out. I can leave his service, find another master, or another slaga to pair with. Get out of this cursed land. She knows this.

I say, is it the risk.

She says, no, it is not that either. I stopped caring about that a long time ago.

I say, is it because you hate to watch me take slaves.

She says, yes. In a way.

I say, why?

She says, this man that you are right now, you are not really this man.

She and Odin must be conspiring. She says her words and Odin dips them in his tar-cauldron and then plasters the hot word-tar onto me. The tar sticks to me, viscous and black and unremovable.

Sometimes you argue with someone and you know that you are wrong. But you have to guard your honor, so you argue with them until the bitter end. You have to look hard for weapons, for things that can help you in your fight against them. You pull rocks up from the ground, you pull up the roots of trees. You soil yourself digging through the word-earth. You have to dig and dig. But you know. You know that you are wrong. You are wrong the moment you start to dig.

She is smart. She herself is a spinner of fate. Already I can feel my tide begin to turn, my spinning coin begin to waver. Here comes my fate, flooding. I argue, I refute her, but I sense a tiny turn in me, the turn of a tiny rudder.

I lay there next to her. There is a long pause, long enough to let me settle into what has been said. The mood changes.

We are turning. I can feel it. Unferth and Wealhtheow swivel on a hinge. We will not go back to how we were.

I do not want it to be over. I look into her face, angular and strong and sure. She still holds onto the strength and rootedness that Hrothgar once had. She is small as a sparrow and thin as a branch, never swung a sword. She is miserable, hopeless. And still she has the strength to tell her lover: leave, for your own good.

I reach up. I touch her neck, her collarbone, and I ask her with my eyes, until the morning? And at this she shows the last sliver of the soft Wealhtheow that I have discovered. She shudders from the sorrow, she nods, quickly and surely, her eyes clutched and watering, to tell me that, yes, we can take in one more night. One more night before, while smiling in sweet bitterness, the spinners will murmur to us, soothe us as they spin our fate-threads away from each other like the two gentle, rolling wakes behind a single quiet-paddling waterbird.

Ð   Ð   Ð

I wake. Horse hooves.

Someone walking around outside the cave. I look toward the entrance. White light and a man's form. I squint at the morning light.

Hrothgar's voice: it's just you and me, Unferth.

I draw my sword. I'm on my feet.

I say, did you hurt her.

No, but I might kill her. Hurt her? Do I want everyone to know? Why do you think it's just me here?

I cannot hope to win a fight against Hrothgar. I say, I'll go and never come back.

He says, you could not go far enough.

I prepare myself. Heft my shield. Sword out.

The white-rimmed figure moves, holds something up. I squint to see. Twang-whistle-thud. An arrow cuts into my shield-rim. Sticks there.

Forward. Twang-whistle, the arrow flying by my left ear-hole. Probably would have cut the ear in half if I still had it.

I am fast. I get to him just as he pulls his huge sword from its scabbard. I slam him with my shield, knocking him off balance.

Run. Toward his horse. Scream at it. Slash its hindquarters. The horse shrieks and sprints off. I jump onto Leaf Litter, bury my heels into his flanks.

Twang-whistle. A piercing pain in my side. I pull out the shallow-buried arrow. Blocked by a rib.

Whistle. The last arrow goes over my head.

Ð   Ð   Ð

The man is a farmer. It looks like he will take good care of the horse. I scratch Leaf on the nose. Leaf cocks his head to the side and lifts his hooves nervously and watches me as I go. Sorry, friend, you're not going to like it down there.

Hrothgar is on foot so I have a few hours in his city before he'll get here. I buy things to make torches: cloth, pitch, stakes. I doubt that there is anything but meat down there so I buy the last of the season's fruit, both dried and fresh, and some cheese. I buy a new sharpening stone.

I will need more than just a sword and a shield down there. I buy a spearhead and three spear shafts. I buy three javelin tips from the smith. I will make my own javelin shafts.

I will need equipment to make traps. I do not know how to build something like Rrodi did to trap Grendel, but I know generally what went into it. I buy trap barbs and rope and wire. The farmer who makes them says that I will need extra of all of them if I'm going to make anything of complexity. I pause for a moment and look at him. I think, maybe I'll learn. I take extra.

I don't want to get lost in there. Not at first. The woman who makes twine in this city is old, lives in an unlivable house of dirt. I walk into her house, looking over my shoulder for Hrothgar. I tell her that I need the longest piece of twine she's got. She says, I just make one long length and cut it up and sell it, and I say, how long is your length right now. She picks up the coil. I wish it was longer. I give her Hrothgar's arm ring and I take the whole length of twine. She holds the arm-ring in both hands like some child. She says, I'm going to buy up all the mead, everywhere. I think, a good way to spend it, for you. If I were making bets with a man, he would have to stack his money good and high if I was the one betting on you making it through the winter. Three to one, at least.

I leave town, travel half the day, spend the night in a farm-house. Surprisingly, I haven't before met the man of the house. He has beer; we drink deep. He says, what is your profession.

I am twenty-five so I should have an answer but I hesitate. The silence tips the man off that there is something wrong about me. I am well-armed. He is suddenly wary; he eyes my sheathed sword and looks out his window for someone he knows, someone that he could shout to.

I must say something. I must respond to him or he will yell out. I do not know what to say, and so, calmly as I can, I say, I am a slaga.

The sound of it. The sound of that word.

The man believes it. He asks me questions that men often asked of Wulfgar. What have you slain, where have you been, who taught you. What is the closest you have come to death.

I can answer these. Yes, there was indeed a time that I was closest to death, there are things that I have slain, there are places I have traveled to. I was taught by Wulfgar the Strategist. I tell him of the orcneas, of fighting the draugr, of Yngvarr and Svala and Wulfgar.

The man is fat. His jollity reddens his cheeks and he drinks the beer with me and pours me extra and does not ask for payment for it. It is good to treat slaga well. They have it rough.

He says, Grendel. You aren't here for Grendel, are you.

He does not know that I was part of the group that tried to kill him. All of the slaga have left since then, giving up on Hrothgar, and this man thinks I am new.

I hesitate. I think, am I after Grendel?

I sit and I look into my beer. It is vibrant brown, like the brown mood created by the fáh, our ill-fated meeting.

Why else would a slaga be here? I finally say, yes, I am after Grendel.

He says, did you bring an army of slaga, or is it just yourself.

He knows that old men cannot sway young men. And so he says, sarcastically but with just the slightest tone of hope, with just the slightest riff that shows that he might be proud of me, he says, you shall be a celebrated man when you reach Odin's corpse-hall, and the other slaga who have tried to bring Grendel down will greet you and pat you on the back and say, what did the monster do to you? How did it eat you? When it ate you, did it start with your feet, too?

I smile and so does he. He thinks that I smile because I think his prediction is wrong but no, I smile because I think that his prediction is, for the most part, right.

That night I lay on a straw bed in the man's house. I am again coming to another barrier, another doorway, another gate. I imagine the entrance to the huge cave. Again, I think: I do not know what lies behind the barrier but I know that it is important. Some men fall into this other place. Some men go through this barrier and do not come back.

Đ   Đ   Đ

It is midday when I reach the entrance of the cave. I put my lopsided leather bag down and I unstrap the spear shafts from my back and I unsling my shield. I sit down on a rock, resting before I go in.

The weather is turning cold. The autumn sun sits low in the sky. It looks feeble, dim.

I want to knock something over, or push everything off me. I want to be burdenless, thoughtless. No family, no friends, no loves. No children, no wives, no brothers or mothers. Nowhere to be, no reputation, no fame, no master. No king to run from.

I'm shaking. I lift my hand, try to steady it. Can't.

Caves are dark sunrises. They blot up from out of the ground, rising in orbs. You can walk into these shadow-dawns. You can empty yourself into them.

It is something that my black hair, my black beard could blend into. Like I grew up there. Cool cave-breath shudders out of its black, perfect entrance. It breathes out, breathes in.

Hello, void. The last five years have been no good. Besides Wealhtheow, they have been no good.

I stand up. I pick up my leather bag and my spear shafts and my shield and I walk down into the cave.

Where are you going, Unferth?

To the only place that will keep me safe from Hrothgar. Or maybe somewhere else. Maybe to pick a fight with Grendel, if he's down there. Maybe to my death. Maybe just into a cave, a big cave. Maybe I'm going to another world. Maybe I'm going to Valhalla. It does not matter where.

This, this here is what matters. Right here, this: I can feel my thread. I can feel my fate-thread. I am walking right on top of it. It is thick, wooly, taut. Slide your foot forward. Slide your other foot forward. Can you feel the yarn on your heels?

Where are you going? A bad question, Unferth-who-was. It doesn't matter. It has never mattered. Here's where I'm going:

See that thread? Wherever it leads.

Ð   Ð   Ð

The world was made from the body of the giant Ymir. The soil was made from his flesh, the rocks and mountains from his bones. The sea was made from his blood and the sky from his skull and his brains were thrown and scattered in the air to create clouds. I do not know what the caves of the world are. Maybe they are the nose, the mouth, the ears, the veins.

I unravel my twine as I go so that I will not get lost. I make marks on the walls, naming the passageways and rooms. Thor's Breath because the wind is strong in this room. Giant's Bed for this room because of the large flat stone that rises from the floor. Trunk of Yggdrasil because this room connects to many other rooms. I make marks on the walls of other passages that tell me, to Thor's Breath, to the Trunk of Yggdrasil.

The cave is massive. I explore each passage that branches from the Trunk of Yggdrasil. Half of these branches have ten or twenty more branching passages, which then further fork and branch and wind. There are tight spaces between some of the tunnels. I hesitate to go through them.

One of these squeezes entices me. I look into it and I can see, just barely, a blue light on the other side. I extinguish my torch and hold my breath to look and listen. No noise. A blue glow slides over the wet rock. The color of a shallow sea in summer. Maybe I've found one of Loki's hiding spots. He's always running from some god, trying to hide himself away from the trouble he's caused.

I later run into orcneas. I hide from them. I hide from everything.

Wandering, I come to a troll-room. Littered with bones and debris. I listen at the door for anything inside. Silence. I go in. I run my hand over the smoothed rock floor where generation after generation of trolls have slept. Who knows if the trolls are the biggest thing down here or if they fear something even bigger or more deadly than themselves.

The scraping of something on rock.

I look back toward the passage that I came through. Something is coming home.

I go rigid. He trudges in, sits.

Troll. An ugly, bent-backed mixture of a man and a pig and a bat. He is naked. Thick, the bulk of three or four men. Blue-white skin. He stands like a man does. His cock dangles and swings. Stubby legs and large, long bulked arms. Huge ears on his head. Big flaps of ruffled, pointed flesh that catch cave-noises. A man's lips. A mouth full of stubby teeth. No eyes. A huge, piggish snout, fleshy, broad, many-nostriled. The snout is long like a pig's but ends in a flower of skin like the nose of a bat. The skin-flaps of the nose dangle, loose.

He carries the skin of an orcnea, the remains of prey. Weeks old. He sucks the orcnea hide like an infant would its thumb. The troll drools, broods on some monster-thought.

He stops chewing. Silence. He angles his head toward me, listening. I make no noise. I am absolutely still. The room is nearly silent. The only noise is the delicate whisper of my torch.

Oh. My torch.

He snorts. He drops his orcnea corpse toy and fists his way toward me, snuffling and drooling, knuckles to the ground.

Run.

He pursues. His arms do his running, shooting ahead to grab ridges in the cave walls and then hurling his body forward. I am fast. But the troll is built for chasing down prey in a cave.

I sprint into utter darkness, the wind-muffled torchlight barely strong enough to light my way. Each moment I am newly amazed that I have not run into rock. I know that the Trunk of Yggdrasil is coming up soon and if I can make it there then maybe I can slip into one of the side-passages and

An up-jutting rock catches my foot. In the air, pawing darkness. I hit the floor, rolling, sliding, stunned. Here he comes.

I lay still.

The troll comes to a stop not a spear's length away. I hear his breaths scraping their way out of his craggy, twisted windpipe.

His breaths stop. He listens for me.

I hold my breath.

I dropped my torch as I fell. It sits, an arm's length away, burning.

The torch crackles, sends out a flame-pop.

The troll pounces on it, so near that it grazes my boot. The troll grabs up the torch with his huge hands and shoves the torch into his mouth.

Darkness.

A shriek, almost human. The whoosh of something thrown followed by a wooden knock on the rock wall behind me. The extinguished torch on the stone floor. Rolling back and forth.

The troll turns his bulk in the darkness, his feet scratching the stone floor. He breathes deeply. Like he's trying to reassure himself.

The troll moves on, long-hunting, prowling for something to tear and gnaw and carry with him like a favorite toy.

Đ   Đ   Đ

Time to eat. If you've got a salamander and a bat and a crab, you've got a good meal. There is a viscous yellow paste that grows on the wet stalactites and stalagmites and if you boil it long enough it dissolves into broth. You can drop your chunks of meat into the broth. It doesn't taste good. But you can will it down. There is a red moss that grows on the ceiling of many of the chambers of the cave. I throw headless spear shafts at the moss to knock it down. You can't ever eat the stuff. It's too tough. But it makes for something to chew on and it tastes nice and earthy. The bitterness of beer and the sharpness of a root. It turns my spit blood-red.

A world of predators and prey down here just as there is on the surface. The translucent salamanders and shrimp and fish and crabs eat the insects. And they eat the mice that wander into the cave or the unfortunate bats that fall from the ceiling. The crabs even eat the bat spoor. Orcneas and haugbui then eat the salamanders and the crabs and the shrimp and the fish. And the trolls eat the orcneas and sometimes a haugbui. The trolls eventually die and the cycle repeats.

I have learned the routes that the orcneas take. I set snare traps along their paths. You can't hunt them because they travel in large packs. But if you lay a trap and catch one, the rest will leave it behind. Then you can go and harvest your meat.

You can do a thousand things with the body of an orcnea. Their springy sinews can be used to make trap or bait lines. Their eyeballs are good for eating. At first you see them as all slime and skin and bone. Then you see them as little stringy tool-bags.

I come back to Giant's Bed from a long day of hunting, exploring. Time to lie down. Blow out that torch. Light is precious.

Ð   Ð   Ð

You and me, Unferth, it is just you and me now. Unferth and Unferth. Welcome to the cave and the darkness that I call home, Unferth. Let me show you its wonders and its terrors and its ability to press upon a man. And then I will show you the magic of the cave, the magic that lets a man's lost soul gather like dew, remaking him like a slow-growing stalagmite.

Wake, Unferth. What will I do today, you ask. But there is no day. There is no day and no night. Day and night run together like a sunset and its sea-reflected image.

I am getting lower and lower on torches and I know that I must either learn to see in the dark or find a way of creating light without using fire. The spot that I found with the blue light is deep in the cave. I only have two torches left and they will get me down there to the blue but not back to the surface again. Will I need to get back to the surface again?

It is sometimes the way of a man to ignore something that he ought not to ignore simply because he doesn't feel like thinking about it. I am a man who does this. And so down I go with my two torches, descending into the depth to visit the blue light. I descend and I descend and it takes me a long time. It is warmer down here.

Down and down and down. My last torch. I am getting close. Maybe this blue light is made by some huge beast that hunts by light in the heart of this labyrinth. Who knows how the beast is formed or how it moves. Maybe it's a huge millipede with a poisonous bite and blue lights on its head. Maybe it's a bird with blue-glowing feathers that glides through the darkness, taking its prey with long, obsidian talons. Maybe it's my dead brother, eternally prowling the caves for me. Maybe he has asked wise Odin where I am and Odin told him and so my brother searches for me in this world-recess with his eyes that were blue in life and now glow blue in death.

I approach the hole. Depthless blue light. Not caring, I drop my torch at my feet. It falls into a puddle. It hisses and sputters out.

The blue light pulls me like a bug to a campfire. I drop my weapons, all except my seax, a long battle-knife for cramped fighting. I crawl forward into the hole.

It's a squeeze. I can barely move my arms. I'm as vulnerable as a legless horse. But the light grows stronger. The thin tunnel is long. I crawl and crawl and the light grows stronger. I think, for just a moment, that I see it ripple, see the light pulse. I stop for a moment and listen.

Dripping behind me. The eternal cave-drip, which began before man and will go on after him. In front of me: the faintest fluttering. Like the air is rearranging itself, scratching itself or performing some task. Maybe the air down here has learned to move, to blow itself around. Who knows what the world has learned about itself down in these caves. And, if so, who knows what it wants, what it can do.

I keep crawling. A breeze. I am making too much noise but there is no way to avoid it. I try to squeeze my body over one last rock. I have to turn my head to the side to get through. My chest gets caught so I exhale all of my air and I slowly squeeze my chest through the pinch, inching ever so slightly. Don't get stuck. My chest goes through and I breathe again and I slip the rest of my body past. I look up.

Glowing blue rods hanging from the roof of the cave. Like a thousand oceanwater icicles have found a home and decided to stay here in eternal company.

I stand up and my face touches something. Sticky, gooey, cold. I put my hand up to brush it off but my hand gets caught by more of the stickiness so I just stand there for a moment with my face and hand covered in this mysterious goop, trying to figure out what it is. I look. The slime is clear, almost invisible. It dangles from the blue glowing rods.

I remain, hand and face cradled by this slime. I feel the slightest of tugs. The slime-strands gently pull me toward the ceiling. I let my arm go lax and the slime-strand keeps it suspended in the air. The slime pulls it upward, gently.

The light-making creatures themselves are moving, wriggling

around. They are reeling in like fishermen these gooey strands that grasp my hand and face. They heave in the line, pulling their bodies up like retracting worms, and then reach their bodies out again to grab more of their line, and then heave in the line again. I smile. It feels like the tiny delight that you get when a seal comes to your boat to get a better look at you, or when a tree drops its small fruit right onto your head, or, as you rest in a field, when a butterfly lands right on the tip of your boot.

I use my seax to gently cut the goo lines stuck to my hand and face. I kneel so I don't get caught in them again. I sit down and watch. Hello, goo-worms. What are you doing down here?

There are constellations underground. The glowing stars of the sky are not only in the sky. Stars are everywhere. There are stars that dance in campfires, there are stars that sparkle from within rocks, stars that wink at you from the tops of waves, that pulse in the blue bodies of underground worms. Stars are not a thing themselves, they are a thing that is in other things. They are like a law, or a memory: anywhere you go, they are there. They have found it already.

A fluttering noise. Insects. There are moths flying through this room. In the next room, a moth-roost. The moths line the cave ceiling like mold on bread.

A moth flying to the roost gets caught by one of the goo-lines. The worm, which is ironically itself fishing, starts to pull in its catch. The moth flutters and struggles and gets itself caught in more of the slime-lines and the owners of these slime-lines pull up, up. The moth reaches the top. Five of the worms extend their black jaws and start to feed. The moth bats its wings furiously and then stops.

Part Two

I wish that Wulfgar could see them.

Ð   Ð   Ð

Odin gave up his eye to know everything. Losing an eye is no small thing. I know many men that would not give up an eye to know everything. They would say, I don't want to know everything. They would say, and one eye would leave one of my sides vulnerable on the battlefield.

These men are justified. But then, if you know everything, won't you win any fight?

Odin has two crows, named Thought and Memory. The crows go out into the world and then come back and sit on his shoulders and whisper what they've learned to him. They tell him all of the world's goings-on. Through them Odin sees all of the past and all of the present and all of the future: Ragnarok and the end of the world, even his own death.

Thought and Memory visit me, too. They whisper to me like they whisper to Odin. But they are not bound to tell me the truth like they are to Odin. No, they tease me. They pull lies and rumors from my own mind and cover them in honey and dangle them in front of me.

Wulfgar is alive, says Memory.

Use caution here. When you are remembering, you should always ask Thought what he has to say. It is trouble to listen to Memory when he talks about your memories. But I listen anyway. The more you ignore Memory, the more he squawks.

165

He is alive, says Memory.

I know that this is wrong. Thought knows. He argues with the other crow. I did not see Wulfgar die but he is dead, says Thought. Thought says, Grendel ate him or he killed himself and then Grendel ate him. He could not have cut himself out of Grendel's skinflap because that flap was inches thick. Wulfgar has been devoured and the only things left of him are his cracked bones, which were shat out and now sit hollow and brittle in some swamp. Some frog has made a hatchery out of his eye socket.

Thought always puts forth his reasons, Memory always ignores them. Memory always says, we did not see him die. We did not see him die.

The two birds argue and argue. I am hounded by their squawking on either side of my head for the thousandth time as I walk through the cave, ducking under low ceilings and hopping over the rises and falls of the cave floor. The glow-worms light my way.

I run the cave passages, wearing a path of smoothness into the rock floor. I have been here a long time. If you can get away from that troll when it comes hunting, you can survive in this cave.

The glow-worms ride on me. I use the sticky strands that they dangled in the darkness. I have wrapped these strands around my helmet and then again over the bodies of the worms so that they are stuck there by their own strands of slime. Put on the helmet and you've got a torch that burns on insects. I'm more than a little proud of this invention.

I feed the worms well and they grow. They become brighter than a torch. My helmet has the great serpent Midgard engraved into the metal, which runs along the center, from the top of the nose to the back of the skull. I put two of the glow-worms on each side of Midgard, running front-to-back. But the biggest glow-worm, which I have named Bug, sits directly on top of Midgard. I have named him Bug because he is a bug. He is huge. The worm basks in his glory as the best and brightest of the glow-worms. He is first fed.

I have been up long today. Tonight. This portion of eternity. It is time to sleep. I return to Giant's Bed, my home. I take off my helmet and put it under an orcnea skin to black out the room and I collapse onto my bedding made from the hide of a young haugbui that had a bad death. I lay on its furry skin and I apologize to it every time that I lay on it because I was the cause of its bad death. But the feeling of guilt is starting to go away because I am better at killing small haugbui now.

I lay on my side. I always sleep on my side. I let out a sigh and I bend my knees just so and I bend my elbows too, curling up, and my muscles relax and the contours of the cave floor and the haugbui skin cradle me.

There is a tiny stream that runs through this room and falls into a bottomless hole. This sprinkling cave-rain sings me to sleep as it comes from somewhere and goes nowhere.

Unferth. You take comfort in being nowhere. In wrapping yourself in darkness.

Puzzle that one apart.

Or don't.

Ð　　Ð　　Ð

There are places in the world with enough personality to make you the place and they the visitor, you the thing and they the man. They put their cuts or their chips into you as a traveler might do to a rock that he passes on the road.

The cave's marks are on me, its teeth are in me. I cry and stalactites form on the hairs of my beard, on the end of my nose, tan and crusty. I shit. When I turn around I see the stalagmites that have plop-plopped out of my ass. I am a many-tunneled labyrinth of cave-tubes and wet passages that take water from here to there, dripping and running and churning and then disappearing into a black void.

I've been down here a long time. A year? Two? Five? You cannot judge time in the cave. You could count your sleeps, I suppose. But why care about time when there are no seasons?

I try to guess. A year of living in the cave, maybe. A year of eating orcneas and haugbui and that red ceiling-hung moss and that scum that grows on the wet rocks. A year of feeding bat and orcnea meat to my glow-worms to keep them shining and to keep the world lit. A year in and I finally decide to see how deep it goes.

Deep, so deep. Days deep. I descend and descend. Much of the cave does not go deep. It stays near the surface, crisscrossing horizontally. But some paths go deep if you wish to follow. Follow the water.

Most of the water of this earth-throat runs out and away from the cave in small streams that wind their way through tiny passages that are too small to fit through. The only waterways that I can fit through are those that terminate in a great fall. Follow a stream and then it falls into a black abyss. Find another stream, follow it through winding passages for a day, and yet again it falls into an abyss. Follow another stream steeply downhill, steady yourself with orcnea teeth on the bottom of your boots for traction. Descend and descend.

I go through a passage that opens up into a formless void. Not a tunnel, but a void. I see nothing. Empty below, empty to the right, empty to the left. The only thing that stretches in front of me is a roof. My voice does not echo; the chamber is too large. It is like a sky that goes down instead of up. An under-sky. I look down and I expect to see stars, the moon.

I steady myself over the hole. The water from the passage runs down and down and then falls out and ceases to be.

There is a vague noise, dim and full and deep. Distant falling water. Maybe this is where the hæftworld meets Yggdrasil and where the tree sucks the water from our world to feed its massive leaves and branches. I pull out a spare glow-worm. I always carry extra. I lean over the edge of the void, dangling the glow-worm from my hand. It wiggles. I drop it.

Down it falls, end over end. Far. I see it splash, the tiniest of splashes. If my vision were not as keen as it is there is no way that I could see it. But there it is, writhing in the water. That is a long way down.

It drifts. A lonely blue mark. Distant, lazily bobbing end over end, floating away and out of this world. There is a current.

I want to go down there. Have a look. Turn over a few rocks. I want to know if there is something under me, maybe some undecayed body part of Ymir, the giant whose body was used to create the hæftworld. A huge toenail. An eyeball.

There was a current, a downstream. There must be an upstream. And if there is an upstream then there might be some part that drains into that chamber more gradually than all of the drops that I have found so far. I note which direction the upstream is. Let's take a look in that direction. As soon as I am ready.

I go up again to get supplies for a longer journey. I kill more orcneas and I dry their eyeballs and I stockpile more food: red moss, slime, bats, crabs. I sharpen my sword and my seax and I feed the glow-worms on my helmet and I pack eight more glow-worms in an orcnea skull. I grab up handfuls of moths for them to eat.

Back down. The cave branches and branches again and I keep to where I think the most gradual slope might be, a slope that goes toward the direction that I saw the current coming from.

After two sleeps, I find a promising passage. It spirals down and down like it was bored into the earth by some tunneling mole. I descend and descend. The tunnel dead ends into a pool of water. Not very wide, but deep and clear. I leave my small bag of equipment. I take off my boots. I take off my sword, keeping my little seax, small and sharp, strapped across my lower back. I take my helmet and my spare glow-worms.

I dive down into it and follow it out into a larger body of water and then I swim up, up. I see the surface rippling above me and I go to it. I break the surface.

This is it. All I can see in front of me is water. It is blue-tinged from the light of my glow-worms. A dark sea. Endless. Calm. What the world must have been like before anything existed.

I tread water for a moment, taking in my surroundings. There is a wall of stone behind me, from where I came in. To my left, far away across the dark light, is a slash of light. Coming from a jagged crack in the distance. Not sunlight. It pulses. Brighter, dimmer. Orange.

I need to mark where I came in. I take a glow-worm from the orcnea skull that I carry. I smash the worm against the wall and I spread its glowing guts over the rock.

Ð   Ð   Ð

I swim toward that orange fissure. It looked small from where I came in. It is not small. It is far.

It takes a while. But I am a good swimmer when I need to be and the water is calm.

I swim. The orange scar grows as I approach. I swim for a while, take a break, tread water. I hope there are no eoten in here. I taste the water. Fresh. Are there freshwater eoten? Who knows how deep this lake goes. I look back to make sure I can still see where I came in. The guts still glow.

I turn around and start swimming gain. The orange glow emanates from a huge gash in solid rock. It looks like there is a beach, a slight shore, just in front of the gash. The cut in the rock goes all the way down to the beach, and then stretches upward, towering over this buried lake like some beacon.

I drag myself all the way through the wide under-sea, breathing heavily by the time I reach the crack.

My swimming feet find ground. I walk onto the black sand beach, dripping. The fissure stands tall in front of me. It starts at the beach floor and reaches upward the length of a hundred of myselves, stacked, feet-on-head. Immense. It takes a very impressive thing to impress a Northman, and I am impressed. Orange-yellow light comes from it, oranging the lakewater in front of it. Bright. I shade my eyes. I am pulled. I am drawn. This gash in the world must have been hewn by some god. Some god with the might to strike this deep, the might to wound the world at its core. Some god-made axe-wound.

I approach. The rocks around the fissure are unlike cave rocks, black and jagged instead of tan and worn.

Hot air pours out of it. Churning heat-waves that writhe and wave and float up and out of the gash. I unstrap and put down my glow-worm helmet. I set it on the sand. I walk forward.

I stop. I stand and stare. Warmth.

There is a rightness to it. Like when you are splitting wood and you swing your axe down and you know that it is a good swing even before the axe hits the log, and then you look down and, yes, the log is split as even as a half-moon. Like when you are listening to a man play a lyre and you think that you have heard his song before but you are not sure and then the refrain comes and, yes, you recognize this song, it's a beautiful song, and you know that the coming refrain will put nothing but beauty into your ears.

The black sand puffs out from the weight of my feet. It's not mud and it's not sand. Softer than both. If the world has fur, this is it.

Heat pours from the gash, wobbling and waving as it ascends. I step closer. Warmer. I step again. Hot.

I look up. It towers. Massive. Red and orange and solemn. Light and heat and power. Who knows how long this earth-wound has been rumbling and venting. Festering.

I feel it rumble. I stand still and listen to the deep groan. It rumbles, stops. Rumbles again, stops. I look down at my feet. Rumble, rumble, and the grains of earth-fur shake and bounce on my feet.

I raise my head again toward the earth-wound. My feet guide me forward. They step closer and the sound grows. As if the wound reacts to my approach. Another step. A louder rumble. Deep. The pitch goes deeper and deeper and deeper until it cannot be heard, until it is just a shaking of the ground. A giant snarls.

I stop, fearing its anger. I am close to the rock wall and the opening of the gash. It is so hot. The light from inside the gash bathes my face, my beard, my hair in orange. I raise my hands up in front of me, palms forward. I plead with it. I say, can I touch.

I stand there a moment, feet staggered, arms raised, palms forward. I wait for an answer.

Moments pass.

Ymir sighs. The wound lets out one long, sonorous moan like a man does when his pain is too much for him, when he has reached the end of his endurance, when he is on the cusp of giving in.

Left hand first, then right. I touch the rock wall. I run my hands over it. It is hot and rough. It vibrates like a purring cat.

My mother tells me, the first things were poison and frost.

We are inside our home. Sometimes, she talks to me deep into the night. She knows that I never want to sleep and usually she makes me go to sleep anyway but sometimes it seems like she does not want me to. Tonight is one of those nights. So we stay up and she tells me stories and sings me quiet, murmuring songs.

It feels like I have to look down a deep well to see these old memories. Sometimes I can't remember them at all. You can only see down a well when the sun is at the right angle. But, sun or not, you can always hear those memories splashing around.

She says, and then warmth crept up and threw the frost back, chunk by chunk, until there was room to create a giant. And from this warmth, Ymir gathered himself together in the way that water droplets grab each other.

As she says this, she pinches her thumbs and fingers together on each hand and then brings each pinched hand together so that the tips of her fingers touch.

Odin was already around by then, she says. Whenever she mentions Odin, she puts eight fingers, four in front of four, on the ground to symbolize his horse, Sleipnir, who has eight legs. She says, the gods and the giants were in a feud, and he and his brothers killed the giant Ymir. And then the gods sculpted Ymir's body to create the earth: oceans and rivers from blood, rocks and mountains from bones, sky from his skull, clouds from his brains, soil from his flesh.

I listen. I wonder, in that childish way, purely and earnestly, if Ymir is still alive.

My child-mind thinks: no, he is dead because if you take away a sheep's blood and take its brain and put it somewhere else, like in the sky, it dies.

The heat. My hands begin to burn as I run them over the rock.

It is bright inside the gash. I squint until my eyes are used to the light. I force myself to glance in. There is movement.

I put my head into the gash. Hot, hot.

I turn my eyes downward. Lava.

Rumbling, a sound so low. Hot. Baking my face. Lava. There

is yellow-orange blood flowing down there. A steady flow, measured. Viscous. A river of thick, orange water.

Look at this pumping blood. Ymir is not dead. Ymir is alive. Odin struck him but he is not dead.

I was wrong about Ymir. The whole world was wrong about Ymir. We all think he's dead. But I stand here. I stand at the edge of Ymir's heart. I can see it beat.

Ymir is alive.

What other things am I wrong about? What other things do I believe that I should not? I picture Hrunting at the bottom of that lake, choked by seaweed. Hrunting, thrown in that lake by a man who thought himself no man. I picture Beowulf, big and bulging. Beowulf, dismissed by me, who thought himself better. Grendel. Everyone's fear of him. My fear of him. Grendel, feared by a man who now has no reason to fear because fear requires risk and risk requires the chance of losing something.

Ymir lets out another sigh. The ground rumbles. I pull my right hand off of the wall, bringing my hand to my chest. I can feel something. There is something in there, something beneath my skin. It roils. It wakes.

I had never considered Beowulf.

Hope hatches from its white shell.

Ð   Ð   Ð

You can put off your fate. The spinners will allow it for some time. You can hide behind a royal name, an easy craft, a failure.

You can hide under the black of mourning, under sickness. You can even hide yourself behind a sword.

You know, Unferth, of the hiding that I'm talking about.

But eventually the fates, those motherly spinners, will pull you out of hiding. Their threads are attached to you, body and soul.

I feel their tugging. Grendel.

I realize, I haven't killed anything bigger than a baby haugbui. I'm not ready for Grendel. But maybe something else. Yes, something else must be done first. Before Grendel. Don't test the boat on the sea until you've tested it on the river.

I have seen the cave's wonders: the rooms of spindly crystals so delicate that they are broken by breath. The endless stone chambers that are as tall as any tree but so narrow that you can barely fit a foot into them. The waterfalls and the stone columns and the rivers and lakes and small, pearl-hued salamanders. I have endured its loneliness, its endless silence, its slips and falls and cuts and squeezes and haunted passages through which haugbui mourns and troll screams reach after me as I run, panting. I do not get lost. It is not because I have a map or because I keep track of where I was coming from. I just know the cave. I know every nook. I could draw a map. This is my cave.

The call of some eoten echoes, bouncing and reverberating and echoing back. Low, gurgling. A chill down my back. The sound of a troll.

The troll that I still run from, the troll that steals orcneas out of my traps, the troll that prowls like a nightmare.

It is my cave. Almost.

Here is the way that fates are made. The spinners weave this into you and that into you and they weave you over here and over there and they weave you near other people and then they weave you apart. And then at some point the spinners will change their weave. They will start to weave your various threads together. Your upbringing, your loves, your memories, your strengths and your weaknesses. They will weave every part of you together for one event, one event that will test each part of you. And when all of your fate-threads finally come together in this way, the spinners will hand the weave over to you. It is your turn. You will be free from the fate-threads for just a moment: the moment that it takes for you to decide whether to defy your king, the moment that it takes for you try to convince a girl's parents that she should be your wife, the moment when you pull up and aim your bow at the deer that could feed your starving family. And right then, the spinners will notify Odin and he will turn his head toward you and they will all watch to see what you do with your threadless moment.

Đ   Đ   Đ

Arm.

Pick up the heavy chainmail, think about wearing it. Faster without it.

I imagine the troll's jaws. Wear it.

Strap on the sword belt. It is a good thing to take your weapons out and hold them, spin them before you use them. Pull the blade from its scabbard and check the edge though I know that it is already sharp. Slide it back into the scabbard. Draw my seax, which is so slender and deadly that it could fit between the scales of a snake.

Shield. Will it do any good?

I decide to bring it. Strap it to my back.

Helmet next. I greet Bug. I run my finger over his blue-glowing body. He contracts slightly. No food today, my wormy friend. Have a shit, cut your hair, if you have any. Today we must be light and limber.

I strap on the helm and I shake my head around, testing the fit. The glow-worm light moves over the ceiling and the walls.

Spears. Pick them up, three altogether. Grab my Thor's hammer necklace, put it on, remember him. Bad to forget the gods before you head out. Bad to remember them right before you fight. Better to remember them now.

Have you thought up how to kill this thing, Unferth?

A fall trap would not work because trolls are too quick. He would just grab the cave walls before he falls and then come and kill me. I could use a net but he is so big that he may break out of it and then it is me and my sword against him and his two crushing fists and he would kill me. Poison is good for a big eoten but I have no poison to put on a weapon and to use poison you must have time to let it do its work. He would just kill me.

You cannot blind a troll like you can blind orcneas because trolls have no eyes. No one knows how they move through the utter blackness. Magic, some say. I think it's their ears. They can hear even the whispers of stone, the quiet muttering of flesh.

To his lair. He will hunt soon. I know his rhythms.

A memory enters my mind. The troll carrying that orcnea

carcass, dry and decayed. Cradling it like a little girl carries her doll. I push it away. Pound that fear flat.

He can hear. He can hear very well. So I clap and yell and bang on my shield.

I yell, where are you, troll. This is my cave, troll. The salamanders and the crabs and the insects are tired of your moaning. Can you hear me, troll. Even the bats are tired of your screeching. I met an orcnea named Hrugir who says you ate his brother. He's going to give me nine whole pebbles for killing you.

I bang my sword on my shield. Clang, clang. Clang, clang, clang. Stop. Listen. Wait.

Silence.

I am giddy: that I-care-not tone that you can get despite any amount of danger. You just have to be in the right mood. You could be doing this to a fyrdraca, challenging it to lure it out of its lair, and still your giddiness would falter less than Grendel's eternal grin.

Caves drink noise, and if you pour enough into its throat, it will vomit out an eoten, snarling and hungry. Drink.

Clap. Yell. Stop. Listen.

Silence.

Where is he? I take a step forward.

A low pitch and then a high pitch, one cry and then another. Like he mourns.

Sob, troll. Maybe you know what the fates are dishing up for you.

Boom, scrape, boom. The booms are his feet hitting the cave floor. The scrapes are his calloused hands. They grab the cave walls and hurl his mass forward. As they let go to grab a new spot, their coarse grip scrapes the rock wall. Scrape.

Boom, scrape, boom.

Silence. A moment passes. He is deciding which way to go. If I make one noise…

I yell, I'm this way, you blind bastard.

Boom, scrape, boom.

One more time. To make sure that he knows where I am. And to make sure that I am ready. I hope you are ready, I yell. But there is a weakness in my voice and it feels like I am saying it to myself.

Bounding nearer. The rocks shake and the chambers thunder. Nearer, nearer. He's here.

I turn. I run.

His sand-palmed hands scratching the cave walls, his stubby feet slapping the floor.

I sprint through the twisting cave chambers, bringing them light and then leaving them in darkness.

The tunnel straightens out: the Trunk of Yggdrasil. It is long and flat. Come, troll. Follow me. Catch me.

I need him to pick up speed and momentum. I must time it exactly. I must not be one moment-sliver off.

There he is, turning the last corner. I am right in front of him. He lets out a troll-moan that says, I will feast on you. It says, I will tear off every bit.

I sprint, boots grabbing, arms heaving. Where is it.

The cave swallows our sound but we are like gods at war, thunderous. The jingling of chainmail, the boom of troll-feet.

He is catching up. I hear the saliva in his mouth.

Where is it? Where is it? I see it. I drop.

Part Two

Sliding over the cave floor, armor scratching the stone in a deafening scrape. Sparks illuminate the chamber. Metal lightning.

I slide to the rock sticking up from the floor that I tripped over the first time I ran from this troll. Feet first. My foot catches the rock. I grab the prepared shafts. I'm up again, kneeling, and there, in my hands, are three spears. Bound together to make one large, lethal spike. I ram them against that up-jutting stone, stomping them down and securing them with my foot. He hurtles toward me, full-speed. Just like hunting boar.

I bring my head up to look at him. An eyeful of troll. I aim the triple-spear faster than flight.

It is not fast enough. Instead of getting him up higher, in the heart or the throat, I get him right through the belly.

The troll hits the triple-spear with great force. The shock breaks one of the spear shafts but the others stay true.

Impaled, he falls, rolls onto his side, toward me. I dodge to the right.

I draw my sword. It sings that metal-alive song. I pull my shield from over my shoulder. I approach. A foe-walk.

He rolls, rolls. Blood flinging out of him. Up again as fast as he went down. He does not even make a sound of pain. Here he comes, belly full of spears.

I come upon him, stone-faced.

He lunges forward and grabs my shield. He thinks that it is part of me, wrenching it out of my hands and lifting it into the air and smashing it down onto the floor, shattering it. It is no more.

Spears through his belly, shield fragment gripped in his hand, he stands there, unsure. I swing my sword at his leg to hamstring him. If I can get away, I can let him bleed out. But just after I swing, I think, Unferth, you can't hamstring a beast that uses his arms as his legs.

I cut his leg deep but he does not even notice. I try to step away. He flails toward me and grabs my shin. Down I go.

We are on the floor, sliding around on his blood. He drags me around by the ankle. He brings up his other hand, palm open, to grab me, but I point my sword at his palm as it comes. The blade goes through the palm. Still he pushes, sliding his palm further down on the blade. I push back but it is not as hard as he pushes. The pommel of the sword buries itself in my chest between two ribs. I hear them cracking.

The troll gives this up and draws his sword-stuck hand back, pulling the blade out of my hands. He still has hold of my leg with his other hand. He swings me by the leg up into the air. He yanks me down, slamming me to the rock floor, and the force of it punches my air out. My helmet hits the floor, saving my skull. I hear the wet pop of glow-worms. Glow-worm goop splatters and swirls into the troll blood that coats and slipperies the room. Unbreathing, I draw my seax, short and sharp.

I bury the seax in the wrist of the hand gripping my foot. It doesn't let go. I pull it out again and slash across the wrist. I hear the blade strumming and snapping his tendons. His grip loosens. I yank away. I am free.

Up, I push myself, still unable to breathe. I am on my feet. I run through puddles of blood. Get away.

The whoosh of something through the air. His sword-pierced hand slaps me on the ass. My muscle writhes in agony and quits. On the floor again, swimming in troll-blood.

He comes. I push myself away, crawling with my arms. Splashing through the blood. He pursues, also crawling. His gnarled, sworded hand grabs my foot. I feel the sword's hard metal against my heel.

I am pulled, pulled over the rock floor. I scratch at the floor for something to grip, breaking fingernails. There is so much troll-blood that nothing can be gripped. I cut at his foot-grabbing hand. I slash as hard as I can with my seax but it is not enough.

Hot, salty troll-blood in my boots, my beard, my mouth, my eyes.

He pulls me in close, onto his chest as he lays on his back. His sworded hand cannot grip me very well. His other slashed hand is useless, too, but his upper arms are not. So he pulls me into a hug. To crush me.

His bluish, hairy skin. Clammy. His face, morbid and eyeless. Disgust and twist. His breath is tangy and overripe. His arm hairs scratch my face, my eyes. He presses me in. His thunderous heartbeat.

He has me around the chest, bear-hugging. He tightens his grip, bending my broken ribs. I scream, fast and urgent. My kicking feet knock on the spear shafts that stick out of his belly. I writhe, squirm, flail, but he squeezes harder. This boar hunt is all wrong: this boar uses Beowulf's squeeze on me.

I still hold my seax in my right arm, but my right arm is pinned along with my body. I can only move my elbow. So I plunge the seax into him. Plunge, withdraw, plunge. I feel the blood welling out over my hand. The seax is my last hope. Do not let it slip.

Plunge, withdraw, plunge. Wriggle and twist the blade inside his belly. He squeezes me tighter. His full strength collects, builds in those arms. They are snuffing me out. My ribs are giving. Cracking and popping.

I gasp. It will be my last. I am fading. It must be his neck or his brain. The seax blade must go into something vital. It is in my right hand, but my right arm is pinned. I must get it to the left hand, which is free. It is impossible. But I must do it.

He squeezes harder. My vision goes to black.

I think, he will die too.

Darker, darker. Concentrate your mind back. Bring it back. I can still see, barely, and it is a sudden movement that wakes me: he opens his jaws, pulling his arms up and pushing his head down to bite my head. I wake at the sight of teeth.

Forlorn. Pitiful. But I try it. I fling my seax. I bend my elbow and fling it up and over, trying to get it to my left hand, which can reach his neck. The seax flies over my back and the flat of the blade hits the troll in the face, pinging on his teeth. It goes handle-first into his gaping maw. The troll coughs, flinging bloody spittle into my eyes. The blade slides around in his mouth, cutting, stabbing as he tries to tongue it out. I stick my hand in between slams of chomping teeth. I get it by the blade. His tongue pushes on the hilt, sending it stabbing into my hand. I remove my impaled hand. The seax falls out into the troll-blood on the cave floor.

I moan. I thrust my cut hand into the blood, thrashing the liquid around for what seems like an eternity. I find it. I grab it by the blade, blood-warmed.

It is too late. His jaws.

He goes for my neck. To kill me.

I squirm. I squirm with more power than anything has ever squirmed before. I writhe my body. I throw it to the left, cramming my right shoulder forward into his mouth.

My shoulder, instead of my neck, is bitten. The teeth break through the chainmail. Screams. Pain immeasurable. I shudder. A death-throe.

I hold the seax by the blade. It slices into my palm. Fingers to the fuller. I strike. Down-piercing. I shove it into the troll's ear. It catches on something hard. I pull it away again. The blade cuts deep into my hand. I bring it down.

Into his neck, cutting his windpipe. The troll does not even notice. He can't breathe. A cut to the windpipe can kill quickly. But not quickly enough. He will kill me before he suffocates. I have botched the cut. I moan in agony. I kick my legs.

The grip. The force of it. The power. One after another, my ribs snap. Pop, pop. They sliver and sheer apart from each other, cutting into my flesh. Crack, crack, snap. My heart falters. The bone-cage is breaking. The troll thrashes his biting head back and forth, his teeth buried in my shoulder. Ripping my flesh. I scream. Desperate and hollow and futile. My hand is bleeding from holding the seax. Its grip weakens.

I'm going to die.

I must have a better grip.

I am going to die.

I drop the seax.

The same hand intercepts, grabbing it mid-air, this time by the handle. The troll releases my shoulder and pulls his head back, open-mouthed. He tries to breathe. I bring my seax up and I look into the troll's eyeless face. He leans forward to take another bite. His jaws coming for my head. No escaping them. My left hand brings the seax up under his jaw, right at his throat, right into his vulnerable throat, as he bends his head forward to bite and crush my skull. I push on his neck with the blade to keep his head away but he is unstoppable. He pushes forward. He crams my head into his mouth, his tongue in my eyes. My seax at his neck.

I put the rest of myself into one cutting motion. I put the rest into drawing that seax to the side, slicing that throat.

A barrel-full of blood wells out over my hand and arm. He bites my head. The bite closes and closes. Crushing my head. I scream out. I have killed him. I'm dying. He's dead. I have killed him. He isn't dying. I hear the crushing of my skull. The bone-dome groans, grinds against itself.

The bite loosens. Little by little. As the blood flows out of him. His head drops. His arms release me. They flop to the floor, splashing in his blood. I am free. I gasp. A hard-won breath.

I lay motionless, face down on his chest, head on his sweaty skin. I listen to his heart flutter and then pause. It beats again, flutters, stops.

Đ   Đ   Đ

Still lying on his body.

I miss him, somehow. He made me feel a thing that I have not felt since being with my brother. A pressure. Good pressure, like someone pushing on your shield.

He is getting cold. I want to warm him.

Part Two

Đ   Đ   Đ

Still on top of him. Shallow, pained breaths.

I imagine what the three spinners are saying about me now.

I like to think that they tried to kill me but it went wrong. I hope that they are throwing the blame around, playing catch with it like sisters standing over a broken egg.

Did we just let a man, on his own, kill a troll? asks the first spinner.

It was all over when he got his seax in his other hand, says the second spinner. It wasn't me who let that happen.

Nor me, says the third.

The first says, I was spinning the arms of the troll tighter around Unferth's body.

And I was trying to splash troll blood in his eyes, says the second.

Well, it wasn't me, says the third. I was weaving fast as I could to crush his skull in the troll-mouth.

The second says, well, how did he kill this troll, sisters? Look at our weave. It's all wrong now. We are going to have to wait until Grendel to kill him.

I bask on his corpse. My smile gets bigger. And then I chuckle. Who knows why. The giggle wiggles out of me.

The chuckle grows. Laughing now, and it hurts. My laugh turns into some bubbling, hawking thing, like a choking cat. I laugh at this strange noise. I laugh and cough in pain, making myself laugh, making myself cough, laughing at myself, whooping in terrible pain.

Gods, my ribs hurt. My chest is broken.

But it swells in pride. I have never known anything like this. I have killed eoten before, yes, but never on my own, never by my own design. Never anything this powerful. I think, it's going to take me half a year to recover from this. But when the rudder is mended, when the oars are replaced, when all the strakes are recalked, I'll steer out to sea.

Maybe you can trick the spinners. Maybe there are places that the fabric can be bent or stretched or cut. Maybe you can embroider things on top of the thread. Maybe you can dye it. Maybe I have been weaving too and only now is my own pattern coming together, only now is it taking shape.

I rise. Like a waking troll. I turn over slowly, heavily. I open my eyes. I stand. I square my shoulders. I lift my head. I tilt it back. All the way back. I sound out a moan. A mournful call. Deep and guttural. It echoes. My call says, hello, world-in-the-dark. I have awoken.

Đ   Đ   Đ

I could die. I will likely die. The ribs will heal and the hand will heal but the bite to the shoulder will probably kill me because the wound will fester.

I must start a fire. I pick up the fragments of my shield and I break off the shafts of the spears sticking out of the troll's belly. I will use these bits for firewood. I pick up my sword, now mangled and bent from the troll thrashing it around. I remove one of the troll's teeth for a trophy.

I head back to Giant's Bed, limping and leaning. There are now two glow-worms on my helmet instead of three. One was smashed. But not Bug. So it is darker but I know the way; I could find it in the dark. I limp along. Fearful of the pain that I must soon inflict on myself.

I start a fire to cauterize the bite-wounds. I strike my steel against my flint, shooting out a spark that ignites a pile of the red moss, my wooden shield-fragments underneath.

I put my seax into the fire until it is yellow-hot. I am afraid.

I stick it into the deepest of the bite-wounds. Deep, very deep. Searing pain all the way down to my balls.

I wake up. I think I fainted. I see that I have cauterized it well but I also dropped the seax. It fell and burned the top of my leg. There are six more to go. Stoke the fire, put the seax back in.

Breathe. Six more.

I heal and I rest. Ribs take a long time to heal. Months. Life-times. But these durations are all the same inside a cave.

And yet this time seems rare, valuable, like I should set it down in my mind to be remembered. I am again paying attention to the formations of the cave: its rock-drips, the flowering crystals, the abyssal blackness. I pay attention again because I know that I will soon leave.

I pack up my things: a seax, a bent sword, a haugbui skin, a troll tooth. I put on my glow-worm helmet and I step to the exit of Giant's Bed and I cast one last glance around at the little stream and at the corner where I used to sleep.

I begin the ascent. Up and up. The air seems to get heavier. It is too thick, too moist. I feel the slightest change in temperature and then, finally, I hear it.

It is something other than the sound of my own footsteps, my own breaths.

A bird. Singing. A light ahead, bright and constant, shining on the cave walls. I turn the corner. I look out. That is the sky.

I hesitate. It has been a long time since I have seen the sky. I think for just a moment: I will fall up there, I will fall into that sky.

It is red. The sky was blue before. I walk out of the cave and onto the grass. I nearly gasp. The grass is unbelievably soft.

A red sky. I turn and look around. There is the sun. I forget how bright the sun is. I look right at it and it burns my eyes and they water.

I am still trying to figure out why the sky is red and then I remember that the sky sometimes turns red at sunrise or sunset. Yes, and sunrise and sunset happen when the sun comes up or goes down.

There is day up here. And night.

That's why it is red. It is a sunset. The sun sinks and sinks. Look at that glowing orb sink. It drops at a sprint. Compared to the creation of stalactites and stalagmites, the sun flies like an arrow. If the sun is how men measure time, they measure almost nothing at all.

I sit. I can see a hundred, a thousand times farther than I ever did in the cave. Over there, way over there, the mountains rise and tower. Caveless stalagmites.

The wind. I remember: there is rain and there are clouds, too. Storms. There are seasons. Everything comes to life in the spring. The summer is warm and you can get a sunburn if you stay in the sun too long. Then fall comes and the trees lose their leaves and it is time for harvest. And then winter comes and with it comes the ice. And the snow. The sound of walking on snow.

Twilight. I look at the distant mountains. There are trees. There are trees on those mountains and near those trees are flowers that bloom in the spring. Butterflies will flop and weave to the flowers and then perch on them, slow-moving their wings, showing them off to the sun.

Butterflies. There are butterflies.

Đ   Đ   Đ

A man who spends a long time in a cave is unlike other men. If you watch closely enough, you see that he puts his back to trees when he can, and he always sits in the corner of a room. He is unused to having nothing protecting his flank.

He stoops under or around branches instead of pushing them to the side. If a door is half-open, he will slide through it instead of opening it further. He does this because he is from a world that cannot be moved, that cannot be bent or opened or closed.

The moon is out. It has been so long since I have seen the moon. I am attracted to it; I feel like I could fly up to it. Or, I just need to find the right tunnel.

Hrothgar's hall and Grendel, too, pull me, but I can't go there yet. There is something that I must retrieve first.

At night I dream that I am down there with it. It has lived these years as I have lived: alone, in a dark, cold place, shut away. But there, still. It is remembered. It knows this. It knows that it will eventually be called out of the dark to do what it has to do. For now it sits, waiting with bright eyes. Bright because it knows that, before long, it will sing again.

I walk. I know the way there.

It is winter and the traveling is hard but I have been hardened more. It is too cold for my glow-worms out in this snow so I keep them in an orcnea skull close to my body. I feed them leftover bats and I eat snow and warm it to water in my mouth and spit it over them to moisten them and to give them something to drink. I don't need them anymore. But I keep them.

There are so many things that I have forgotten. I expect each footfall to land on something hard but there is snow. The air can move and blow. The animals have eyes.

I can trap anything now. I feed myself and my glow-worms on rabbit and deer. I don't see anyone else, save the man that gives me passage on his trade ship. I give two deer in exchange.

After three weeks of traveling, I am there.

I set my gear down and walk out onto the ice. I remember exactly where it landed. I stomp my foot to check the thickness. That is one thick sheet of ice.

I look around at the ice, worried. I hope this pond is not very deep. I set up a camp next to a fallen tree. The moon is out so I can see fairly well. I look into another tree standing tall in front of me. An owl, white and quiet.

I wake up. I squint. Still unused to the brightness.

I look out at that ice. It looks cold. It looks very cold.

I will need to build a fire. A huge fire. I look for wood. There is a tree near my camp, fifty paces up the hill behind me, that must have been newly struck by Thor's thunderbolts because it has been shattered. Fresh, unrotted pieces of wood are strewn all around over the snow. That lightning strike must have been in the last week.

Does lightning strike during the winter?

Do rocks float?

I gather the wood bits to make the fire. I make the fire at the pond's edge and then I walk out to the exact spot in the pond. I clear the snow away. I walk back to the edge of the pond and I stoke the fire and I pick up my bent sword. I bring it out onto the ice and I rig up a fire out on the middle of the pond using the sword as a cradle for the wood so that the wood does not get wet from the melting ice. It doesn't work perfectly but it works well enough and the ice starts to melt.

I do this for a long time. By mid-day, the ice has finally melted through. I chip it away with the bent sword to round out and expand the hole. Water underneath. Black.

How will I see down there. I did not think of this. Can't take fire down there.

I walk back to the camp and look in the orcnea skull. Two worms in there: Bug and another. Sorry to bring you to a frosty end, nameless glow-worm, but you are needed. I grab him.

I fan the fire to get it raging and hot. I take off my coat and then my clothes and set them on a log. Freeze-hounds and frost-giants. It is cold.

I am already shivering. I yank off my boots and I step onto the snow. I grab the glow-worm. I run naked across the snow-covered ice of the pond and I come to the side of the hole and as I am about to dive in I think, Unferth, you are a purebred fool.

Head-first. Cold shock. A blade. My body retreats, huddling itself together. I resist it. I swim down into the cold and the dark. My eyes. The cold water hurts my eyes.

I have my glow-worm in my hand so I can see, barely, but it is so dark. I swim down, down. Where is the bottom. It is so deep.

I swim down and down and the depth hurts my ears. I did not know the pond was so deep. I am running out of air.

I paddle down further, bringing the muddy bottom into view. I need enough air to get back up. I decide to turn around.

I see it. In the corner of my eye. A shine. A glitter in the dark, barely there. I turn my head to look but I lose it. My chest burns. I must return to the surface.

The glow-worm is slick and slimy and hard to hold onto. As I turn my body back around to swim to the surface, it slips out of my hand and falls like a rock, a rock that sinks, to the bottom. Unferth, you fool.

I swim up. Up and up. I can see the hole that I made in the ice. It is so far up there, terribly far. But the swimming is easier because I am going up and I have both of my hands to swim with.

I reach the surface. I gasp in the cold air and I hold onto the ice. I think, you blundered. Now you have to use Bug to light your way. And now he'll die too.

I hang on to the ice to catch my breath, getting colder and colder. Spasming like a dying man. Losing control of my body.

I think, but the glow-worm will light my way. It is not in my hand but it does not need to be in my hand because I dropped it near my quarry.

But it will not stay glowing for long in this cold. It was fading even as I swam down.

I must try again.

Needles in my skin. Violently shaking. I have to get out of here. Go down and get it and get out.

I need to get as much breath as I can. I suck in deep breaths of pain. Ice forms on my hair, my black beard, my eyebrows. I set my teeth. I groan. The coldness. The ice-knives and man-skewers. My feet throb. Losing sensation.

Down again. I foot-push off of the ice at the surface of the pond, shooting myself down.

Down and down, looking for the glow-worm.

I see it: a forlorn blue light resting on the black mud.

I reach it and pick it up, stiff and dead. My air is running out quickly. My feet touch the muddy pond bottom. I look around for the glint of metal. Bring me to you, battle-singer.

I wave the glow-worm around. I ask Odin to tell me where it is.

A quiet reply in my head: you hid it. You find it.

A flick. The smallest light-snap. Like the crackle of a burning log.

I swim over and send the mud swirling as I pull it out. I carry it to the surface, breaking the water with a huge breath. I moan in agony and heave it up and out of the water. I throw it toward the fire. It whistles in flight. It pings on the ice and slides to the log that I put my clothes on. I gasp and suck in the cold air. I plant my hands onto the ice to heave myself out of the hole. I don't have the strength. I am too cold. I can't move. I can't pull myself out.

If there is one time you can't die, Unferth, it is now.

I try again, pushing up on the ice with my elbows. I heave my knee up and out and then pull the rest of my frozen flesh out and stand up to run to the fire. I have no sensation anywhere. I fall. I crawl. An eternity of crawling. Snow all over me, sticking to me. A white-covered snow-man. The fire, the fire. I pull myself up next to it. Hot, hot. I am being stung. The ice and fire compete to see who can hurt me more.

My mouth spasms and chatters. I cannot smile. So instead I smile in my mind. I look up and over at the recovered Hrunting, sharper than ice, hotter than blood. It cannot smile either but I know that it is smiling too. We smile together. The rattle of ice in my hair and my beard. The crackling fire.

My ability to speak comes back. I say, I am glad to see you.

I warm myself by the fire, huddled in furs. I give the sword a few minutes to get used to me. And then I pick it up and inspect the hilt and blade. It will need to be re-gripped. The blade needs polishing. But it will be as much the sword it ever was. I hold it out in front of me, tip in the snow, my hand on its ratty, rotted grip. I say, I'm sorry. I'm sorry for before. For making you do those things.

Speaking flatly, like you would speak to a familiar friend, I ask, do you want to come with me.

Part Two

Fire makes the sword, and a sword can whisper through fire. The campfire pops, shooting embers out at me, burning me, and I flinch away. I take this to mean, yes. I will come. But do not forget that I have my own code and my own will. Do not forget that I am sharp on both sides.

Part Three

____

Unferth and Beowulf

I am on a hunt for half of me. The half I lost eight years ago. I don't care if that other half is dead. I will cut Grendel open and fish it out. I will eat Grendel's raw, corrupted, still-warm brain if that's where my other half resides. In my mind, I am cutting Grendel down, carving him up. I am cutting off his legs, his arms, bathing in his blood. I am gutting his corpse and pulling myself inside it to look for my other half, to play and paw in Grendel's hollow belly like a cat in a bag.

It is not an obsession. It has matured. An obsession in its adult form. It has broken from its cocoon and now spreads its wings to harden in the sun.

Years of my life have come and gone, and they were years. But these, right now. These are days. These are the days. These are my days. These days are the days to remember or the days to die in. These days are straight and true. They fly by like arrows, simple and lethal. They streak and whistle through the air, through the rest of a blurred world, a world of chaff. They streak toward the final fight. They have one target, one purpose.

Spring slowly pulls the season out of winter's reach. The snow melts. Across the hæftworld, the warm weather wakes the eoten or sends them into hibernation, whichever their nature prefers. Those that wake rouse their eoten family. The nesting matriarchs roll themselves over so that their young can suckle, or they go out and kill something to drag back to their den. And then they lead their newborn young out from their dark broods and into the wide-ranging marches. As the young come into the brightness, they squint their swollen fetal eyes. Those bulging, hungry eyes pore over the marches and forests that they will prowl. Who knows how large these younglings will grow or where they will go on their monster-errands.

I travel back to Hrothgar's hall, Heorot, with Hrunting slung over my back. Out on the marches, crossing the rivers and fjords, picking my way to avoid roads and river crossings. Eoten are not the only things that prowl.

The Geats and Danes and Svear open their doors to the melting whiteness. They look out over the rolling marches. They wonder what the hæftworld has spawned during the cold winter, what new twists it has wrought. Any eoten can mate with any other eoten, some slaga say. And so one generation of eoten is not the same as the next: a ketta may spawn an orcnea. A troll, if it lives near the sea, may give birth to a scinnum or scuccum. Eoten also give birth to new things, strange things that have never come around before. Things like Nunemator, like Grendel. A haugbui might gestate some huge centipede that eats its way out of its mother, killing her. A troll could birth some slime-covered, black slug. Some abomination with pincers and suckers and tentacles and long antennae. The beast writhes in birthing agony, struggles to live but dies the next afternoon, a failed brood. Cut the corpse open and its black organs are mangled, twisted around each other like fibers in a rope. Imagine being an eoten mother, having no idea what is going to worm its way out from between your legs, or when.

When the spring starts to wriggle out from under the snow, men go out to survey their snowy fields. As they leave their homes they look back at their wives and children and they think, winter is ending. I will not be around the home now.

The men will have to be out there, planting or hunting or raiding. As they return to their homes after the day's work, they hope that the bodies of their families are warm and not cold. Any day your family still lives is a good day. And if their families are ever dead when the men come home, they become mercenaries or outlaws or slaga, or who knows, some say that these men go into caves and slowly become eoten. Whatever their nature prefers.

A small village on my way to Hrothgar's high hall. I am seen as I walk in from the outskirts of the village. I am met by three men, two with spears and one with an axe. They are nervous. Of course they are. I've been living in a cave. I look like I'd eat your children.

I say, what year is it.

The men with spears look at the man with the axe. The man with the axe looks at me.

He says, where are you coming from?

I say, what year is it.

One of the spearmen, with patches of hair missing, tells me.

I say, by the beard of Thor. I was in that cave for three years. I am thirty-three years old.

I ask about the Grinder. The men relax because they think, he must be a slaga, this explains his roughness. The man with the axe, who is also thicker and bald with a braided red beard says, yes, he's still there. Wealhtheow still sends for men to kill him.

I say, Wealhtheow. Is Hrothgar no longer king?

The patch-haired man gives the thick man a look. His look says that he is interested in what the thick man has to say, as if the truth is a moldable thing here.

Yes, he is still king, he says. But he is broken. He does not come out of his home anymore, and Wealhtheow rules. But she is breaking, too. Grendel still haunts Heorot. And also there are rumors of invasion by the Jutes. And the Svear.

Wealhtheow. I imagine her plagued by her drunk husband. I imagine her sending word to other lords and slaga, pleading for help to kill the Grinder. None of them come. Instead, they plot to take her lands.

I imagine Wealhtheow alone in the mornings. She dresses herself. She puts on her word-armor. She battles day-in and day-out with unruly thanes who don't want to be told what to do by a woman. Does she think of me. Does she know that I am coming. Maybe she's bribed the spinners to bring someone to help. Maybe she's promised her next child to them.

I say to the men, better keep moving. I turn around, start to walk.

The thick man says, where are you coming from.

I keep walking. I am still adjusting to the sun so I squint at him. I point to the ground.

Đ   Đ   Đ

Climbing a hill, the one that Wulfgar and I once climbed, the last before Heorot comes into view. The snow has melted. The green marches are fresh and muddy.

Hrunting on my back. I am wearing Svala's Thor's hammer necklace, and my clothes are made of black orcnea hides, banded and pieced together. On top of them sits my chainmail. I have an orcnea skull, small and vicious-looking, slung over my shoulder with Bug in it. I wear my helmet, dented and scratched but still useful. It frames my eyes in grey metal. My skin is pale from my time inside the cave. My black hair is long. I have it pulled back to show my missing ear. Ear or not, I have my own handsomeness. I am harshly handsome, Wealhtheow once said, and my brown eyes do not let up. I am tall. Life in the cave has made me thin and ropey. I have a black beard, long and full. A man's beard. I braid little orcnea bones into it: ribs and fingerbones. It is a good thing to have trophies on your face.

The wind blows over the hill. I feel its push. I crest the hill. I see it.

I am in the wrong place. This isn't Hrothgar's city. It is too small. The city is twice this size.

I look around, re-check my landmarks. This is it. I am sure.

Hrothgar. Where are all of your people?

Ð   Ð   Ð

You can tell if a city has been recently attacked by eoten. Look for dogs. If there are no dogs, something has been prowling. Something big is eating well.

I enter the city. No dogs. The people of the city are haunted, jumpy, ready to flee. Their eyes wide. The whites of their eyes say, I am prey. They walk through the mud and try to keep their feet from getting too deep into it. Like they do not want to be the slowest when the thing comes around to feed.

Eoten cast a pall. Every other kind of disaster that kills people strikes and then leaves. Floods, fires, earthquakes, wars. They happen and then they do not happen again for years and so yes, people die, but when it is over it is over. Time to rebuild.

But when an eoten gets a taste for man-flesh: that is a disaster that can persist for years, centuries, as long as the eoten is still alive. They go away sometimes, maybe for a day or a week or a year, but they will come back. They always remember where they can feed.

You can rebuild. But the eoten is on the face of every newborn child, on the door of every new building constructed. Mothers have children and they think: this, this newborn baby. This child could be eaten. Men build houses. When they finish, they get a sense of pride. But then they look at the door and hesitate. They think, this house right here. This house might be destroyed by the eoten's fists.

Though disasters kill hundreds at a time, more than a stalking eoten would eat in a year, the eoten is still worse. The number of people killed is not as potent as the knowledge that the killing is intentional, that the beast is hunting. The number itself is not as potent as knowing that there is a thing out there that hungers for your viscera, that spends its huddled sleeps dreaming of making you scream and squeal. This is the thing that keeps you awake at night, that cuts your feasts short. Every time you leave your home, you think, will it be me today? Every decision you make, you think, will I live long enough to see this come to fruition?

This makes a nest in your mind, deposits fear into your eyes and ears. You go over a hill and, just for a moment, you see the monster. And then it becomes a tree stump. You get up from your bed and go outside to piss. There it is. Movement on the ground. And then you see a scurrying rodent. You stalk a deer, hunting. A groan howls behind you. You turn quickly and nock your arrow and draw it back. Your eyes fly around, searching for the eoten. You look up to see two big branches rubbing each other. Creaking in the wind.

I walk through the muddy lanes on my way to Heorot. I take my time. I look around at the people, really look at them. Scared. Men and women and a few elderly. They trudge through the mud. They do their work. They give me strange glances, which I deserve. I see the front door of Heorot, repaired a hundred times. I wonder what Wealhtheow will do when she sees me. I wonder how she looks.

Heorot is guarded by two men. They ask me my business. I say, I am a slaga. Unferth.

One of the men goes around to the back of the hall to tell someone that I'm here. The remaining man casts his gaze away from my face. He won't meet my eyes. He doesn't want to know me. He has seen other slaga, other warriors approach Heorot's doors. He has heard their vows to kill Grendel. He has cleaned up their gory bits afterward. To him I am already dead.

The other guard comes back, says, Hrothgar and Wealhtheow will receive you.

The doors to Heorot are scratched, like a giant cat has pawed at them to get its owner to open up. The guards drag them open, slowly. The iron hinges wail. Long and low.

Dark inside. A contagious dark that ebbs out. It reaches and grabs, beckoning. I wonder if Hrothgar will try to kill me. I enter.

Heorot is clawed, blood-stained. It has been repaired, but there is not much you can do about deep scratches in the wood. The pillars holding up the hall are all stained with red. There are guards around, sitting. Lounging. One of us will have to clean him off the floor tomorrow, they are thinking. Heads it will be you, tails it will be me.

Wealhtheow and Hrothgar have been told I am here. They have taken their places on their thrones. Hrothgar looks like he'll fall out of his. Wealhtheow's back is rigid against her chair's back, her arms are on its armrests, her legs flush with its legs. Like she has been bound to the chair. Like it grips her. She wears a dress the color of a dark sea. Her skin is pallid and she is too skinny. Worst of all is her head, which leans back in a strange way, lazily, bored, resting on the chair's high back. She looks down her face at me. I almost do not recognize her. But she recognizes me: her eyes widen a queenly amount, the most that they can without seeming surprised. I look like a wild man. Good.

I go to Hrothgar. Show him deference. He says, rise. I look him over. He holds a drinking horn of wine. Very drunk. When a Northman says that another Northman is very drunk, he means very, very drunk. His head is tilted downward, opposite of Wealhtheow's. He looks at me from under his brow. Slurring it out, he says, tie this man to a post and get me my bow.

The guards, half of them drunk, look at each other.

Wealhtheow stands up. Her movements show the bones beneath her clothing. Her face used to be a hard thing, sharp and dangerously beautiful. Now her features jut and fall off like dried-up waterfalls. Before, her eyes were angled and cutting. Now their sockets are hollow, deep, like they could hold water. Before, her nose was the prow of a ship, which could cut its own path through packed ice. Now it droops like a dead branch. Tears, years of tears, weigh on her eyes. I try to smile for her.

The silence of the hall reaches into my throat. Maybe it's seeing Wealhtheow. But I push it out. I say, he can be killed.

It is maybe the most pathetic thing that has ever been said in Hrothgar's hall. Unless you consider the snoring that starts to buzz and haw out of Hrothgar's mouth and nose.

Wealhtheow picks the conversation up easily, intuitively. She must have heard this before. She stays formal. Acts like she doesn't know me.

She says, we will hear you. Weakness in her voice. Desperation.

She smiles timidly at the guards. They do not smile back. Tension in the air. Their rule is precarious, grasping. She knows that the townspeople, that everyone she rules wants her dead. They think that the two are a curse. The only value that their people now see for Hrothgar and Wealhtheow is that the couple could make a good sacrifice.

I say, you know the story of the binding of Fenrir the wolf, and she says, yes, but you already tried binding Grendel. I know she's going to say this so I cut in and I flatly ask, but was Fenrir really bound.

She pauses. She says, no.

I tell her my plan.

She makes excuses to not let me do it. Is it a show for her

guards or is she serious? She says, you'll smash up my hall. She says, I won't be able to find any men to help you. She says, and your plan needs Beowulf but Beowulf wouldn't ever come. He never did and he will not now.

I say, you could never get Beowulf to come. But I can.

Dismissively, Wealhtheow says, how? What could you give him that I could not?

I say, an insult.

With a voice slow and deliberate, like it's some proclamation of importance, she says, may-be. Now she is acting.

I say, I'm tired.

She nods, tells one of her guards to find me a place in the warrior-hall. I bow. I look at her before I turn around. She flashes me our old hand signal, crossing one finger over the other, which means to meet out at our old spot tonight. I raise an eyebrow to acknowledge.

I start walking out. Hrothgar's snores halt. He wakes, snortingly, snuffling, sucking the drool back into his mouth.

He booms, shouting, Unferth.

I halt.

He must not be as drunk as he looks.

Before I turn to face him, I cast a glance around, looking for a way out. Guards at the door. It doesn't look good.

I look to him. My head turns and orcnea bones jingle and sway in my beard.

Hrothgar slurs his words. He says, if you fail, I'm going to kill you myself.

Hrothgar must detect the resigned look on my face, the look that says, I am going to die doing this, because all Hrothgar does is nod, frown in approval, and flick his fingers to motion me out.

Ð   Ð   Ð

I get to the cave early. Our usual routine was to arrive just before dark but I don't know how the place looks because I haven't been there for three years. So I get there early. I want to make sure there isn't some dead animal in there and, yes, there is. I drag the ratty deer carcass out and toss it away.

I gingerly lay my cloak down. I reach into my orcnea skull and pull out a flower. If it can be called that. A first flower of spring. Tiny, just a bud. Hasn't opened yet. I think about trying to force it open. I wonder, is it ready in there. I take out my seax and start to pry down one of the delicate protective green leaves. But then I think, don't do that. You'll tear it. I bet it's like a scab, not ready to be removed until it doesn't have to be forced. And this is the only flower I've got. The only almost-flower.

I lay it down in the center of my cloak, which is on the floor for her to sit on.

I think about starting a fire. But then I think: she would like to see Bug. So I look into the orcnea skull that I've brought along and there is Bug, glowing as ever. I take him out with both hands, carefully, and drip some water onto him to make sure he is comfortable and moist. I cup him in my hands. I hold my hands up to the roof of the cave, bringing him near it. He puts his head up to it like he's sniffing it. He pokes around. This little rock-bit? That little rock-bit? He pulls his tail up to the roof and latches onto it. I pull my hands back down, gently. Bug hangs there like he did when I first found him, glowing like a blue icicle.

Fires are good. But she will like Bug.

I have filled a waterskin with some beer. I hang this up by its strap.

Ready.

I greet her. Embrace her. There is nothing on her bones. I show her into the cave and I watch her eyes as she first sees the glow-worm. A smile takes shape on her face. She walks around Bug, ducking because the cave roof is low. She says, what is it.

I say, a worm. I say, his name is Bug.

I tell her about how I found it and how I attached the worms to my helmet to make an ever-glowing torch out of them. She pokes it. Bug curls up. She is fascinated. Painfully endearing, Wealhtheow says, squishy. My heart swoops and soars. She turns and looks at me with her crow-walked eyes. She holds her gaze. There we are again. Three years gone like that. Like we've skipped right over them and are picking up what we were talking about just a moment ago.

She looks at me, top-to-bottom. At my scars, my orcnea hide clothing. She takes in what I must have seen and done in that cave over three years. Was it dangerous, she asks. I nod. She looks jealous. Tell me, she says. She is still standing, stooped because of the low roof. I stand, stooped, as well, unable to move. This is how Wealhtheow is. All look to her to guide the event. So you don't sit down. No, you find yourself and her stooping, uncomfortable, locking eyes.

You expect most to ask about danger because they want to be

entertained or because they want to measure the man. Measure his boldness, the danger he faced. Not Wealhtheow. No, she asks because she is jealous. She wishes she could have been there, too.

I tell her about the orcneas that can chew you to bone and the chasms that open into great abysses. I tell her about rocks frosted with crystals that you could shatter with a breath. I tell her about having no sun and no daytime and no seasons. I tell her about the troll. About the desperate troll fight, the feel of the troll's moist skin and thick hair and the last-ditch effort to get my seax into my left hand so that I could cut his throat.

Danes sometimes try to figure out what you actually did when they listen to your stories or boasts. They ask how you managed something, or point out that what you've done could never happen. But their women want to believe you, whatever you say. What did you do then, they ask. Or, what happened next. Wealhtheow does this. She says, how did you feel after you killed it. I say, well, I think that I wanted to die.

All the talk about eoten reminds her of Grendel. The wonder and curiosity drains out of her. Her face changes, prepares itself for danger. Like she has just drawn her sword. She sits down on my cloak and she sees the unopened flower that I have left on it. She holds it up and looks at the puny bud. She says, they will kill him. She says, they think that Hrothgar is the cause. They are going to sacrifice him.

This happens. Bad harvest, bad weather, a persistent eoten. Kill the king. Give his cursed blood to the gods and they will let up.

If Hrothgar dies, the land will rumble. One of Hrothgar's sons will become king but this will stir ambitions in neighboring kings.

They know that a new king is a vulnerable king and they will make war. I do not care about what happens to Hrothgar. But Wealhtheow would be made a slave. Or executed.

She stiffens, says, can the Grinder be killed. The tone of her voice as she says this. She is at the end of her endurance.

When has a man ever been asked if his rival can be killed, and then kills that rival? Never, because if a man's rival can possibly be seen as unkillable, the man doesn't end up winning. He ends up dead. I try to decide whether to cheer her up or to spare her the false hope.

I give her an answer that I would give to a fellow slaga. I say, I think that he can be killed. But I do not think that we can kill him.

My face must be saying something because she says, what.

I don't respond.

She says, tell me.

I want to pull her in and kiss her. I am silent, trying to stretch out our moment, sad as this moment is. When you know your death is coming, you clutch onto things a little longer. You think, this could be the last time I do this, the last time I feel that.

I say things. Scattered comments, unrelated things. To get her to go. I don't tell her to go, but she understands. Go, before I crack.

Wealhtheow kisses me on the cheek, steps out. I watch her walk away. I put the worm away.

Darkness. I sit in it. I draw it around myself like a cold blanket.

There are times when you might be loved. Or you might not. You might be a good man, you might be a bad man. You might make it into a good afterlife. Or you might not.

Part Three

Ð   Ð   Ð

I hear one of the spinners. Her voice. Or maybe it is the little girl who peeled the bark of Yggdrasil. She sings to me. The melody rises in pitch. Soft but powerful. A solemn tune from a tiny throat.

I know this song. She tells the story of Fenrir the wolf. My mother once told me this story. In it, the gods subdued a thing of infinite strength, something that no one thought could be bested.

The little girl says, the gods bred Fenrir the wolf themselves. He was raised by Odin and Thor and they fed him and fed him, mice and then rats and then rabbits and then whole sheep and finally whole boars. He was raised by the gods, so he grew big like the gods. But Fenrir grew too much, grew to be too powerful, more powerful than Odin, than even Thor. They knew that Fenrir would eventually kill them if he had a chance. He was, after all, a wolf.

I say back to the little girl, Grendel's might, too, is unmatched.

She nods, says, but the gods came up with a trick. They thought that they might be able to make bonds to hold Fenrir. Loki tricked Fenrir into testing the strength of the bonds and then locked Fenrir into them. But that trick did not work. The metal snapped. Fenrir is one strong wolf. He broke these bonds, as well as stronger bonds reinforced with the heaviest metals.

She says, but then the gods had an idea. Instead of metal, they made the fetters out of the spit of a bird, the breath of a fish, the beard of a woman, the noise that a cat makes when it walks.

She says, nothing. Nothing could hold Fenrir. So nothing is what they used to hold him.

Ð   Ð   Ð

The next day. Time to send a letter to Beowulf. There are two men in Hrothgar's city that know how to read and write. Hrothgar and another man. I am shown to this other man. His name is Ulf. I go to his hovel and take a look at him. He is disfigured, hunched over, squirrely, a little older than me. I know this type of man. No good in battle or out in the field. The oddities of people like him are caught at birth and the babies are usually sacrificed to the gods because they will live pointless lives. But some make it through childhood one way or another, a sentimental mother or a year of good harvest, and the ones that make it to adulthood become this other type of thing, this other kind of person. They live lives of seclusion and dishonor because they cannot do anything worthwhile. But the women of this city bring this man food, so he endures and drives himself mad out here in his secluded hut, coming into town only for weddings or to preside over funerals, the only things that his monkishness contributes to, the only things he can do.

But sometimes these men eventually become useful. Seclusion pulls you away from other men, sets your mind apart. This separation brings your mind closer to those of the gods. These are the men who tell us what the gods are saying or thinking. You can go to them and ask them things and they will tell you either the answer that you had all along but did not realize or they will tell you something so outlandish that you say, that's not it, and in saying this you discover your answer. If you hear someone else's bad idea, you can usually come up with your own good idea.

I have myself spent time alone and so I feel a certain kinship with these seers. There is an uncrossable fjord between us because I am not stunted like they are. I am useful. But I know their world.

I go into his hut. It is like a bone-yard, full of skeletons. They are assembled to look like the animals they were. Or they are hodge-podged, mouse skulls on top of bird skeletons or bat skeletons strung up under the skull of a bear. Human skulls sitting on top of wolf jawbones.

The little man looks up at me. A pained look. Big eyes and a twisted nose. Half of his face looks like it melted and re-froze, drooping lower than the rest. The pain of his life, the pain of having no way to win honor and no way to get rich and no way to impress women, is burned onto his face. I feel sorry for the dead, even though they are in the corpse-hall. But I feel even worse for men who live with no hope of that high-gabled place. The hæft-world.

He says, I've heard of you. I play along. I jokingly say, yes. He hasn't.

He flashes this little smile that means something, but what I cannot tell.

I say, Hrothgar wants me to dictate a letter.

He has no neck; he nods with his whole body. He hobbles over to his desk, the only clean thing in his hovel. He reaches for a calf skin hide and a quill and a jar with black clay in it. He pours water into it and stirs it around. He sharpens the quill with a knife and then he says, where is the letter going.

I say, to Beowulf. Of the Geats.

He thinks for a moment and he says, none of the Geats know how to read.

Is he playing? I can't tell. Beowulf cannot read, that is certain. I shrug.

He says, I'll read the letter to the messenger, too, in case.

He looks over at me and says, well.

I say, I don't know how to do this.

He smiles in amusement. He says, just act as if I am Beowulf.

I try to imagine Beowulf in front of me. It's strange, trying to play-act. I feel like a child. Embarrassed.

I shake it off. I puff out my chest and stand up straight. Beowulf, I say.

The little hunchback writes something on the calf skin. A strange kind of power I feel. The words there. Put down in ink. They stay. They don't float in the air and go away. A finality to it. A terrible invention. You cannot ever go back on anything that you say. This thing will ruin every king that ever comes to power.

Ulf has written Beowulf's name. I want to get closer to his desk to see the writing. I approach. He looks at me, frowns, then smiles. I must look absurd. Probably with an idiot's expression. I have only ever thought that there was magic in two things: snow and writing.

Beowulf might not know who sent this letter. I say, Ulf, should I say who I am. I feel strange calling Ulf by his name.

Ulf says, you can. Or I can write it at the bottom of the letter, where he will eventually find it. I say, no, if the bottom comes later and the top comes sooner then write it at the top. He smiles. He says, fine, fine.

He writes things on the calf skin. Words, I suppose. I say, which one is my name. He points to one of the words. I look at it. It looks spiny. I say, which one is Beowulf's name. He points to another word. It looks like my name, just a little different. Like how trees look different. While one branches here, another branches there. This one has more branches, this one has fewer.

I say, so he will know that this is from me?

Sure of himself, too sure, it seems to me, he says, yes.

I nod. I try to determine if he's playing some trick. No, he knows I would bash his face in. I nod again. I say, alright.

I say, Beowulf. Your father was old and I bet he's dead now. Ulf writes.

I say, wait, stop writing. I say, Ulf, is there a way to start out a letter. Like when you bow to a king or shake hands with a man. Do you need to greet him a certain way. Ulf smiles mischievously and reads from the paper. He reads, your father was old and I bet he's dead now. Ulf hides the smile, says, the way you've just greeted him is fine. I look at Ulf under a furrowed brow. I say, alright. I say, you can start writing again. He says, fine, fine. I think. I say, Beowulf, are you the king of the Geats yet. Do you still eat like a pregnant pig. I hope that all of your sport hunting hasn't made you incapable of hunting something worth a fight, something that Thor would want you to hunt.

Thor is probably his favorite god. He's the strongest. Thick-skulled.

I stop and think. I say, Hrothgar has asked you to come kill Grendel but you haven't and now Grendel has killed all of the slaga around except me and there is no one else to face him. We tried to kill Grendel but he killed Wulfgar. And Wealhtheow is suffering.

Ulf stops at the mention of Wealhtheow. He looks up at me. Maybe I shouldn't have said that. About Wealhtheow.

Too late, it's already written. Terrible invention.

I try to temper what I said about Wealhtheow so I say, I don't care about Wealhtheow or any of these weak Danes. But I want to kill Grendel because he killed Wulfgar. I killed a troll and I have a plan to kill Grendel. Come help me kill Grendel. Hrothgar will give you all of his gold.

Ulf looks up at me. He says, is that true.

I wonder if writing something down will show you if it's true or not. I decide that it won't. I say, yes. He will.

Ulf says, that man is lost.

I say, alright. Goodbye Beowulf.

I say, I'm done. I stand there while Ulf does other things to the calf skin – sprinkles something onto it like he's spicing a meal. Folds it. I wonder if it is a good letter. I want to ask Ulf if it is but I don't want to seem like a fool. He finishes folding it and he puts it into an oiled pouch that keeps the letter safe from water and he says, I'll give it to a man to deliver.

Still I am waiting to hear whether it was a good letter but he doesn't even mention it. Finally he says, do you need anything else. I want to say, what did you think of the letter.

Maybe I can ask him to write my name down again. I want to look at it some more. I want to carry it around. I want to carve it into my shield or my boot or into some rock. But I don't ask him.

I walk out of his hut into the rainy air. The only thing that I needed to say to Beowulf was that last bit. That last thing about gold would have done it. I should have put the gold part at the top of the letter. Beowulf might not even get to that part. He won't get through the whole thing. He'll probably wipe his ass with it.

Ð   Ð   Ð

Total darkness. A cave. No, not a cave. I'm bouncing around inside something. I touch the wall. It is warm, rough. Animal hide. Bouncing, up and down and up and down. Whatever I am in, it is moving. Running.

A repetitive noise, muffled. I stand up, putting my arms out, but the movement knocks me over.

I listen to the noise. Grunting. Breathing.

The container stops moving. Stillness.

The container spins, round and round.

Dizzy, laying on the rough, warm, rounded floor. The ceiling opens up and light comes in. A dark orb looking down at me. Grendel's face.

A hand reaches out of the darkness beside me, grabs my arm. Frightened, I jump.

Wulfgar's face out of the black. Haggard. Bloodied. Trembling. Wide-eyed.

He shakes me. Urgency in his voice. He says, do you have anything sharp.

I wake in a cold sweat. In Hrothgar's warrior-hall packed with snoring thanes. I slog outside into the dawning morning. Fair. Crisp. I look up at Heorot standing tall and long and broad on the single hill of Hrothgar's city. I climb the hill and remove long-bladed Hrunting and set it down. I sit on Heorot's stone doorstep. The rising sun cuts a swathe out of the horizon.

I hold out my hand. It shakes.

Wulfgar stuffed into Grendel's flesh-bag. The look on his face. It said, what is this thing. And then it realized what was going on and it said, no, no, no. Not this. Anything. Anything else.

Waiting in there. To be eaten. Grendel's muffled breathing. The touch of his flesh-bag skin. The darkness. The expectation of death. It would bring some small comfort to know of a more terrible thing. A more terrible way to die.

I let my head fall into my hands. I shut my eyes.

I sit for a long time.

There isn't one.

Before. Ten years old. Terrified. Scratching and banging at the door. My father pushing against it. With all his strength. Keeping them outside. A woodcutter's axe in his hand.

My eyes are closed. Shaking in fear. Running my fingers over my mother's hair. The only way she knows to calm me down.

Crying. She wraps me in hides, stuffs me into the corner of the room. To hide me. She says, quiet. I say, I'm too scared. A knife in her hand. She grabs a handful of her hair. Cuts it. Hands it to me. Shoves my wrapped body into the corner.

The door splintering. My father yelling.

Now. Sitting on Heorot's doorstep. I reach under my shirt. I take out a little leather pouch.

I don't do this often. Grow up, Unferth.

I open the pouch.
It is still soft.

Ð   Ð   Ð

Rrodi, the Woad from some island land to the northwest, tall and bald with a reach as long as a lightning bolt. He used a spear to make his reach doubly long. He designed the trap that was supposed to catch Grendel and hold him tight as we pushed him into the deep. And then, as the fight went to pieces, Rrodi saw its futility and put me on my horse and got me out. A good man. Let's get Rrodi.

I find him on a pig farm not far from Heorot.

Between breaths he asks, can you not find some other way to win fame.

I say, is wrestling pigs a good way.

He stands. Remains standing. He says, you are playing my pride.

Pride. Spend three years scraping goop off of rocks and running from trolls and having week-long conversations with yourself about crabs. And then you will know how absurd it is to have pride. Pride has no place in the hæftworld.

Pride. The weakness of every Northman. Almost every North-man.

Ð   Ð   Ð

I look out at the sea from Heorot's hill. High-cresting waves march toward the distant coastline. Who knows where waves come from or how they grow so large. Midgard, the world serpent, encircles the world with his scaled body to keep the oceans from flowing out into oblivion. I have heard that waves are created by Midgard's heartbeat. And that sometimes he flexes his body or adjusts his position and that is what makes the big waves.

The sea breeze. Some scent of decay. I will see you soon, Wulfgar. Maybe a month, if things go right. I look forward to drinking with you again, or talking coarsely about sex with the shield-maidens of the corpse-hall. I look forward to you saying, pick this one some night, she's spirited. Or, careful of that one, she demands hours out of you, your cock will be raw for weeks afterward. I look forward to fighting with you in each day's battle and to recounting our feats to the other and comparing them, bragging about them, making our smallest dagger thrusts into unblockable, flesh-rending chops.

I look over the sea. Yes. I am done here. I am ready to continue.

The wind picks up, whipping at Rrodi and me. The clouds pass quickly. Today, they have somewhere to go.

Rrodi says, here comes your friend.

I follow his gaze off to the right. At a strait that runs between the mainland and an island. There is a ship. It's Geatish. Beowulf's people.

The spinners who sit at the base of the tree of Yggdrasil weave the ship closer. Their fate-threads descend from the sky. Huge, long, wispy ropes attached to the prow of the ship. Pulling it forward.

Never have I been so happy to see a man I hated. I can see him all the way from here. Standing on his ship. A beast. A muscle under a helmet. The ship rides those huge Midgard-shudders, cresting them and falling and splitting the water with its keel, tearing through, impetuous. Beowulf stands on its deck. Huge in his war-gear. Standing like a master of sea and land and sky. A feeling of fullness in my chest. The feeling worms its way up to my eyes, watering them.

Beowulf. Glorious Beowulf.

The fates are cruel in this way. It is always the thing that you most hate or that you cannot bear to confront that comes sailing its way back to you. And then once it finally returns, you've either got to tame it or swallow it down.

Can't swallow this one. Too big.

Ð   Ð   Ð

Hrothgar hosts a feast to celebrate their arrival. The city gets ready. By this I mean that the women cook and the men start drinking.

I peek from behind Heorot to get a glimpse of Beowulf and his troop as they settle into their lodging. Beowulf prepares for the feast. He grabs the cross-post of the door to his lodge. He uses this cross-post to pull himself up. He pulls himself up and lets himself drop and pulls himself up again. He stops, inspects his muscles. Preening like a bird.

I found a mirror about a week ago. One of Wealhtheow's, probably. It is simple. Just a sliver of polished bronze.

I'm still around the corner from Beowulf. I bob my head around to see if anyone is looking and then I pull the bronze mirror out from a pocket. I use it to take an account of myself. I'm surprised at how scarred my face is each time I do this.

Tonight, Hrothgar will decide how we go about killing Grendel. Will decide who will be in charge.

At this feast, when people look from Beowulf to me, will they count me his equal?

Let's braid some more orcnea bones into that beard.

Ð   Ð   Ð

I do not insult men that I like. I do not insult men that I respect in this way or in that way. I do not insult men who are just out of luck or men who boast about something that is worth boasting about. I do not insult anyone who says less than he does, or, if he says more than he does, says it in an entertaining way.

Hrothgar may be a failure of a man but at least he knows this, at least he doesn't boast to hide it. You look into Hrothgar's eyes and you know that he has fallen from his crown. He hits his woman. Men who hit their women only do it because they will get pummeled if they hit anyone else. But he doesn't claim to be a better man than you. So I don't insult Hrothgar.

Wulfgar. Now there's a man who was likely to boast himself bigger than he actually was. But it didn't matter if Wulfgar boasted. We all knew Wulfgar to be a generous man. And worthy. When you know that a man is generous, you let him have his boasts because you know that he will pay you back in compliments or in subtle looks that say, you are my brother, my son. And, Wulfgar's boasts made me laugh.

But Beowulf. Now that man is different.

The feast. Hrothgar is drunk. But merry. Maybe he's taken heart now that Beowulf has come. Wealhtheow is not convinced. She sits. Broods. She is thinking, this should be a funeral and not a party. A funeral for these peacocks. Perched on Hrothgar's benches, warbling, eating, warbling some more. Fifteen of them, fifteen Geats. Not a slaga among them.

A bang on the table. Beowulf stands up. Massive. Taller than even me, broader than anyone. His chainmail sits on him like dewdrops on an ox. The air rushes in and out of his nostrils. His hair and beard are both in great length. They fall, hair flowing and beard frizzing. Both down to his chest. The hair on his arms is bushy and thick. He even has hair on the underside of his arms. A blonde bear.

Beowulf speaks slowly. As you would imagine a large man might. He says, a good feast. But now it is time to talk of what we will do tonight.

He raises his drinking horn. Our eyes follow it.

I groan. Time for a boast.

Beowulf says, there is something I say everywhere I go and before every boast I make.

He stands there like some statue.

He says, my father was a great man and full of bravery. You could drink his blood or his saliva and become brave. I am not my father. But I have been in many battles, both with him before he died and after he was gone. I am no fledgling in the nest. So listen.

He says, I will now formally make my boast.

Formally make my boast. I want to vomit on his face.

Hrothgar listens. Sits forward in his chair. I think, Hrothgar: how many times have you heard a speech like this. How many times have you foretold the speech-giver's blood all over Heorot's planks and wooden columns, his severed head on the ground, tongue lolling in his mouth.

Maybe Grendel is doing all of my work for me. Showing all of the boasters what they are really made of. Maybe Grendel is me if I'd lived in the cave a hundred years.

Now that is a thing to think on.

Beowulf says, you have heard of me. I have taken up my father's throne, defended my forts, devastated my enemies. I have become a king in my own right, giving arm rings and torques and swords out to my thanes. He motions to his preening birds.

He says, I would challenge the Grinder to combat if he had a mind of his own. But he doesn't so I'll announce the challenge to you, fellow Northmen. Consider the challenge made.

He says, there are men who lie to themselves and say that they are happy to farm or do other trades. But we know that these are lies. Men want to win fame through combat. We want glory through combat and we want for men look up to us and we want our pick of the women and we want to sit in our high halls and show our generosity by handing out arm-rings of gold and silver to our thanes. And we want to do it all over again the next day.

He says, this is what all men want and this is what I will get. I'm made for it. I've yet to know anything as good as a fight.

I can't help it.

I say, but Beowulf, I've yet to know anything as good as roasting a fool in front of a king.

A general hush. A few scattered giggles. Beowulf doesn't know what to do.

I say, boast. Boast and brag and strut. But if you fight him, if you fight him, you will die.

Beowulf must speak to save face. He holds his ire, pins it down. It is rude to behave in front of a king like I'm behaving and he doesn't want to draw Hrothgar's disapproval. I have an advantage. I don't care.

Beowulf shoots a glance at Hrothgar. I take the opportunity to shoot one at Wealhtheow. My look says, help, if you can.

I can't tell her. But I will it into her mind: help me stop them from throwing their lives away. They are fools but I need their muscle to kill Grendel. I must convince Hrothgar that Beowulf cannot kill Grendel without my help, my plan.

Beowulf ignores me. He keeps bragging. He looks at Hrothgar, says, you have heard of the swimming contest between me and Breca. We swam for an entire day, neither man able to pull away from the other. The finish, an island out to sea, was in view before a storm came and the waves parted us and the great churn stirred the monsters out of the deep and they came to eat me. But I killed them. Nine brimwylf, nine sea-wolves, each longer than the height of three men.

I say, I saw a swimming contest between you and Breca. Is this the same contest?

Beowulf holds his tongue. I say, you could hardly even swim, Geat.

Time for a little bravado. I relax my shoulders and walk forward with a slow stride. Beowulf stands, one foot propped on one of the benches. I saunter over to him. I look around at the thanes in the hall while I speak. In a lazy voice I say, is this the swimming contest that almost got you both killed? I'd never seen such misplaced pride. You and Breca have been friends since childhood. You know that he's a better swimmer than you, you must have always known. What were you swimming for? It was pure foolhardiness that made you set out on that dangerous sea. Foolhardiness and vanity.

Vain. The worst thing a man can be. Beowulf scoffs, shakes his head.

I say, you shake your head now, but yes, you are vain. Show them your mirror, Beowulf.

There it is, sticking out of his belt. A little bronze disc. I point at it. How did that get there? He turns, looks, pulls it out, flings it onto the floor. Ping, clang.

He is redder than a bleeding sunset. Piping.

The hall rumbles with the deep laughter of hard men.

I have this in hand.

Hrothgar leans forward in his stupor and almost says something to Beowulf, as if he wants to give him a chance to speak. But Wealhtheow crosses her arm over his waist, hushing him. Thank you, Wealhtheow.

I turn back to the listening thanes. I say, you even wore chainmail in that swimming contest. How can a man that reckless kill the Grinder? Grendel learns each time he fights us. He saw through our trap years ago. He anticipated it and countered it. For all we know, the Grinder may be smarter than Beowulf. I would bet on it.

I pound my hand on the table and say, a man with a mind must plan the fight. I say, we need a man with a mind.

The thanes shout, aye. They are merry now. Confident. This is what people come to feasts for, to see something exciting happen. The greatest feasts are those that are followed by a funeral or two.

I've cut Beowulf deep. Very deep. Poor Beowulf.

He says, yes, your last plan failed, and I guess you have a plan this time, too? Beowulf turns to Hrothgar and says, get rid of this man. He's bad luck. He was bad luck for Wulfgar.

I say, there is no worse luck than putting a man in charge who has not planned the killing of one eoten in his life.

Beowulf says, but I have killed many men.

Something comes to him. In his eyes. He has an idea. He says, and I have killed the right men. He looks at me, pointedly.

Confusion. The look Beowulf is now giving me says, you know what I'm talking about. But I have no idea. Killed the right men.

Beowulf knows.

No. He is going to say it. He knows. How does he know. It must have been Hygelac, the man on our boar hunt. Beowulf's uncle. He knew it. He knew who my parents were. Who my brother was.

My mind churns and churns for something to distract him, something to stop him from saying it. I start to speak but Beowulf booms out:

You killed your brother. You and you only. Led him to a foolish death, I heard.

I am impaled.

Silence.

Murmurs, dissenting voices. They turn to shouts. The heat of shame. A man who has killed his brother? Worse than a queen who has poisoned her king.

The room turns against me. To a man.

I look to Hrothgar. I shout above the insults. I shout, Hrothgar, they need me. To kill Grendel. I yell, there is not one slaga among them.

Who knows, Hrothgar may want to put me in charge. But honor is supreme. If a king cannot uphold honor, he cannot uphold his rule.

Wealhtheow's face says, I am sorry.

Hrothgar points to Beowulf and says, rid us of this eoten tonight, Beowulf, bear-paw of the Geats, and you will have anything you ask.

Ð   Ð   Ð

I said, you can't swim as far as me.

He said, yes I can, Unferth.

This is how it starts. It ends with dragging your dead little brother out of the water, his skin pale and clammy, water coming from his mouth. You drag his heavy corpse onto the beach, heavy like he has drunk the whole sea. His eyes lolling. And then you go to your parents to tell them what you've done.

A week later, with my mother. I said, it won't be the same, will it.

Yes it will, Unferth.

Can you have another baby?

No, I haven't been able since your brother.

Then how will it be the same?

Part Three

We can make it the same.

Father said that I killed my better half.

You can't swim as far as me, Breca.

Yes I can, Beowulf.

Did Beowulf and Breca deserve something different from us?

Lucky escapes. Reasonless tragedies. These are the things that separate those who rise from those who fall.

There have been no days since my brother's drowning that have been free from his heavy ghost, his fish-belly skin.

Ð   Ð   Ð

The no-moon is out. Only the stars tonight. Darkness thick around me. This is not a darkness that prevents you from seeing things that will make you trip. This is darkness that throws things in your way. The hæftworld is a hungry thing, and its hunger is rampant tonight. I can feel it. It is out for blood.

The ocean out there is black. Thick. Like it could clot.

I stand behind Heorot, next to the outer wall that we peeked through before, eight years ago, watching Grendel as he wrecked around inside it. I wait here for Grendel to come and devastate the Geats who wait for him inside.

I think, there is a lot of blood inside Beowulf. Grendel will think that too.

I look out at the blood-sea that licks the sand off of the beaches. It is all black-on-grey out there but I can still make it out in the distance. I walk and turn the corner of Heorot to look out over the marches. A falling star. The sound of summer insects. Are you watching, Odin? I imagine him sitting down for the show, saying, bring me ale.

Grendel. He comes. I have never before spotted him from so far away. Long-loping. Beautifully. Like a wolf but with a longer stride, his lengthy arms and legs reaching out. Relaxed but swift. The hair on my arms springs up.

He comes. Swift grace. Implacable as the ocean. Natural as the swaying of a branch. Maybe men are the intruders in this world. On Ymir's body. Maybe Ymir grows these eoten in a womb and then births them out to hunt us because he wants us gone. Many of us are, after all, descendants of the gods who fought with him.

Maybe he makes this type of eoten, that type of eoten, to get rid of us. Maybe Grendel is his favorite eoten and maybe the reason that I never found Grendel's lair is because Ymir hides him. Maybe Ymir opens his body up to let Grendel out and then closes around him again when Grendel returns. Maybe Ymir tells him, bring us back some men in your skin-flap. We'll drink their blood. And then I will sing you a song that is older than everything but myself. And then we will sleep until I craft the morning.

He comes. Straight through the city, the muddy lanes. Not caring for the homes he passes. Heorot only.

He closes the distance. A stalking cat. Low-bodied. Smooth strides. Quiet.

His smell. A fetid fog. Flesh and blood. Rot. Sharp-smelling. Like when you kill a pig and take the fatty meat off of its belly and fry it up over the fire. And blood, the smell of blood. The smell is moist. It clings to my skin and burns my nostrils. You can escape the grasp of anything but a smell.

I retreat back around the corner of Heorot and I vomit fiercely, splashing my dinner into the mud. I can hear the men inside Heorot vomiting.

I continue to hurl. First food and then bile. I try to ignore it. I take the wooden plug out of the spy-hole that Wulfgar made those years ago in Heorot's wall. I look inside.

The Geats are all armed, all puking. Fear on Beowulf's face. He thinks, what is this thing.

A rumble at the front door. The thanes stop. They look at the door. Not even I can help from feeling pity for them. The breeze stops. The ocean stops. A halt to the rhythms of the world. Odin, Thor, Midgard, the wind-making eagle watch so intently that they forget their duties.

Crash. The shiver and splinter of wood. The door flies at Grendel's touch. It goes crashing into Heorot, ruining one of the thanes. The men rush Grendel. The eoten wades into them like a hungry bear into a salmon-river.

He swings his clawed arm up and out, impales a man, brings the man up to his toothed maw. Grendel takes a bite, ripping the man apart. The monster's eyes catch fire. Poof. They light up like a fanned flame that has found its footing. He laughs greedily, springs forward to dodge away from the other men. Grendel lands at the back of Heorot, near my eye-hole. I expect a thunderous boom from such a great landing. But he lands like a cat. Barely the creak of a board. Quietly, he turns around to face the men.

He is huge. He has grown even larger. How does something eat enough to reach such a size. How does a man hope to stand against this power-monger. His thorn-fur is crusted over. Half-decayed animal carcasses are pinned to it, stuck in it. Along with spoor and offal.

He roars in glee. Like a yelping dog. The breath comes and goes from his toothy mouth in great rushes.

He stands there and savors the moment. His back is to me but I see his shoulders rise and fall. He clacks his finger-talons together in some pre-fight routine, some habit.

Forward, brave Northmen. They know they are dead. But forward they go. Grendel swats away those on his right. They fly and roll away. Those on his left close with him. They stab. They are strong. Fierce men. But Grendel's hide is thick, his body-thorns tough and stubborn. Their blows do nothing but get stuck in his hair-spears. Grendel picks one of them up by the waist. The thane makes his final roar. He anticipates that Grendel will eat him so the thane puts his sword out in front of him to cut into Grendel's mouth. But Grendel sees it coming. He just breaks the man against a wooden pillar. A smile of superiority across his knobby face.

Beowulf the opportunist. He's coming now. Now that Grendel is distracted. Let us see how good you really are, Beowulf.

That is one fast man. He has run out of Grendel's field of vision, coming around behind him. He leaps onto Grendel's spine-covered back, his long arms wrapping halfway around Grendel's enormous torso. The Grinder rears up. His face like a woman with a spider in her cleavage. He reaches back to pluck Beowulf off but Beowulf's thanes keep him busy. They stab with spears. They try to get a rope around Grendel's leg so they can pull him down. Grendel kicks at them and thrashes at the spears, knocking them away.

They swarm. They learn quickly that his speed must be countered with numbers, with distractions, so he cannot make his crushing attacks. Beowulf holds on to the Grinder's back-spines. The points jab into him. He bleeds. He can't do much because of the spines. But still he holds. He grabs one of the big spines, long and thick as a man's arm. He pulls. His face contorts, turns red. Spittle flies out of Beowulf's mouth. The spine comes off from Grendel's back with a great suction-pop. With the spine comes blood and skin.

Grendel hoots. A scream of pleasure and pain. The thanes grab at Grendel's hands to stop him from plucking Beowulf off his back. Two men hold each hand. The others have a rope around Grendel's leg. Thor, they are winning. They may kill him.

I've got to go in and do my part or I will never live in peace.

I leave the wall and step forward but just as I do this there is a desperate scream. I hear Beowulf yell, hurry. Beowulf yells, he learns quickly.

I go back to the hole. Grendel has a look on his face that curdles blood. Pure joy. Maniacal and malignant. Two thanes pull on each of Grendel's fists. He cannot move his fists quickly so he cannot smash them. But he can still move them. He slowly pulls his hands close together, locking his gnarled knuckles together. All of the six heavy thanes are right in front of him. Standing in front of him, holding his hands in place. He knows what they're doing. He knows that they're trying to pull him down.

So he lets them. His fists out in front, thanes dangling from them, he pulls them to his body and lets his legs go limp. He falls on top of them.

The yells of doomed men. Impalement. Grendel flat on his belly on top of the thanes. Hands and feet reaching out from under his spines, shuddering in death-throes.

Beowulf rips off another of Grendel's back-spines. The eoten roars again and reaches back with his free hands and grabs Beowulf off of his back. He throws the man forward. Beowulf soars through the air. An impossible bird. His thick skull hits a crossbeam. The wood cracks. Beowulf falls and hits the floor and a table falls on top of him.

Grendel stands up. He roars. Six thanes impaled on his chest-spikes. Arms and legs dangle from the corpse-walker like on some frilly dress. Loose pieces of flesh fall to the ground.

He hungers. The saliva ropes down from Grendel's mouth. He turns his arm to let his flesh-bag drop. The horror-bag. The nightmare-sack.

The remaining thanes know they have lost. But they try to make the best end that they can. Some of the knocked-away thanes are back on their feet and rushing with swords and shields or with spears, stools, whatever they can find. Grendel opens them up. He breaks them in half. He drinks their blood. He stuffs them into his bag in one piece or in many pieces. It doesn't matter. In they go. Two of the men are still alive. They scream as Grendel stuffs them in with pieces of their friends.

He giggles. His eyes are bright now, fueled by the blood of men. The torches of the hall are puny candles in comparison. He giggles as he collects the flesh. The air rushes and whistles around his grotesquely long, pointed teeth, which stick out of his mouth at odd angles. I am still vomiting. Nothing comes out.

Grendel leaves, bounds out, his flesh-bag full of quarter-men, half-men, full men. The sack's leathery bulk drags on the ground at his side. The fight has awoken the village. They shriek in their homes as Grendel bounds by. The yelping glee recedes. Eventually all I can see of Grendel is the light from his eyes. The light hits the thorns around his face and casts sharp shadows on the ground before him.

I run around to the front of Heorot. I enter. Blood and vomit and Grendel-spit. Two of Grendel's thorns on the ground.

The table, upside down. A huge table for feasting. Rising and falling.

Ð　　　Ð　　　Ð

The next day, full of grey clouds and stark green grass and black mud. I'm in Heorot, examining the carnage while Hrothgar's slaves clean up the mess. Hrothgar's slaves and Wealhtheow.

I walk to her. She scrubs blood from a scratch in the floor. She seems to have shrunk even further. She stops scrubbing, sits up, looks at me. Her hair is a strong shade of blonde. Dark blonde. Wholesome, like barley.

I look around for Hrothgar, don't see him. I crouch down next to her.

I ask, why is it always Heorot. Only Heorot. I ask and don't expect to be answered.

She stops scrubbing. She looks into the floor. A word pushes on her lips, prying its way out. She doesn't want to encourage me. Encourage us. She keeps it in.

I run my finger in the groove of the Grendel-writing, the claw-scratch. I wait for her to speak further. She starts scrubbing again.

I say, why do you think. Why do you think he goes after only Heorot.

I can tell by looking into her face that she has wondered. She's been thinking about it. While scrubbing the unremovable blood from Heorot's planks, time after time, she has to have scrubbed up some idea.

She stops. Tears building in her eyes. She says, he is getting smarter. He knows us now. Knows Hrothgar. Even knew your friend's name, Wulfgar.

She says, he is no mindless eoten. He is deliberate as you or me. Aware.

I say, yes. But why Heorot.

She sits. She says, what is the one thing we do in Heorot that we do not do anywhere else.

I say, we feast.

She scrubs. She says, he's mocking us. Mocking our feasts. In his own way.

Ð   Ð   Ð

Beowulf is awake.

Rrodi and I walk, heavy-striding. I think, it is time. Yes, this feels right. I am following my fate-thread. There it is, laid on the ground in front of me. Beowulf woke and now, if he hasn't been knocked into an idiot, he will have to help me. He will have to try again if he is going to preserve his honor. And Hrothgar is so despondent now that we won't even have to tell him that we're going to do it. He won't care. Beowulf, you're going to have to put your pride aside, because this fight is going to be gloryless. We're not going to boast before the fight. They'll know our fear. We're not going to ask for gold. We're not going to feast and get fat before the fight. We'd vomit it up anyway.

Here's what we're going to do, Beowulf. We're going to hone ourselves. We're going to prepare Heorot. We're going to pray to the gods. I'm going to pray to Odin and you're going to pray to Thor and somebody should pray to Loki, too, because we will need his luck. And then we're going to lure Grendel to Heorot and we're going to spring our trap. Yes, every other plan, every other attempt at killing Grendel, including the plan laid out by the best eoten hunter in the north, Wulfgar, has failed. But I might as well be dead if I don't kill Grendel because this monster has taken from me myself, my real father, Wulfgar. He has taken the shine out of luminous Wealhtheow. And you might as well be dead with the dishonor of this loss. If you go away with this shame, you'd probably drink yourself into worthlessness and become some turd of a king just like Hrothgar. You're smart enough to know this. I hope.

We enter the room. Beowulf's two surviving thanes, shamed at being knocked out but not killed. Breca and Helga. They look at me. Thinking of a way to blame me for this. They can't.

Helga says, get out.

Beowulf is there on a bed, roughed up but alive. A huge welt on his forehead. Maybe his skull broke. Cracked. But he's got alert eyes. It looks like the injury hasn't made him more of a bland simpleton braggart than he was before. He looks at me. Disgust. He says, oh yes, this bastard.

I look at Beowulf. I say, yes. This bastard.

I stand. Beowulf looks me up and down with new eyes. His eyes go over to Rrodi. An impressive man, so menacing and starkly white and starkly bald with starkly black eyebrows that Beowulf himself looks intimidated.

I have obviously come to say something to Beowulf but I want to be rude. So I don't talk. I let them talk first. I expect one of Beowulf's thanes to tell us to get out again and I expect that I'll have to shout them silent but this doesn't happen because, to my surprise, Beowulf is the first to speak.

He says, alright.

I stand.

Again, more urgently, he says, alright.

I say, a gloryless fight.

He nods. He knows that I've been running this through my head. What else would Unferth think about?

I say, if only one of the two of us lives, he can claim the entire plan as his own.

Beowulf nods.

I continue, and we'll do it all exactly how I say. You're going to do what I say.

And your thanes will help, too.

Anger in his voice. He says, alright, alright.

I doubt him. I say, do you know what that means, Geat? It means that if I tell you that your job in killing Grendel is to comb my hair and scratch my balls, then you'll do it.

Beowulf says, alright, you shit-eater.

So compliant. Lost. Like a child. I want to smile.

I say, alright. I turn and walk out into the grey air. Rrodi catches up to me and looks at my face. I finally let that grin out of my throat. He smiles with yellow teeth.

I say, alright.

I think I've finally tamed him.

Here is what it takes to tame Beowulf.

Defeat.

And contact between his head and a very thick piece of wood.

Ð   Ð   Ð

The next evening. I'm tired of eating meals in Hrothgar's damned haunted hall. So me and Helga and Breca and Rrodi and Beowulf take our food up to the small cave that Wealhtheow and I used. We eat up there where the breeze and the stars and the gods can find us. It's good to let them know what we're up to. What we're planning. That we'll probably ask for their help. Warm them up to the idea.

Our first time together as a group, as a team of slaga.

It's a good meal. Steak of beef. The company is fine if not reserved. A thing that I love about men is that after they fight with each other, they can quickly become friends. Better friends, even, than they would otherwise be.

We toss around ideas. Ways to kill Grendel. All but Rrodi want to avoid direct combat. Helga says, what about a trap. Lead him to a spot, drop a rock on him. Or dig a pit and put spikes in it.

Breca says, burn him. Trap him in Heorot and burn it.

Beowulf says, we could lead him to a troll-den. They could kill him.

I shake my head. Rrodi says, we all know that those won't work.

It must be a fight. With us. Grendel will get away from anything you put in front of him unless it is your own body. Also. I want to bury my sword in his side myself.

Rrodi says, the first problem. It is hard to penetrate his skin.

Hrunting can do it but Hrunting is just one small sword. I would give it to Beowulf to use but I doubt that the brute really knows how to swing a sword.

Beowulf is strong. But I do not know how to use him. Get him up on Grendel's shoulders and have him choke the beast. I try to imagine it. All I can see is Beowulf in pieces. Chewed and ripped.

I say, I don't have it fully formed yet. But I have a plan. In flat-tone, I ask, do you know the binding of Fenrir the wolf.

Beowulf says, of course we know. But binding has been tried. Grendel is too strong for any trap.

I say, and Fenrir, too, was too strong for any trap. But he was trapped.

Beowulf says, well, I guess then that you have the right ingredients for Fenrir's trap?

And by this Beowulf means those nothings that were used to bind Fenrir. The breath of a fish, the spit of a bird, the roots of a mountain, the sound that a cat makes as it walks.

I say, there are more nothings than just those.

I lie. I say, I know at least six more.

I look at Beowulf like he should know what I'm talking about. He Grunts. Scowls. A big, angry beast.

I say, the men who live in the cold north have forty names for ice. Those who live east, in vast forests of pine, have sixty names for one type of tree. Sit with a rock long enough and it will become a hundred types of itself. We all have our ice, our tree, our rock.

Mine is the dark.

I say, there is eclipse-dark. There is night-dark, with the moon. And then there is cave-dark, true-dark. I lived in cave-dark for years.

Helga says, if we are fighting him in the dark then are we not bound by the darkness, too. Are we not blind, too.

I say, no.

Helga scoffs.

I say, I have a friend that will help us.

Breca gives a stern brow. He says, but Grendel can sometimes see in the dark, too. When his eyes glow. His eyes light up when he eats manflesh.

Silence round the circle. The campfire pops. Licks the air.

I say, well, don't get eaten.

Here is how you know you are a slaga. You tell your friends, don't get eaten.

Đ   Đ   Đ

Me and Rrodi and Beowulf and Helga and Breca outside Heorot. Rrodi has given up his farm shirt and now stands shirt-less, sharpening his spear. His skin is white. He is tall. Tall as me but more muscled. His chest a big, rounded thing. The brown hair on his chest and in his eyebrows sets the rest of his whiteness apart. White as chalk. Looks like a man from a myth. He found an ash tree and felled it and is making a spear from it. He will make three spears, each of a different length. The longest is more than twice as tall as he is. Who uses such a spear? I watch him honing the shaft, sees me watching. I look away but he has seen me in my wonderment. He smiles. In his strange accent, he says, this is the spear for the big ones.

Beowulf. Bear-man. Stands with a welt on his forehead so pronounced and purple that you can't take your eyes off of it. But he's up and around, eating more than a pack of starving wolves, probably shitting head-sized turds. A huge man. A lumbering knot of muscle.

Three of Hrothgar's men approach, hauling buckets of muddy gravel up the hill to Heorot. I motion them to follow me. I open the doors. We go into Heorot.

There are holes and cracks and gaps between the planks in any hall. It is noon so the sunlight penetrates these holes all over Heorot. I tell the men: we are going to patch the holes so that you cannot see any light when you stand inside. I want to be able to stand in here at noon on a sunny day and not see my hand in front of my face.

The men look at me like I am mad. But I am a slaga and slaga are strange. And do they want to disobey their king? Then patch the holes. The men go outside to climb up on Heorot's roof to start patching. It is dangerous work because Heorot's roof is tall. The four of us go up there to help them. Everyone but Beowulf. His balance hasn't fully returned.

Hrothgar comes to see how we are faring. For once I see him without a cup in his hand.

His eyes find us on the roof. He says, get off, I'll get other men to do that.

I say, we are not above working.

He says, I don't mind you working. I mind you dying. If you're going to die, I want you to die against Grendel.

Me and Rrodi go into the hall. Heorot is big. Long as forty of me laid head-to-feet. Wide as twenty laid the same way. A fire pit in the middle. An all-wood floor. The only all-wood floor I've seen. Tall ceiling that comes to a point in the middle. Long benches and chairs and tables, two thrones. A few footstools. A small door on one side of the building, for normal use. For feasts: two big doors at the far end. Grand doors. Big enough for Grendel.

I say, we should take all of the benches and all of the tables out or we will trip on them. We should leave the big doors open, let Grendel in and then close the doors behind him. Don't let him break them down on his way in and send them flying at us.

I look up at the rafters and at the men slopping mud into the holes. The mud comes dripping down through them, splattering Heorot's planked floor. Some of the holes in the roof are too big and will need to be shored up with planks. The mud drips. Plopping noises.

What am I missing. I look over at Rrodi, trying to read his face, his mind. I gave all the details of my plan last night.

I say, do you think it is a good plan.

A mud glob falls onto the toe of my boot.

Rrodi shrugs. He says, I do not know. Things can go wrong with any plan.

He pauses, thinks.
He says, I trust your judgment. You trained with Wulfgar.
Slop, drip. Heorot cries mud.

Đ   Đ   Đ

When Grendel is not hunting men, he runs other monster-errands. Stirs up storms. Poisons wells. Sends boulders down the mountain at goat herds. Visits dreams and turns them to dreaded things that make men afraid to sleep.

The sky is purple tonight and red and the clouds are low. I smell his rot.

I stand. Grendel leans over, bending down to look at me. I look into his face, human but not. A hand comes reaching out of Grendel's mouth, and then another hand, both covered in strings of saliva. They push Grendel's jaws open and out of his throat comes Wulfgar, his eyes glowing like Grendel's. Wulfgar talks in a wheeze. He says, come here.

I go over to him. His upper half hangs from Grendel's mouth.

He grabs my head with both hands. His jaw opens unnaturally wide. His cheeks are in tatters, strings of flesh. He breathes out and his breath plays these flesh-strings like a lyre. They vibrate in his breath-wind. The music is discordant. I pull back, try to get out of his grip. I cannot get away. He is too strong. I feel his hot breath on my face. He pulls me to his mouth. His teeth close on my skull. The pressure. I am back in the mouth of the troll.

Part Three

Đ   Đ   Đ

The four of us. Standing in Heorot's darkness. It does not feel like a cave. Like I want it to feel. I want it to feel like there could be an orcnea pack this way, a troll-den that way, an underground lake beneath me.

It doesn't. It's too hot. I smell the death-sea. The sounds of the city outside. Chickens. Children. No perfect silence. No time-dropped waterlets.

It is a fake darkness, built by men. But it is darkness nonetheless. Truly dark. It has taken three days to patch and re-patch Heorot, but it is black.

I yell out, we are done in here. Hrothgar's men pick up the animal pelts that are nailed to the bottom of the big doors to Heorot, on the outside, that keep light from getting in. They pick up these pelts and hold them in the air so the doors won't catch on them while other men pull the them open.

We walk outside. I turn around toward the building. Are you ready to face the Grinder again, Heorot? You have known Grendel, his speed and power and craven gluttony. Does your knowledge, does the blood that has been ground into your planks and pillars make you more or less afraid of him?

As for me? Well, I myself have killed fast-feeding orcneas, unstoppable draugr. I lived in a cave full of darkness and eoten for three years. I killed a troll. I have slain fear again and again and again. I have faced death more times than I can remember.

As for me? I am terrified.

Ð   Ð   Ð

We cut down trees, split the boards, hone them, shape them into practice staves. We've got a long staff, the length of three men, and many short ones the length of swords or axes.

We move to a clearing in the woods. The sun is out today, bathing the meadow in bright light that catches the trees and grass, firing the green around us. The greenfire reaches out at us in long, slender blades from the trees, the ground.

I'm Grendel. I've got the long staff. Rrodi and Helga and Breca and Beowulf have the short ones. The goal is to hit me with their sticks and dodge away before I hit them with mine. The length of mine gives a natural advantage. As I watched Beowulf and his thanes fail, I thought, they die so quickly. You have to find a way to last. Armor won't help you. All you can do is hit him and then dodge away.

We fight. We take bruises. Beowulf, who could kill me with that stick, is very bad. Like he's never used a weapon. He holds the thing like a child holds a rotted fish.

I stop the game.

I realize something. I've never seen Beowulf use a weapon. He always just uses his hands.

I say to everyone, take a break.

I draw Breca aside.

I say to him, is Beowulf no good with weapons? Surely he has been trained?

Breca gives a knowing smile. He bobs his wide head up and down, says, yes, trained. Any good? No. Can't use one at all. Can't shoot a bow either. Can't even row a boat. Strange, eh? Hygelac almost disowned him. What good is a warrior who can't use a weapon?

Breca says, and then Beowulf killed two men with one punch. That settled it.

The next day. I go to Hrothgar's smith. He stands in an open, shaded smithy. A large tree grows high over the forge, sheltering it. The lowest branches are dead and blackened. The man is out of work for the moment so he's cleaning up his shop. A blacksmith who cleans. A good sign.

He looks like any other smith. Legs thick and arms thicker. Short-cropped beard, not so long that it catches sparks but long and full enough to block the heat of the forge. Like me, he has dark hair. I can tell from sight that he is a direct man. Sometimes you can tell. I don't even say hello. I say, I need gloves.

He says, smiths don't make gloves, tanners do.

I say, but I don't want leather gloves. I want metal gloves.

He says, chainmail gloves?

I think about Grendel's spines and Beowulf's strength. I imagine the spines against the metal. I say, no, they must be plates, chain isn't strong enough.

The man says, metal plates? You couldn't move your hands with plate gloves. He says this with finality, like he's done with me. I stand in front of him. He stands in front of me. Again, he says, you can't move with metal plates.

I leave.

I go and visit one of the city's fishermen. I return to the smith in the time it would take you to have a shit. The smith continues his cleaning. He frowns when he sees that it's me. He sees what I've got in my hand. His face says, what is that lunatic going to do with that.

I plod through the mud to him. He sits down on a stump behind his anvil. I go right up to the anvil and I lift up what I'm carrying to eye level. I drop the lobster down onto the anvil. Caught this morning. Still alive. It lifts its claws at him, clicking.

Strangely eloquent, I say, there are many things that animals and eoten have that men could learn from.

The smithy looks at me like I'm a madman. I say, get up and look.

The man probably thinks I'm a loon who lives in the woods and talks to animals. His eyes go to the bones braided into my beard.

He gets up. His slow saunter says, I'm taking my time because idiots don't rush me.

I'm used to this by now. Yes, yes, get over my strangeness. Let's come to the point.

He rotates the animal in his hands. Stops and stares at the tail of the slow-moving, dying lobster.

The tail of a lobster is made of a hard shell, a shell that is broken up into many plates. Not one long plate. These plates overlap each other to cover the entire tail. They protect it. And yet their positions give the tail enough flexibility to move around. I grab its tail and I wiggle it up and down. I look at the smith and I say, well, this lobster has plates, and he can move. I say, this lobster is a better smith than you.

The look on his face. I want to say, I bet you've never had anyone come and drop seafood onto your anvil.

I say, lobsters have armor. Crabs have armor. Turtles have armor. And they can move.

The smith says, they don't have hands.

But he picks up the lobster and takes out a knife and sticks it under one of the tail plates. He lifts the plate up to look inside.

He looks good and long.

He moves its tail up and down.

I've got him.

He turns around and starts rummaging through some scrap metal. Clangs and clatters. He says, get gloves made from the tanner first. I'll use those as a model. He says, for Beowulf? I nod. He says, big hands will make it easier.

I nod. I say, and they need spikes or blades on the palm so that he can grip.

He says, will they stand up under the pressure? And Grendel's spines?

Shrug.

He says, why doesn't Beowulf use a sword?

Shrug.

He says, I doubt it will work.

I say nothing.

Shrug. This time it's him.

Anything to kill him.

Ð   Ð   Ð

Later that night. We are again sitting around the hearth in our cave outside of town. Our lair, our collusion-hole. Away from Heorot. From the blood-hearth that waits for us, that waits for Grendel.

The summer is out. The ocean's wind is warm and these warm rivulets breeze over us and enfold our fire, pushing it higher and wider. We put deer meat on spits and roast it over the fire. The meat drips and sizzles and browns. It is dark in this cave but the fire offers a ring of light. We sit inside the ring, closely, like we know each other well.

The meat's barely cooked. But Beowulf rips it up like a wolf, burning his mouth on the steaming meat. He pushes the hot chunks down his gullet with his fingers. We cook and serve out the rest. There is plenty to go around. Helga pulls out skins of mead that she's sneaked away from Hrothgar's stores and because mead is made from honey she says, I've been a busy bee.

We eat. Beowulf consumes an entire haunch. We drink our mead. As tradition dictates, now it is time for boasts. Rrodi looks at me discreetly. He is thinking, Unferth won't like this.

They will all want to hear a boast from Beowulf of course.

But then, out of that rare-speaking mouth, Rrodi says, what about un-boasts.

Un-boasts? And then I realize what he's trying to do. A sly soul.

Helga agrees, says, yes, un-boasts, let's hear failures.

At this moment I decide that I like her.

Beowulf was about to go first before and so Beowulf has to go first now. That hairy child-like face, those eyes searching around for something to get their master out of this bind. Silence. No one's pulling you out of this one, you suckling pig.

I twist my boot heel, grinding a pebble.

His eyes travel the circle. And then around again. Finally they come to rest upon me. Yes. That is it. Yes, Beowulf, that story. You know the story. That's the one to tell. It's a good one. And the only failure you remember, probably.

I laugh inside my chest, inside my neck, at Beowulf's absurd, insecure pride. Just tell it, you strutting, preening bird. He looks at me like he's a rabbit in a cage. I look at him like you'd look at a rabbit in a cage.

Well, he says. He bends forward and looks from side to side at us, at Breca and Helga who haven't seen Beowulf do anything but gloat.

Well, he mumbles, starting again.

He mumbles, well, Breca was there but he didn't see much.

Beowulf says nothing of my presence. Fine with me. As long as he tells it true. I'll make sure of that.

He points to Breca. He says, we had a swimming match, but.

He pauses.

He says, but I did not know how to swim.

As Beowulf says this he raises his arms up and brings them down onto his legs like a frustrated child. Huge arms dangling hopelessly. Ridiculous on such a huge man. We cannot help but snicker, smile.

Beowulf sees this, sees that maybe he's succeeding at this thing that is to him so strange and difficult. He gets some confidence. It's all he needs.

He says, I had done it before, swimming, but I forgot how. I pushed with my arms but the water just moved out of the way. My arms dug down into the water and caught the dirt. It probably flew into the air but I didn't see it.

At this point I interrupt him and say, you sent up clods bigger than your own fists and they rained down on all of us watching and your aunt yowled like a cat in a bath.

Beowulf chuckles, his chest pushing up in two great rises.

He says, I knew where we were going, where the finish was, but you all know that my vision is bad. I tried to follow Breca. But eventually something caught onto my leg, bit me.

Beowulf works himself up. He play-acts, putting some enthusiasm into it. A child's enthusiasm.

He says, I yelled. I yelled at the thing, I will kill you.

What else could he say?

Beowulf says, and so I killed it. As he says this he claps and rubs his hands together like he's squishing something.

He says, but more eoten kept coming, attracted by that dead one. I kept ripping their bodies apart or folding them in half or twisting them until they broke. They were very slippery.

He smiles an innocent smile. He says, and then I got slapped in the face by the tail of a shark.

I look back at Beowulf. I see something there. On his cheek. Am I seeing it right?

I have heard of a thing called a Fylgja, which inhabits someone's body and then passes on to someone else when that person dies. It takes the person's spirit with them to the new person.

Maybe, when your friend dies, they don't really die. Not fully. Maybe a part of them moves on, changes shape. Maybe it finds another body.

The Fylgja, who was your old friend, dives into this new body.

But you don't always see the Fylgja in that new person. You don't always see your old friend in them. You think, they can't be in that person. That person is too dumb, too ugly, too proud.

So you ignore them and the Fylgja-friend inside them.

This thing, this Fylgja, is tiny. It sits in that body and wishes and hopes for you to take notice of it, hopes for you to take notice of this person that it has picked out for you. Maybe the Fylgja can do a little thing, something small, to get you to notice. Maybe it can bend a sunbeam, flick a flame to dodge and dance, make a water droplet stir and twinkle. It does these things to catch your eye, to draw your eye to a face. You find yourself seeing into someone when you otherwise would not have. You start to wonder why. And then you see what the Fylgja wanted you to see. All it took was a second glance.

Beowulf. He has that look of mischief. The look of mischief that Wulfgar used to shoot me before saying something sly. That small twitch between his eye and the corner of his mouth.

That small twitch.

Ð   Ð   Ð

There are eoten that breed naturally, like other animals. As with insects, you can find orcnea eggs in an orcnea den. You see troll pups clinging to their mothers, following them down long, dark caves and chasms.

There are other eoten that are different. They hatch from an orcnea egg but they're furry, not slimy. They are different from their parents. Some eoten come out of the belly of a troll but shaped like a snake and not a troll. They grow up as half-breeds, the top half like one eoten and the bottom half like another. Or maybe they are like one in every way except they are as big as the other. Maybe they are what happen when one type of eoten breeds with another. The world creates these things, creates them every day.

But there are some eoten that are unlike anything that came before. Some eoten, Wulfgar said, spring from rock. You can see the ore in their eyes, the minerals on their skin. They rise from the swamp, trudging with soggy, flopping feet. They wiggle out of the sea's sand, hard-shelled. Usually, there are things that are wrong with these strange eoten. They are mockeries of living things. Though there seems to be nothing wrong with them, they screech and howl in pain. Sometimes they are ill-proportioned. Their heads are too small. Or their limbs are swollen and purple. Sometimes their left halves are bigger than their right halves. Sometimes they have both feathers and scales, like they could not decide whether they should fly or swim. Sometimes all you find are their pitiful corpses because they couldn't defend themselves against even seagulls, housecats.

But sometimes, these strangelings are unstoppable. Nunemator. Grendel.

Grendel's needle-teeth, his spiney fur, his talons. Those gluttonous eyes that flame up when he feeds on the flesh of men. That flesh-bag, which helps him carry off his hoard. Grendel, what happened to make you? Does your mother lurk out there, too? Did she form you in her womb, giving you that flesh-bag so that you could take your meat home to her? Or are you parentless, a child of rotted wood and fog and fear?

Ð   Ð   Ð

We need deer skins to make drums, at least ten drums, so we are all chasing the deer around. You couldn't really call it a hunt.

We finally round a few up. We take them down with arrows and javelins. They go down pawing.

I approach to finish off one of the deer. Its eyes are huge. Black orbs.

The things that get closer to your eyes are somehow even closer to you than the things that touch you on your arms, your legs, your chest.

I look into those black eyes and I think, how far is it into those eyes before I am right there touching the soul of that deer?

In childhood, your fate hovers high above you. Distant, so distant, like clouds. But these clouds get lower and lower as you pass through your life and then finally the impossible happens. Finally, at the end, at your death, you reach up and touch these clouds of fate.

I am feeling for my fate, reaching out for it, reaching up into the air. There is mist up there. It collects on my fingers, my palms.

Ð   Ð   Ð

We are practicing. I tell that to Wealhtheow. I tell her, we are practicing, and she thinks that by practice I mean that we are running every possible contingency: if I die, if Helga dies, if Breca dies, if Rrodi dies, if Beowulf dies. What then? Then we do this, we do that. Then this person takes on the role of that person. This is what Wealhtheow assumes we practice. This is what anyone would assume.

But if you've ever seen Grendel fight, you know that any detailed plan against Grendel is a failed plan. The fight changes from moment to moment. So instead of specific plans we practice things loosely. Helga and Rrodi: try to keep Grendel busy, try to distract him. Breca: as my partner, you and I are trying to wound him if we can, but if he turns his attention to us, run away. Beowulf: go for the kill. But if you don't see a good opportunity, wait until you do. Even if we are dying. Even if we are getting eaten up. Wait until something opens up and then do it: choke him like you did the boar, rip off his jaw, ram your fingers into his eyes. Ram your fist up his asshole, even. Anything to get by those spines.

But this I tell them, above all: do not let Beowulf die or become seriously injured. Take the killing blow for him, jump into the Grinder's mouth when he's about to stick Beowulf in. Beowulf is the only one who can bring down the Grinder.

We wrestle with Beowulf to get him ready. His strength beats us all: Helga body-slammed, Rrodi choked out, Breca in a painful hold. At one point I'm on Beowulf's back, feet off the ground trying to get a choke. Failing. Beowulf laughs, says, you could give up now. Or I could fall on you and crush your ribcage.

He's too strong. I can't teach him anything useful because I am only teaching him to beat weaklings. Grendel is no weakling.

And then I have an idea. I get up, motion him to follow. I say, let's try something else. I say, if we are ever in a situation when it is my strength against yours, when we are fighting for position or to get in or out of a hold, you must go loose, letting me act like I am the stronger one.

He hesitates, nods.

We struggle, sweat. Difficult to wrestle a man the size of a bear, but it can be done. I push him around, bringing my fake strength to bear on his fake weakness. He forgets himself and uses his strength sometimes but we all say, hey, hey, and he stops. I arm-lock him, twist him around, choke him. Grass flying through the air. Now I'm winning. This is fun.

He's angry, frustrated.

He stops, says, this is not fair at all.

I take that to mean: now we are getting somewhere.

Đ   Đ   Đ

Gleipnir, the shackle that bound Fenrir the wolf, was made by dwarves. The dwarves made it out of the sound that a cat makes when it walks, the roots of a mountain, the beard of a woman, the spittle of a bird, the tail of a bear, the breath of a fish. But none of these things exist. So what did the dwarves really do to fashion this shackle? How would you make one, if you had to?

I have found out how. I am making a shackle out of nothing. Watch me collect this and that, make plans for this and that. There really are nothings that can bind, absences that can hold, voids that can pin you down. They are around us, everywhere. They are hard to find because they are, by their nature, invisible.

Living in a cave, among perpetual nothingness, among perpetual darkness, will turn your mind inside-out. When this happens, when your mind turns inside-out, you start seeing these nothings as they really are. You start thinking of holes and caves as filling the ground instead of emptying it. You think of the air not as being open and thingless. No. It has its own waves, its own currents. It has wind. It is a sea, just like the sea of water. It is the sea of the sun.

You see that your friend's death did not create a void. No. Your friend's death dug you a well. From which you can draw water.

Ð   Ð   Ð

Ranged round the fire, the five of us.

Beowulf is still eating. Look at him chew. He swallows and then roots around like a boar for his next piece of food, snorting as he wolfs it down. It's endearing, almost.

Helga and Rrodi have taken to each other. I don't know if I've ever seen a more ferocious-looking couple, Rrodi's scowl and baldness with Helga's big-chested, big-legged power. Tonight may be their last chance to take advantage of their time together, get a hump in before it is time to face the Grinder. They have no illusions about living through it.

But they don't keep themselves separate. We are a five-slaga group here. We sit in our circle.

Beowulf and Breca got tangled up in each other today. I

thought that would have been impossible. It isn't, not with a bear like Beowulf. His muscles are already huge, and they swell up more when he uses them. Breca got him into a tangled hold and as Beowulf struggled to get out, the more he struggled, the more his muscles swelled up until they finally locked the two men together, a jumble of arms and legs. There was nothing we could do but wait for the swelling to leave Beowulf's muscles. Laughed in buckets.

Breca says, it happened when we were children once, too. Though our bodies were not quite in the same positions. Hygleac, Beowulf's uncle, brought out some lard and greased us up. Squeezed me out.

With a wink, Helga says, maybe we should let Grendel eat Beowulf and then have Beowulf get himself caught in the monster's gullet and push around in it until his muscles swell up and he gets so big that Grendel chokes.

We've been through so many ways to kill Grendel. We pass the time by coming up with absurd strategies. Wait until the moon is on the horizon, huge, and then pull it down on him. Harvest honey for twenty years and get him stuck in a big barrel of it. Breed and train two hundred dogs to pile onto him and rip him up.

Silence.

We will face him tomorrow night. The terror is hard to ignore.

Rrodi says, we have the best plan you could devise.

I say, I am not sure.

Rrodi says, no. We are ready.

Beowulf nods. In his simple-but-sage way, Beowulf says, there are many men who can kill things. But they are special who can unite men to kill things.

If Beowulf had a tail, it would be wagging. A tail would suit him.

Rrodi nods.

Beowulf leans over and puts his hand on my shoulder. With his other hand he lifts his drinking horn. He says, to Unferth, Un-smart.

To Un-smart, they say, grinning. All but Beowulf. On his face is something smaller, more reserved. I would almost say, tender.

He gives me a long look. The kind of long look you give when you are piecing together something new about someone, adding onto or altering how you see them. The expression you have when you look at your mentor, your father, your older brother. I've looked at Wulfgar like that. And I've been looked at like that. It's been twenty years since I've been looked at like that.

Odin, Thor, do not let him die. Any of them.

Is this how mothers feel?

It is like I have four children, all going off to war. But I'm leading them.

Ð   Ð   Ð

I am looking for Thor, looking for him in the mud, the blades of grass, the fiery flicks and flops of my torch. I think of the spinners and what they are doing now, if they are asleep or if they are watching us, watching what we carry.

The no-moon is out. No moonlight, but we know the way. Back to that patch of ground upon which I had my first fáh, on top of that hill with that sickly tree.

We reach the hill and we walk up it, trudgingly, still half-drunk. We have been walking most of the night. The sun will soon cut an orange slash between earth and sky. The wind has died. The only noises are those of our breath.

We reach the top of the hill. Breca and Helga dig a pit and get a fire going. We sit down in a circle under the tree. Rrodi puts the baby down at the trunk of the tree.

We sit in silence for a moment, watching the baby whine and writhe. An impulse bubbles up from within me, a voice that reaches up through my bowels and into my lungs and then out of my throat: some guttural noise. I chant. A low chant. A noise that great fishes make to each other out in the bottomless sea.

Rrodi joins me, murmuring. Then Helga and Breca and finally Beowulf. We moan and murmur. I see them. But I do not. Like people in a dream: they appear to me in some other form, but I know that it is them.

Wulfgar watches us. He sits in that master's repose, leaning out a window of the corpse-hall, one arm resting on a friend's shoulder, the other with a horn of beer. He sips it, sizes me up, sizes us up. He neither smiles nor frowns.

He looks around at us. I follow his eyes: me, Rrodi to my left, followed by Breca and Helga and Beowulf.

Rrodi, the fierce Woad. Expert with traps, master of spears. Experienced.

Breca, an unrivaled athlete who can run forever, fight forever. A true Northman.

Helga, sharp-minded, a tactician, and strong in her own right.

Beowulf, both hammer and anvil. Pounder, ruiner, fear of men and monster.

And there too, is Odin, and next to him is Heimdall, followed by Freya and finally Thor.

Who says it? I do not know. But someone says, from the body of Ymir sprang Yggdrasil the world tree. And from Ymir's body came the hæftworld.

I stand up and grab the baby by the leg and I hold it over the mud pit. The baby sputtles and cries. The pit, gulping, pulls down on the baby with unseen force. The gods are thirsty.

I unsheathe my short seax.

We do not ask for victory. We deserve it or we don't.

All we want, gods, all we ever want, is your presence. Your attention. Your eye.

I open it by the neck. The god-quench rains down.

Đ　　　Đ　　　Đ

The anxiety is gone now. All that is left is the feeling of lightness. If you are looking forward to something good, you are racked with pain until it arrives. But if you are looking forward to your death, you can choose euphoria.

The pre-battle clarity. The red-soaked pillars of Heorot, each and every one. Each with its own knots, its own woodgrains. I imagine what these wooden pillars looked like as trees. I remember the owl that I saw as I was keeping watch for draugr on that cold night. I wonder where that owl is, whether it has had chicks, whether it starved.

I feel, ever so faintly, Wulfgar's warmth. I am ready to sit next to you again, Wulfgar. I am ready to tell you about that troll I killed. I am thinking of you showing me around the corpse-hall. You will have some joke prepared. Or some trick. You will trip me in front of all the warriors just as I walk into Odin's hall. You will tell me that I did nothing with my life, that I was a failure. And then, after a long silence, that grin will bound across you face and you will clap me on the shoulder and you will say I'm kidding, you little cat turd, it is about time you got here. The company is lousy. Thor's testicles, you little cat turd, you killed a troll.

I think about my brother. If you were alive, brother, you would be here with me. You would be a handsome man, like me. My better half. Maybe you would see me now, calm in this perilous moment. Maybe you would be reassured by my presence. I would be thinking, somehow I will be able to stop Grendel from hurting you.

I reach into my shirt, open the little pouch. I touch what is inside.

I turn Hrunting in my hand as is my custom before I fight.

He is here.

The fire burns low.

We smell him. We vomit as we take our positions inside Heorot. None of us ate anything. It's all yellow bile. We run to our spots, leaving bile-streaks as we go.

Rrodi, Breca, Helga in corners of the hall, myself next to Hrothgar's throne, Beowulf at the center of the room. Standing above the fire. Holding a great bearskin. Ready to drop it onto the fire.

The doors are open. The moonlight slants in. We watch.

Two leaves blow in through the doorway. They collide, fall, hit the floor.

Ymir lets out a low groan. A shudder. From the lowest range of hearing. Grendel's shadow makes its advance. The wind screams behind him as he comes. He lopes forth. I hear the snap and rip of his talons rooting up the soil.

His shadow folds itself through the doorway. Almost imperceptible. He hugs the wall.

Beowulf drops the bearskin onto the fire and at the same time the door to Heorot slams shut from the outside. We are plunged into total, complete darkness. A glimpse of him before the blackout. He is even bigger. Tall as three men. He could jump up and touch the roof of this high-gabled hall.

I hear the wooden crossbar being secured on the outside of the door.

Utterly black.

The whistling breath of the Grinder.

He quiets himself, suppresses his breath so he can hear better.

I hear him turn his head. His spines knock against each other. Hollow.

One drum. Wealhtheow. Pounding away just outside Heorot. My heart sets itself to the tempo. Other drums join. Low. Resonant and full. Chest-swelling.

Do I sense his worry, his sudden doubt?

The drums rouse my soul. My heart brims. Hrunting vibrates in my hand. Ready to sing and dance. Stretched, at their end, my fate-threads hum.

Blind and deaf. All of us. Welcome to Unferth's cave.

I reach over in the dark. To Hrothgar's throne. I feel around on the seat for my helmet, shrouded by a thick cloth. I pull the cloth away and step back from the throne.

Bug. On my helmet, which sits on a dummy head made of straw. He casts out his blue light.

Grendel's fists out of the darkness. Swift. Crashing down onto the head and helmet. The throne shatters. A roar of breaking and cracking.

Darkness.

Grendel lifts up his fists. Coated in glowing worm blood. For all to see.

There are nothings that bind, absences that hold, voids that pin you down. They are more common than you might think.

Live in a cave long enough and your mind will turn inside-out. You will start seeing these nothings as they really are. You will see that it is not what you climb the mountain for, but what you come down for. You will see that your friend's death did not create a void. Your friend's death dug you a well from which you can draw water. Live in a cave long enough and you will see the butterflies when you come out. See them for what they really are.

You will see that darkness is not something that obscures. Darkness reveals. Darkness tells you where the light is.

Vibrant blue streaks thrashing around in the dark. Glowing blue guts on his wrists, his hands. Like shackles.

Nothing can bind Grendel. Nothing is what binds Grendel.

Grendel roars in fury as he realizes what we have done. He turns his head to look for us, to find his enemies. But he cannot see us. We have wrapped ourselves in black.

We descend on his blue-glowing fists. Predators in the darkness. A javelin from Rrodi whistles through the air. It pins itself into his thick side-thorns. Grendel turns toward where the javelin came from, advancing and slashing out. But a spear. Helga's spear. It shoots up in front of him under Grendel's leg-spines at just the right angle to get under them. Grendel gasps and swings his fist at his hidden enemy. She bounds away before he can hit.

The drums pound louder. They must hear the roaring and cracking within. I run like a predatory cat, quiet and sure. Hrunting out. The blade whistles, gleeful. Grendel turns, turns, expecting hits from everywhere. I wait until his back is to me. I rush. I swing, cutting up under his thigh. Spines and blood fall on me. Grendel falters, forced into a kneel. He reaches out for me, groping in the darkness. I am already back and away.

The monster starts lunging forward, blindly swiping with his huge claws. Grendel blindly lunges again, this time toward me. Too fast for me to dodge away.

Another spear, heavy and thick, stops the Grinder. Stops him cold. Just as we rehearsed. It is Rrodi, master of spears.

Grendel stands impaled. Ropes of saliva fall from his mouth onto the huge spear-shaft. Pierced through his lower belly, almost at his groin. His spikes are thick and tough. But he threw his entire weight on that reinforced spear.

Grendel grabs the spear in his belly. He rips it out, cutting his own twisted flesh. He flings the spear across the room. He kicks and hits Rrodi but it is a glancing blow. Rrodi rolls away.

A hammer-fist, Beowulf's, comes down on Grendel's foot. An immense crack. Grendel whines and swats. He hits nothing but keeps going in the direction of his attacker. One of his swipes makes contact with Beowulf. Beowulf rolls and skitters and comes to rest against a wall, stunned. Glowing worm-blood on his chest.

This is all Grendel needs.

Beowulf tries to get up. Grendel is slowed from his wounds, but he closes fast.

Someone.

Breca. Out from the black, putting himself between Grendel and Beowulf.

Grendel grabs for Beowulf and gets Breca. He takes Breca's shield in one hand, keeps grabbing with the other. Helga and Rrodi and I run to him and stab and slice but the Grinder's armor is thick. Very thick. It takes me two swings to get to the flesh.

Finally he catches his prey. We can do nothing. Grendel raises Breca to his maw. Breca still has his sword. He stabs at the Grinder. It is futile. Grendel gets Breca's head and arm into his mouth. He bites and pulls. Twists and rips. He tosses the body aside. It flops and rolls, still clutching the sword.

Grendel moans in pleasure. He swallows the man-flesh. His eyes light like dry tinder. Poof. A flash of light. And then a steady burn. Sickly yellow light. It illuminates all of Heorot, all of us.

Beowulf shuffles away from Grendel as the eoten gluts down the man's childhood friend.

The eoten turns and looks. He takes in his environment.

He looks hungrily between Helga, Rrodi, Beowulf, and me. He breathes out and his teeth whistle. He recognizes me. He says something through the thundering of drums. A slurping voice. Like he is sucking the marrow out of a bone. He slathers it out, says, Wulfgar.

He grins. He lets fall his flesh-bag. Sack of nightmares.

Rrodi is closest and first to attack. He runs, shoots forward. Fleet-footed. Up-thrusting his spear, holding it at the very bottom so he can reach the Grinder's face. He goes for the eye.

He jabs. The spearpoint catches on Grendel's snub nose. The Grinder, swift, sweeps one arm to push the spear away, sweeps the other to hit Rrodi. Rrodi dodges, rolls back. Grendel pursues. Me and Helga and Beowulf chase. Distract him.

Grendel swings and swings. Rrodi dodges. Grendel catches up to him, grabs him by the leg. Grendel moves to bring Rrodi to his mouth. I yell but my yell is lost in the drums. I am upon him. I take my sword into both hands. I slash, up-to-down with all I have. It penetrates his flesh, cuts some ligament. I hear it snap apart. Grendel goes down into a kneel, slamming Rrodi to the floor as he falls. Blood shoots from Rrodi's mouth. He is still.

Grendel lets go of Rrodi. He reaches back around and grabs for me. His talons grasp my sword by the blade. I pull it back and away. The keen blade shears off one of his claws, singing blade-music.

Beowulf's lobster-armored hands grab onto the beast. Grendel tries to pull his arm away but Beowulf grips it with impossible strength. An anchor made of muscle. They are caught in a struggle. I add my force, what little I can, to the effort, putting my shield up on Grendel's leg, pushing to try to knock him over. Helga comes, ramming. Adding her strength. Grendel trips, comes down.

It is a wrestle. Grendel thrashes. Me and Helga and Beowulf slash, stab, pull. Grendel's flailing leg catches me in the gut. I go tumbling. The wind is out of me. I can't breathe. I run back toward Grendel, right back in, because I know that if we hesitate for one moment Grendel will get another of us into his mouth.

Beowulf has a hand on Grendel's talon. Another of the claws comes off. Beowulf stumbles back with it in his hands. He throws it down, throws himself again at Grendel's flailing arm. Finally the eoten gets to his feet. Beowulf holds onto the Grinder's arm as the beast stands to his full height. Beowulf dragged off of his feet and into the air. He dangles from the arm like a ripe fruit.

Grendel pulls Beowulf to his mouth. Beowulf brings his legs up to counter. Still clutching Grendel's right paw, Beowulf puts one heel right onto Grendel's neck and the other heel into the Grinder's armpit. He pushes with his legs, keeping himself from Grendel's jaws.

Helga and I stab and chop. Grendel's right leg is minced. Ribboned. The Grinder reaches for the two of us with his free arm, flailingly. His talon rips open my chest. Blood. The talon finally grips something. Helga's arm. Grendel twists and twirls her like a hunter breaking the neck of a bird. Her feet flying through the air. Twists her around her own arm. He drops her. She is mangled, kicking in pain, her arm utterly destroyed.

It is me and Beowulf.

Beowulf wraps his plate-armored arms around Grendel's spiked arm. Like he is going to rip it off. Beowulf straightens his legs, pushing against Grendel's torso with them as he pulls on the Grinder's arm. Beowulf's muscles ripple and shoot, coiling themselves, extending themselves. The veins on his neck and arms are thick as fingers.

Grendel shrieks in pain, tries to pull Beowulf toward his jaw but cannot, Beowulf is too strong. Grendel runs to one of Heorot's pillars. He slams Beowulf against it, trying to free his arm. A loud crack. Beowulf hangs on.

I am here. I am here. Hacking at the Grinder with whistling Hrunting. Grendel claws at me with his free arm. I dodge, hitting the floor, rolling, ducking.

I yell, pull Beowulf. Rip it off.

Grendel smashes him against the pillar again. The man hangs on. His body blue and red and purple. Grendel shrieks through his teeth. Deafening. My ears ring.

I stab at Grendel's groin and legs. Blood everywhere. I am slipping on it.

I look up to Beowulf. A look of calm. A supplicating look. Like he's asking a child to do him a favor. Eyebrows up at the center. He pulls the arm totally straight. Pulls more.

A great pop, like a breaking boulder. Grendel's shoulder is out of socket.

It is not done. I yell, pull it off, Beowulf. The arm must come off.

He pulls. His face serene, red, vein-crossed. The arm will not come. The flesh is too dense. Grendel heaves forward, slamming Beowulf into the pillar again. Blood flows from the man's skull, nose, ears. Beowulf is breaking.

I must assist Beowulf in ripping off the arm. My thoughts come fast. Sheathe Hrunting. Run toward Grendel. Grab up Breca's shield on the way. Sling his shield over my front. My shield on my back.

Jump. Climb. Up the Grinder's leg, grabbing onto spines, wriggling up his struggling body, cutting and bloodying my hands, my arms, my legs.

He hits me with his free arm, clapping me against his body.

The shields ward the spikes but the compression awakens my old rib-wounds. Cracking. Pain excruciate.

Hold together.

Up to his stomach. I steady myself with his spines.

Grendel's talon slams into me again. Breath and blood out of my mouth. I choke on blood, coughing it up. Hold on, ribs. Grab each other. Brace each other.

Blood clouds my vision. Draw Hrunting from its sheath. Pull it back. Forward toward his dislocated shoulder.

Hack.

Shoulder-spines come off.

Back, the blade moaning. Forward, the blade singing.

Hack.

There is blood.

Back. Forward. All of me.

Hack.

I pull back for a fourth strike.

I look up at Grendel's face in time to see the idea come to him. His thin black lips curl up into a grin.

He leans. He tips forward. I am between a falling wall of spears and the hard ground. Jump, Unferth. Grendel will crush you. Your ribs will break. You will be impaled. Jump now or die.

My fate hovers. The strings sing. Wulfgar is near. He says, finish. Finish.

I pull Hrunting back. It whistles. Low and sad.

I bring it forward with all that I am. It shrieks with a maniac's glee, bites deep into Grendel's shoulder-flesh, spilling the blood of the Grinder.

Falling. Beowulf yells like a man who is pulling a blade out of his own gut. Through my blood I see him extracting Grendel's arm. The sinews give in to the tension, tearing and snapping. Twanging. Thrashing like pain-racked snakes.

Down. Falling.

Grendel shrieks, his mouth open unnaturally wide. The shrieks of a soul-drinker. I hear Wulfgar's voice laced in it, echoing around in it.

We fall, the spiney wall on top of me. The ground rushes up.

I hit the ground and again the air is pushed out of my chest. A slough of blood out of my mouth. My head rings on the wooden floor. It is coming. I turn my head up to watch what will kill me. A last thought.

Spines. A thing falling with them, falling before them, some massive thing attached to them. Beowulf.

He lands, his armored hands holding the Grinder up from the floor. From crushing me. Beowulf has caught the monster.

A den of thorns just grazing my face.

The eoten stands up, hooting and hasping, looking left, right, like a scared deer. Without an arm, he shrinks away from Beowulf. He cries out. A plea. A nightmare mewls for its mother.

The Grinder spots the door. He flings himself against it. It explodes into splinters. He bounds out. Blood pours from his arm-hole in great soaking rushes.

I stand. Unable to believe. I stare at my shaking hands. Stare at the world I am still in.

Beowulf sits on the floor. Just sits. Clutching the bloody arm of the Grinder to his chest like a girl with her doll. Bruised. Covered in Grendel's blood. Wide-eyed. Tears running down his face.

He looks up at me. He cradles the severed arm. Like a child waking from a nightmare, he says, is it over?

Ð   Ð   Ð

The next night: a late-night feast. But not any feast. A feast in Heorot.

We sit with Hrothgar at a huge table. Everyone within a day's walking distance has been invited. They fill the hall. They spill out into the night.

Hrothgar is again himself, though I see a fear in him that may never leave. But tonight he is reassured and he is again at his high table, the forge of man-bonds. He distributes gifts that will reinforce his friendships, rebuild his faltering kingship.

Rrodi is here though his jaw is broken. He sits to my left with Helga, her arm bound up, ruined. She helps him, grinding the food of the feast with her one hand and mixing it with water. He sucks up the soup. He is embarrassed at the handicap but it is about time Rrodi showed himself to be human after all. Between slurps he smiles a cracked smile.

Rrodi and I did not expect to live. How did I live, spinners? Do you now sit at the tree of Yggdrasil and grin at each other at how well you've tricked me?

I felt death deep in my bones. It was my fate, the only way that this feud could end, the way for me to go to the corpse-hall and again see Wulfgar, if that is where he is.

The Grinder

I guess the corpse-hall isn't going anywhere.

To my right sits Beowulf, eating with vigor, splattering chicken grease all over his billowy beard. Grendel and Beowulf are not so different. Were not so different. Me and Beowulf were the only ones to come off without crippling wounds. If my ribs ever heal. Rrodi might mend fully. If he can someday chew.

One of Hrothgar's men tracked Grendel's blood trail this morning, said that the Grinder collapsed out there in the marches, didn't make it back to his den, wherever it was. The man found the Grinder's corpse, crows and wolves pulling off its tainted flesh. We'll go collect his head tomorrow.

Is Wulfgar dead? The spinners have tricked me often, but there are certain things that they cannot obscure from a man. He is dead.

They are both gone. And yet I remain, like some forgotten bit of meat on your plate. Like some arm band left round a treebranch by a summertime lake-bather.

Beowulf breaks off a conversation with Hrothgar and leans over to me, dripping with chicken liquid. He says, what is next for you, Unferth.

I say, it is too bad that Hrothgar did not die in all of this. Wealhtheow might have married me.

Beowulf laughs, spitting chicken.

A thought comes into my mind. I hesitate. I stop. Will I really say what I am about to say? I say, do you Geats need a slaga over there in Geatland.

Beowulf smiles. He says, no. One such as you? You'll dwarf my reputation. You'll be first among the Geats.

I say, no I won't.

I stand up and shout to get everyone's attention. The bones in my beard swing and rattle. To the whole room, I say, Wulfgar, my mentor, inspired this fight. He was the best slaga. We honor him. We drink to him. Cup-bearer, Wealhtheow, take round the walrus tusk full of ale.

I say, but he is dead. So let us drink to Beowulf, the man who fought Grendel and ripped his trophy from his very opponent and hung it above the door.

I point to Grendel's spiked arm, the size of a small woman, which has been nailed to the crossbar above the door. I say, hail the victorious dead Breca, hail Beowulf the Geat, slayer of Grendel, the Grinder.

He can have his fame. He deserves it. More than me.

The hairy men bang on the tables and throw ale on Beowulf and yell and yell, shaking Heorot. The cheering goes on a long time. Beowulf smiles the whole way through. Look at all of these happy Danes. I guess, maybe, there is something in me that wants to cheer, wants to celebrate. Maybe for a moment, for the time it takes for a wave to break, I feel happy.

I can't believe we did it.

They chant Beowulf's name. Wealhtheow brings the drinking horn to us amidst the cheering. Beowulf reaches for it but I push his hands away and say, drink after I drink, you will empty it. Cheering. Beowulf gives three big gurgling chuckles. I take the drinking horn from Wealhtheow and as I bring it up to my lips I look at her, beautiful and bright and sharp. It hurts to look at her and no longer know her.

The hæftworld. My chains are still here. I feel them now and I will always feel them. But good things have happened. And I helped bring them into being.

When the cheering dies down, Beowulf says to me, well, you have given it all to me. What can I do for you.

I say, I miss my horse. I don't have any money. Buy him for me.

Beowulf frowns in approval. He nods.

Just as I am about to look away from him, just then, something lets out a small twinkle, a small twitch in the space between his smiling lip and his wrinkled eye. The Fylgja. Wulfgar's Fylgja.

A bit of roguery flashes onto Beowulf's face. He says, well, you know…

He hesitates, draws out the moment. It is endearing, this cleverness he thinks he has. He says, I guess we could use you in Geatland. Would you give me all the credit over there, too?

He smiles. I hide mine long enough to act the older brother.

He nods, says, I have wars to fight, eoten to kill. It will be good.

He pauses.

He says, to have you.

Another pause, longer.

He struggles to find words. He says, would you like Breca's seat.

Yet another pause.

He says, on my ship. For the ride back.

Honor of honors. An honor you'd give your brother. Breca's seat.

It hits me like a hammer. Sweeps in unanticipated. I try to contain it but it cannot be contained. It catches Beowulf off guard. Wealhtheow turns to look. The room halts.

Tears. A flood of tears.

Part Three

Ð   Ð   Ð

Outside at Breca's pyre. The warrior burns, ascends to the corpse-hall.

The vigil has ended and the fire is dying down. Just me out here. Me and the ash and the lingering warmth.

Go, Breca, and when you see Wulfgar, tell him anything about me. You could tell him about a flaw, a mistake, a shortcoming. You could tell him about any of the ways in which I am a failure, a bad man. Tell him anything.

It would not matter what you tell him about me. He would love to hear it. When you get there, just tell him my name. Just say aloud, Unferth, and that sweet sadness will come over him. Tears will fall down his face. And he will say, I loved warming that man's cold bones. I loved drawing out his hard-won smile.

Acknowledgements

For education and coaching I wish to thank Tom Lorenz, Mary Klayder, Michael Butler, and Ann Rowland. As readers I thank Michael Butler, Kelly Renick, Laurie Winkel, Tom Lorenz, Loren Cressler, Taryn Costello, and Michael Stolzle. For encouragement and various forms of support: Laurie Winkel, Saralyn Reece Hardy, Randall Hardy, Tom Lorenz, Mary Klayder, Leonard Krishtalka, Thornton Thompson, Jesse Niebaum, Taryn Costello, and the late Marynell Reece. I'm very lucky to have you all.